Dead Em~~bers~~

# Dead Embers

## Matt Brolly

**CANELO**

First published in the United Kingdom in 2017 by Canelo

Canelo Digital Publishing Limited
57 Shepherds Lane
Beaconsfield, Bucks HP9 2DU
United Kingdom

A CIP catalogue record for this book is available from the British Library.

Print ISBN 978 1 78863 164 8
Ebook ISBN 978 1 911420 43 9

Look for more great books at www.canelo.co

*For my Mum and Dad, Carla and Joe Brolly.*

# Chapter One

The girl pulled the duvet over her head and tried to return to sleep.

Her skin bristled with heat beneath the cover and she stuck her head back out. 'Mummy?' she whispered, her words lost in the darkness.

Her toys acted as if nothing was happening. She grabbed Laney and studied her face, the glass eyes and stitched smile revealing no sense of fear. A crashing noise came from downstairs and she retreated back further beneath the covers with her doll.

It was hot, and not just because she was wrapped in the duvet. She wanted to leave the room, to make the small journey to Mummy and Daddy's room, but they didn't like her leaving her bed in the middle of the night and she wanted to be a good girl. Mummy would come to her if anything was wrong, she was sure. She listened, but all she could hear was the rapid thumping of her heart.

'What do you think?' she asked Laney, as more noises rose from the depths of the house. The sounds were familiar but she couldn't recall from where. She closed her eyes and pictured the dragon from the book Mummy read to her at bedtime.

She poked Laney's head out of the duvet and turned the doll's face in a circle so she could check nothing was in the room with them. Laney didn't say anything so she stuck her head back out.

The room had changed. She rubbed her eyes. She must be tired. Mummy and Daddy always said she was tired when things were going wrong. Her eyes watered, and the room faded. She glanced down at the nightlight, peering closer at the air which danced around its orange glow. Then the door blew open.

She grabbed Laney closer and started to cough. A strange figure stood in her doorway. He wore a helmet and a funny mask. Behind him, something glowed like her nightlight but much brighter. It had changed the house. The man mumbled something and she struggled to keep her eyes open as he grabbed her from the bed and placed something over her mouth.

# Chapter Two

DCI Michael Lambert sped up the escalator. Sweat dripped from his brow, the result of ill-advised heating throughout the packed underground. He sprinted to the gates, holding his scarf in anticipation of the cold blast of air that would greet him above ground. He hurtled up the steps out onto Oxford Street, falling into a group of tourists who had decided this was the perfect spot to check the maps on their phones.

He barged through them, crossed the road and ran down the side street that led to the restaurant. He was already thirty minutes late. He'd been stuck on the Tube for the last twenty minutes so had been unable to send his apologies. The restaurant was down another flight of stairs. He took them in twos, hoping she was still there. He scanned the room for her as he caught his breath and hung his coat.

DCI Sarah May sat in the far corner watching him with detached amusement, a glass of cold water in her hand. 'You're late,' she said, as he approached the table. Her top lip was curled into a crooked smile, which he knew well but couldn't quite read.

'Damn Tube,' said Lambert, still out of breath.

'I was about to leave. Take a seat, I might change my mind.' She was smiling, but there was an edge to her voice.

Sarah had recently moved from Bristol CID to take a position with the Met. She was originally from London but part of her decision to move had been Lambert. They had been in an on-off relationship for nearly two years now. At the moment it was closer to being off than on.

Lambert ordered some water and tried to apologise again. 'I couldn't get any signal on the Tube,' he said.

Sarah relaxed, murmuring. She gave him one of her intent stares. 'I've only thirty minutes left now, so we should order.'

They went straight to the main course, both choosing the restaurant's speciality, a fish stew.

'How's work?' said Lambert.

Sarah sighed, and he feared he'd said the wrong thing. 'Fine.'

'How are you?' he said, trying again.

Sarah laughed and he relaxed. 'I'm well, Michael. Believe it or not, I'm pleased to see you. It's been nearly a week.'

Lambert nodded. 'I know. It's great seeing you too. Sorry I cancelled the other night.'

'Have you seen Sophie recently?' She kept her eyes fixed on him. He instinctively edged back in his seat. It was no wonder she had such a great reputation as an interrogator.

Sophie was Lambert's estranged wife. Their daughter, Chloe, had died four years previously. Sophie had given birth to another baby girl almost a year ago, but Lambert wasn't the father. Every time Sarah mentioned Sophie in conversation he was reminded of Chloe, and her sister who wasn't his.

'Not for ages,' he said.

'Ages?'

Lambert shrugged. He wanted to tell her about the nights he'd recently spent outside Sophie's house, the house which was still technically his. How he'd sat in his car wondering what he was doing there, acting like a deranged voyeur. It wasn't fair on Sarah, but he didn't know how to explain the homing instinct which continually guided him back there. 'A few weeks, now,' he said, ashamed to be lying.

Sarah examined him again as if seeking truth from his words. 'It would make it easier for all of us if you were honest about how you feel.'

Lambert was thankful the waitress had returned, depositing their meals on the table. 'Thank you,' said Lambert, dipping his spoon into the steaming bowl.

They ate in silence for some time, Lambert enjoying the saltiness of the fish despite the uncomfortable atmosphere.

'I've told you, I understand,' said Sarah.

'I know.'

'That baby – Jane, I mean – is Chloe's sister.'

'Don't you think I know that?' said Lambert, louder than intended.

'Then you know it's OK if you want to go back to Sophie and raise her together.'

Lambert drank his water, the coldness of which was unpleasant in contrast to the stew. 'Anyone would think you're trying to get rid of me.'

Sarah shook her head. Lambert wasn't sure if it was pity or disgust in her look. 'You are an idiot sometimes. I don't want to get rid of you, but I don't want to be second best any longer.'

Lambert didn't know how to respond. He hoped he wasn't treating her that way. She deserved more, and he needed to get his priorities in order. 'I'm sorry if you feel I've been doing that,' he said, a little too late.

Sarah ignored his weak response and continued eating. After she finished, she placed her hands on his. 'I need to go,' she said.

'OK.'

'Think about it?'

'I will,' said Lambert.

He watched her leave the restaurant, and wondered how the hell he was managing to mess everything up.

–

Later that evening, Lambert lay motionless on a metal tray and tried not to think about being buried alive. The machinery which curled around his prone body was close enough to touch. He ignored the feeling of claustrophobia, using self-taught breathing exercises as classical music drifted through his earphones. The piece, Bach's Suite No. three in D major, was interrupted by the harsh tones of the radiographer. 'Please lie as still as possible, Mr Simmons.'

Simmons was the name Chief Superintendent Glenn Tillman, the man who'd arranged this for Lambert, had given the radiographer. At last count, Tillman owed Lambert at least two favours, and the anonymous MRI scan was the first he had called in.

'Comfortable, Mr Simmons?'

'Fine,' said Lambert.

'I don't wish to repeat myself, but it is imperative you lie totally still for the whole scan.'

Lambert sighed, and adjusted his position a final time. 'Fine,' he repeated, his voice rising. He wanted out of the room as quick as possible.

'OK, you'll hear some humming sounds and clicks as the scanner does its job. It's nothing to worry about.'

'Let's get it done, shall we?' It was three am in a private hospital in Surrey. Although they were doing nothing technically illegal, getting caught now would cause Lambert problems.

The machine came to life. Lambert closed his eyes. It was Sarah who had finally persuaded him to take the scan. Lambert had suffered from occasional blackouts since his early twenties, usually during times of stress. The episodes would start with a kaleidoscope of colour before his eyes, followed closely by loss of consciousness. Lambert assumed it was a form of narcolepsy, but had never allowed himself to be formally diagnosed. Over the years he'd managed to contain the condition, but the episodes had intensified recently and Sarah had witnessed it for the first time.

She wanted him to report it to his superiors but such an admission could result in him being taken off rotation, and a permanent mark on his record. Lambert discussed the issue with Tillman – the only senior level officer he could trust – and found himself in a dimly lit hospital corridor seven days later. He still hadn't told Sarah.

'All over,' said the voice in his earphones.

The metal tray made its slow journey back into the light. Lambert realised his eyes were still shut. As he opened them, the first thing he saw was the caricature smile of Glenn Tillman.

'Bit too claustrophobic for you?' he said, hauling Lambert to his feet with one pull of his gigantic arm.

'It would turn anyone claustrophobic,' said Lambert, wondering if his colleague would even fit in the confines of the scanner. Tillman's considerable bulk seemed to be constantly expanding. He did little to hide this fact, his shirt stretching to the seams across his broad chest.

The radiographer joined them. A slight man in his twenties, he shuffled from foot to foot. 'This is all a bit rushed,' he said, handing over some print-outs to Lambert.

'Don't keep us waiting,' said Tillman, staring hard at the man. Tillman had a constant air of impatience and anger about him, as if the slightest thing was likely to set off his rage.

The radiographer blinked rapidly. 'I'm no expert, I need to make that clear.'

'Get on with it,' said Tillman.

'There's nothing here which suggests an abnormality. No sign of a tumour, or blood on the brain. I would suggest speaking to someone better qualified, but I've done hundreds of these now and there's nothing out of the ordinary.'

It was a relief, though it raised as many questions as it answered. Lambert glanced at his superior for a response.

'Are we done?' said Tillman.

'I guess so,' said Lambert.

'Here, take your brain and meet me in the car park,' said Tillman, handing Lambert the scans. 'I need a quick word with our friend.'

–

The vastness of the car park came in stark contrast to the confines of the MRI scanner. Lambert leant against Tillman's car, tying his scarf and buttoning his jacket against the cold of the December morning. He imagined Tillman threatening the radiographer, ensuring his silence. Whatever Tillman's shortcomings, lack of loyalty was not amongst them.

'How you feeling?' said Tillman, breaking the stillness of the night as he stormed from the building, his footsteps sending gravel into the air.

'Fine,' said Lambert, opening the passenger seat.

'We don't need to talk about this any further, do we?'

Lambert grinned. 'No.'

'Tired?'

'No.'

'Good, because something came in when you were having your rest.'

# Chapter Three

An hour later they arrived at a gated community in Chislehurst. Lambert spotted the thick plume of black smoke about a mile away. It took him back to earlier that year when he'd worked on the Watcher case which had involved an explosion at a mansion in Hampstead, North London. It had taken the lives of over thirty party guests, including two serving police officers. He glanced at Tillman, who'd been present at the scene. He knew they were both thinking about Lambert's former partner DS Matilda Kennedy.

'When did you last see her?' asked Lambert.

Tillman's hands tightened on the steering wheel. 'Yesterday,' he said, his tone suggesting the conversation was ended.

Matilda had been undercover at the time of the explosion and suffered serious injuries, including severe burns to the left side of her face. At one point it seemed likely she would lose the use of her left eye, but eventually her vision had returned. She and Tillman were lovers, and Tillman had been ever-present during her convalescence. As far as Lambert was aware, they were still together, though Tillman tended not to share such information with him.

Tillman rounded the corner and the destination came into view. It was a detached property, half the size of the house in Hampstead. Flames were still devouring what was left of the brickwork. Fire crews busied away, spraying jets into the centre of the inferno.

Tillman pulled up and they both showed their ID to a uniformed officer guarding the perimeter tape. 'Who's in charge?' said Tillman.

'DS Croft is the senior officer,' said the uniform, pointing to a woman who was talking to one of the fire officers.

'Chief Superintendent Tillman, DCI Lambert,' said Tillman, approaching Croft as the fire chief walked off.

'Sir?' said Croft, confused.

'You should have been informed, Sergeant,' said Tillman. 'We've been called in on this one. DCI Lambert will be the SIO on this case.'

Lambert raised his eyebrows, confused as to why he was being assigned an arson case. He remained silent, studying the DS, who was caught between confusion and outrage that her position at the scene was about to be hijacked.

'Who is "we"?' Croft demanded, her words laced with insolence.

'NCA,' said Lambert.

Croft shrugged her shoulders, as if the presence of the National Crime Agency at what looked a routine arson case in Chislehurst was expected.

'Lambert, I'll leave this with you,' said Tillman.

Lambert nodded, as Tillman departed back to his car without a further word.

'I'm going to discuss this with my boss,' said Croft, her phone already to her ear.

Lambert edged nearer the building. The fire still raged, absorbing the jets of water being fired into its heart, its structure all but destroyed. The heat made Lambert's skin prickle. He scratched his left thigh, where he'd suffered second degree burns at the Hampstead property.

'Apparently you're in charge,' said Croft, returning.

'It's as much a surprise to me as to you,' said Lambert. He held out his hand. 'Michael Lambert.'

'Gemma Croft.'

Croft was a short, stocky woman, close in age to Lambert. He understood her objection to his presence. 'What can you tell me, Croft?' he asked.

'We received a number of reports of a large explosion in this area, ninety minutes ago, followed by a report of a fire. The fire service reached the scene quickly and managed to rescue one inhabitant, a three-year-old girl, from the first storey.'

Lambert hid his surprise. 'Where is she?'

'She's been taken to the local hospital.'

'Her parents?'

'We can only presume they're inside. There was no sign upstairs when they got the girl out, and the fire service have been unable to enter the building since. Both their mobiles go straight to answerphone.'

Lambert rubbed his lower face. He tried not to think about the three-year-old girl at the hospital. 'Names of the parents?'

'Caroline and Marcus Jardine.'

Lambert tried to recall why the names sounded familiar.

Croft rescued him. 'Has your boss told you nothing? Caroline Jardine is an officer,' she said.

Lambert nodded. 'Shit. She's in the Met?'

'DI Caroline Jardine, sir. She works out of Hackney.'

'Right,' said Lambert, understanding why he'd been assigned to the case. Jardine's involvement would propel the case into the media spotlight, and Tillman's department would have been requested to work on the case. 'Marcus Jardine?' asked Lambert.

'Something big in the city, one of the German banks.'

'They're married?'

'Four years, though Caroline was married before. Connor Linklater, head teacher at a local comp. She'd only been divorced a year before she remarried.'

'You've done your homework,' said Lambert.

'Kind of. Common knowledge in this manor. Linklater and Caroline didn't have an ideal marriage. We were called in on more than one case for domestic disturbance.'

'Ever charged?'

'I'll check, but from memory he was strongly advised to behave, and it was kept low-key, if you know what I mean.'

Lambert knew only too well. He turned to look at the building. The fire was subsiding. The fire chief walked over to him, removing his helmet. 'Lambert?' he asked.

Lambert nodded.

'Chapman. I understand you're in charge now?' he asked, exchanging the briefest of glances with Croft.

Lambert nodded. 'What can you tell me?'

'That little girl was lucky, for one. Seconds after we took her out the building, the fire took the whole top floor. I need confirmation, but I would say there was a detonation when we were inside.'

'A detonation? So not an accident?'

Chapman laughed, lines of grime breaking across his face. 'Unless these people had a bunker of explosives in their house, then I can't see this being accidental. I'm sending my teams in now, we should have a better picture for you soon.'

'Stupid question, but was there any sign of the parents?'

Chapman shook his head. 'By the time we entered, the downstairs was an inferno. We only went upstairs because we saw a light in the window. We checked the other upstairs rooms but no sign. If they were in there, then they were downstairs.'

'Will I be working on this?' asked Croft, as Chapman walked off.

'You were first on the scene, so as long as your gaffer agrees, you can be part of the team. Can you set up an incident room at your station?'

'Can do.'

'I need to get some of my team down here. Not going to be an issue?'

'No,' said Croft.

Lambert called the office and spoke to the newest member of the team, Detective Sergeant Joel Bickland. Bickland had joined the team following the Watcher case and Matilda Kennedy's long-term absence. He was an experienced officer, seconded in from another department of the NCA. Lambert instructed him to get to the scene, and to select two others to work on the case.

'What we looking at?' asked Bickland, who had a faded West Country accent.

'Let's plan for the worse. The three-year-old was rescued from a bedroom. It's likely one or both of her parents were at the scene, unless they have a nanny.'

'Be there in thirty,' said Bickland, hanging up.

'Here you go, sir,' said Croft, handing Lambert a paper beaker filled with oily black liquid.

'Thank you,' said Lambert. 'I think.' He sipped the drink, surprised by the heat and richness of the coffee.

The flames were extinguished. The aroma reminded Lambert of bonfires from his childhood. Despite the devastation caused to the building, the smell comforted him. After a time, a team of fire officers, led by Chapman, entered the building, each wearing breathing apparatus.

'What can you tell me about the fire?' Lambert asked Croft.

'It was in full swing by the time we arrived,' said Croft, standing next to him staring at the house. 'That said, I don't know...'

'What is it?' said Lambert.

'I'll be interested to see what the fire investigator comes back with. It sounded to me as if there were at least two or three separate explosions, like Chapman suggested.'

Lambert shook his head, dragging his stare away from the house. 'Witnesses?' he asked Croft.

'We've gone door to door and we're working on a list of comings and goings from the guard desk. Nothing out of the ordinary yet.'

Lambert scrunched up the paper cup and dropped it to the ground, frustrated by the wait. All he had was a destroyed building and a rescued child. If the fire team ruled out arson, which seemed unlikely, then he could leave the case in Croft's hands.

The fire chief, Chapman, left the property as if he'd been listening to Lambert's thoughts. He approached, removing his breathing gear. 'You'll need to get your crime scene guys in here, and a fire investigator if you have one on your team,' he said.

'Bodies?' asked Lambert.

'Two. Must have got caught inside. They were in the middle of the room, arms wrapped around one another. They've fused together. Horrific.'

'Can you confirm arson?'

Chapman nodded. 'We've found two incendiary devices on the first floor. This was fire was set deliberately by someone who knew what they were doing.'

# Chapter Four

Fire officers secured the interior of the house like prison guards. Lambert stood at the entrance of what once was the living room, as the Scene of Crime Officers inspected the room. Dressed in his own white SOCO uniform, a mask strapped across his face, he surveyed the ruins of the house. Chapman had told him the upper floors – where the child was rescued – were off bounds and unsafe. The SOCOs worked as if oblivious to the literal danger only metres above their heads.

A layer of soot clung to the walls and the floors. In the hallway, wallpaper had blistered and fallen from the walls. The air was laced with smoke. Even with his protective suit and mask, Lambert felt its intrusion. It clung to the exposed flesh on his face, and seeped through his pores. The murkiness of the fumes shrunk the interior. The walls felt squeezed together, unstable and threatening. The SOCOs battled for space in the living room, as the pathologist examined the two melted humans, fused not only to one another but also to the remains of the sofa.

'We found another incendiary device upstairs, undetonated,' said Chapman, tapping Lambert on the shoulder.

Lambert nodded to the front door, following Chapman into the coldness of the December morning. He ripped the mask from his face, welcoming the blast of cold air onto his skin. 'So that's three undetonated? Bit of overkill?'

Chapman removed his helmet, exposing a completely hairless skull which looked polished to a shine. 'You could say that. The house would have still gone up without them. We need to take them in but from what I've seen they were on timers. That would account for the reports of separate detonations.'

Croft returned with Bickland, the female detective dwarfed by her companion. Lambert updated them on Chapman's feedback.

'Jesus Christ,' said Bickland, in his West Country slur.

'Looks like he wanted to make sure the whole house was destroyed. Maybe something was worth destroying but our arsonist friend wasn't sure where it was located,' said Croft.

Chapman rubbed his skull, decorating it with a line of soot. 'Maybe. Personally, I think he was showing off. Why else would he have detonated them at different times? You ever heard of John Orr?'

'Orr?' said Lambert.

'Bit of an arsonist's hero. Ex-fire chief, like me,' he said, with a mirthless chuckle. 'I was only reminded of him because of the nature of the devices. Orr liked to start fires with incendiaries on timers. He used to wrap matches in paper, and secure them with a rubber band. He would then light a cigarette and when it burnt down it would set off the matches. The undetonated device we found upstairs has a similar set up, but is missing the cigarette. This guy has used an electrical device to spark the matches instead, but has forgot to set the timer on this one.'

'You think it was some sort of copycat?' said Lambert.

'That's your job, but if it wasn't a copycat it was certainly a tip of the cap – a tribute.'

'A tribute?' said Bickland, face contorted in disgust. 'He murdered two parents and almost killed that little child.'

Chapman glared at the detective sergeant. 'Something you're going to find out: these people don't care about anything but the flames,' he said, placing his helmet back on and heading towards the house.

Bickland spat on the ground. 'Sounds as if he almost admires him.'

'Charming,' said Croft, looking away.

A breeze had picked up and the stifled confines of the crumbling house no longer seemed so unappealing to Lambert. He folded his arms, jogging on the spot. A thought lingered just out of reach. It had been bothering him ever since Croft told him about the little girl being rescued. 'You two set up an incident room and notify Jardine's ex-husband before the press contact him. Suggest he makes an appearance at the station as soon as possible. Remember that nothing is confirmed yet,' said Lambert, pulling his mask back on and following Chapman inside.

It was probably a reaction to leaving the clear freshness of the air outside, but the smoke seemed thicker than before. The fire team guarding the stairs were blurred images, the details of their faces smudged out by the thickness of the fumes. Lambert was reminded of a scuba diving course he'd taken many years ago on holiday with his estranged wife, Sophie. The unreality beneath the surface was akin to the smoke-filled world he waded through now. Even the SOCOs and fire teams were quiet, echoing the quiet of the deep waters.

Lambert stood once again at the crumbling entrance of the living room. The pathologist was packing up. Lambert stared at the image of the merged couple, imagining what their final moments had been like, the desperate struggle against the heat, the terrible realisation that they would be burned alive. It was then he realised what had been bothering him.

Although Lambert no longer had a child, in his mind he would always be a father. He would never call himself a particularly brave man, but one thing was certain. If his daughter had been in danger, he would have done anything to protect her. He couldn't imagine sitting on a sofa, waiting for flames to devour him when there was the slightest chance that his daughter could have been saved. He would have walked through fire to have saved Chloe, and he hadn't met many parents who wouldn't do the same for their children.

The pathologist packed up her case and walked over to Lambert. 'We haven't been introduced – Lindsey Harrington.'

'DCI Lambert. What can you tell me?'

Harrington pulled off her SOCO hood, revealing a short, trendy haircut which in the smoke-filled dimness made her look younger. 'I think they had the hots for each other,' she said, deadpan. She held Lambert's gaze, not smiling, waiting for an acknowledgement.

'That's the best you've got?' said Lambert, returning the stare.

Harrington remained stony-faced for a few seconds before breaking into a smile. 'Tough crowd. I need some air. Follow me out?'

A crowd had gathered outside the property, cordoned off by police tape. 'Going to be a big one,' said Lambert to the young pathologist, who had just lit up a cigarette. She offered him one, which he declined.

'Might be bigger than you think,' said Harrington. She dragged hard on the cigarette, a number of fine lines appearing at the corner of the eyes.

'Do I want to hear this?'

Harrington shrugged. 'Probably best. Might help with your investigations.' She smiled again, holding his gaze for an uncomfortable period.

'Let me guess,' said Lambert, thinking again about the bodies on the sofa. 'They were dead before the fire started.'

Harrington flicked her cigarette to the ground, maintaining eye contact. 'Who told you?' she said, still deadpan.

Lambert was enjoying the woman's dry sense of humour, the way she tried to test him with her hard stares, but wondered if it became wearisome after a while. 'A guess,' he said, holding up his hands. 'If it was me, I would have run through the flames. Couldn't have been any worse than waiting for them to take hold.'

Harrington lit another cigarette, exhaling the smoke in Lambert's direction, staring at him as she considered this particular wisdom. 'I guess you're right. Not much of a choice though. Can you tell me how they died, Derren?'

'Derren?' said Lambert.

'You know, Derren Brown, that crazy mind reader. Ah...' said Harrington, realising Lambert had been teasing her.

Lambert started laughing, pleased to have got one over on her. 'My powers do not extend that far,' he said.

'Blunt trauma to the back of the head, both victims,' said Harrington, failing to suppress her smile. 'We'll know more later obviously – there was a lot of damaged tissue, as you can imagine – but I'd say each skull took five or six big hits. Hammer, if I had to guess.'

'Time of death?'

'I need to get back to you on that.'

Lambert tried to picture the scene. Did the arsonist catch the pair unawares, breaking in and striking them on the skull before they could react? It would have required great speed. 'I'll be interested to know if the blows to the head were consistent,' he said.

'Same weapon, you mean?'

'Perhaps, or same force. Could you measure for that?'

'Possible. You're thinking there may have been more than one perp?'

'"Perp"? You watch too much TV, Harrington.'

'I like to think I'm on *CSI Miami*. Helps me get through the cold months.'

'What are the chances of you rushing through the post-mortem, Miami?'

Harrington flicked the second cigarette to the floor. 'Should be careful, I could start a fire,' she said.

Lambert raised his eyebrows.

'I like you, Lambert,' said Harrington, lighting her third cigarette, her tone playful, almost mocking. She took a long drag, the tip of the cigarette glowing red. She stared at him again, tilting her head like some Sixties fictional detective. 'So I'll make it my number one priority.'

# Chapter Five

After signing off with the rest of the SOCOs, Lambert headed towards his car. The majority of the crowd had dispersed, leaving just lingering journalists and a couple of passers-by. Lambert recognised one of the remaining faces, but did his best to ignore it. It was Mia Helmer, a senior editor at a national broadsheet. Lambert had come close to arresting her during the Watcher case. As he reached his car, Helmer shuffled away from the pack of reporters and made a beeline towards him.

Lambert ignored her, clicking the car open. He was about to get in when she called out to him. 'DCI Lambert,' she said, almost under her breath, lest she attract the attention of the other reporters.

He sighed, resting his arms on the freezing metal of his car's rooftop. 'Mia Helmer,' he said, as she approached. 'I didn't realise you ever left that gigantic desk of yours,' he said, recalling the glass monstrosity which filled her office.

'It is a tad unusual, but then these are unusual circumstances. Why else would you be here?' Helmer was a slight woman, in her late twenties. Heavily made up, her hair was dragged back into a bun stretching the lineless skin of her face.

'You've not found a replacement for Eustace, then?' Eustace Sackville had been the newspaper's head crime reporter until his wife was murdered by the Watcher.

'No one I'd trust with something like this.'

'Like this?'

'Come on, Lambert. Your press office aren't confirming anything, but we know bodies were found in there. We know it wasn't an accident, either. A senior policewoman and a leading figure in investment banking, burnt to a crisp in their home? Their child being rescued at the last minute? Suspected arson? This could be the story of the year.'

'Slow down, Mia, you're getting way ahead of yourself there,' said Lambert.

'So you're denying Caroline Jardine has just burnt to death in her house?' Helmer stared at him in a similar way to the pathologist, Harrington. Where Harrington's eyes had been full of mischief, Helmer's were cold and lifeless.

'I'm not giving you anything, Mia. Even if I had anything to declare, you'd be the last to know.'

'You're confirming arson, though?'

'Goodbye, Mia,' said Lambert, climbing into his car and shutting the door.

–

He was surprised to find Chief Superintendent Tillman waiting for him at Chislehurst station. 'Thought you'd signed off?' he said to his superior.

'Do we have positive ID yet?' said Tillman, ignoring him. Tillman had changed his clothes since he'd left the scene that morning. The navy pinstripe suit accentuated his considerable size. He played at the tie which was pulled tight against his throat, and wiped a bead of sweat from his forehead.

'Working on it. The fire did some damage.' Lambert pointed to an empty conference room. 'Something you should know, sir.'

Inside, Lambert relayed the information about the attack on the victims prior to the fire.

Tillman sat down, groaning as he fell into the seat. 'I'm not sure if that's worse or better. Better for them, I suppose,' said Tillman. 'He must have known we'd find the bodies. As for that little girl...'

'Possibly he didn't know she was there. Although probably he knew and didn't care.'

Tillman shook his head, loosening his tie. 'Where are we on the post-mortems?'

'The pathologist, Harrington, is going to make it her number one priority, whatever that means,' said Lambert.

'So what now?'

'We have Jardine's ex-husband, Connor Linklater, paying us a visit.'

'When?'

'Within the hour, I hope.'

Tillman paused, shifted from one foot to the other. 'I need you back at HQ for two pm. You have an appointment.'

'You going to give me any more details?'

'Caroline Jardine's boss will be there. And his boss, and some others.'

'Best suit?' said Lambert. With Caroline Jardine being a fellow officer, it was obvious the hierarchy would get involved.

'Your very best,' said Tillman.

Lambert spent the time waiting for Linklater in the incident room, researching Caroline Jardine online. At the age of thirty-eight, Jardine was a well-respected officer in her team. The woman had clearly been going places and Lambert's initial impression was that her death would be met with deep regret across the force. Her most recent investigation had been a long-term case on drug trafficking. Her direct superior was DCI William Barnes. Tillman had mentioned that Barnes would be present at his meeting back at the NCA headquarters later that day.

DS Croft knocked on the glass door of the room, and snuck her head into the opening. 'Sir, Connor Linklater has arrived. We've put him in interview room three. He has his brief with him.'

'Does he now?' said Lambert, shutting his laptop. 'He's aware the interview is voluntary?'

'Of course, sir.'

Although attending the station with a solicitor in tow was far from an admission of guilt, it was a strong indication of how Linklater was treating the situation. His ex-wife had been burnt to death, her child barely surviving, and the man's first thought was to protect himself. It was possible to read too much into the situation, but to Lambert the presence of the solicitor had turned the situation from a general conversation into a confrontation. 'I'll be down now,' he said.

Croft hesitated by the door. Lambert knew what she was waiting for but was interested to see how she phrased it. 'How do you want to do this?' she asked, as casually as possible.

'Where's Bickland?'

'Waiting downstairs.'

'I'll tell you what, Croft. You run the interview with Linklater. Find out where he was last night, what his relationship with his ex-wife was like. I'll keep quiet until needed.'

Croft tried to hide her surprise, but Lambert noticed the subtle widening of her eyes. 'Sir,' she replied, exiting before Lambert had the chance to change his mind.

Lambert spoke to Bickland outside the interview room. 'I want you to watch the interview on camera, Bickland. Analyze Linklater's responses and let me know if there is anything we miss,' he said. If the DS took it badly, he hid it well.

The solicitor stood as Lambert entered the room, introducing his client. Linklater rose to his feet and shook hands with the officers, his face emotionless.

'Thank you for taking the time to come and see us, Mr Linklater,' said Lambert. 'This is DS Croft.'

Linklater nodded as they all sat. Croft placed her case file in front of her and went through the formalities of explaining Linklater's rights and informing the man that the session would be taped. Linklater remained passive throughout, Lambert unable to ascertain the man's mental state from the vague visual clues he offered.

'As you know, we believe the bodies of Caroline Jardine and her husband were found in their house this morning. Their deaths are being treated as suspicious.'

'Believe?' asked Linklater's solicitor.

'Subject to post-mortem identification,' said Lambert.

'For the record, please could you confirm your relationship with Mrs Jardine?' asked Croft.

'She was my ex-wife,' said Linklater, not hesitating with the past tense.

Croft played with the papers on the desk. She pinched her nose, hesitating, making Linklater wait. 'When were you divorced?' she asked, her voice light as if she was making a casual enquiry.

'Four years ago.'

Croft maintained her tone. 'The grounds for divorce?'

Linklater's solicitor sighed. 'Is this really necessary? Surely you already have that information.'

Croft shot the man a look which suggested the question was entirely necessary and the solicitor nodded to his client.

'Divorce by mutual consent.'

'Official grounds, divorce by mutual consent,' said Croft, writing in her notebook before looking up at Linklater. 'However, my records show, Mr Linklater, that we were called out on three separate occasions for domestic disturbance complaints.'

Lambert admired Croft's style. She had disarmed the man within minutes of the interview commencing.

Linklater didn't share such admiration. 'What the hell is this?' he said, getting to his feet.

'Sit down, Mr Linklater,' said Lambert.

'May I remind you, officers, that Mr Linklater has taken the trouble to make his way to the station as soon as he was asked, to offer his assistance. He is here voluntarily, and has just had some terrible news.'

'Taken the trouble,' muttered Lambert under his breath. His ex-wife has burnt to death and he takes the trouble to make an appearance. Lambert ignored the solicitor, as Croft defused the situation.

'I apologise if my question is insensitive, Mr Linklater, but we are investigating a potential murder, and there is a prior history of domestic disturbance,' she said, pausing again, pinching her nose, focusing on Linklater's solicitor. 'We can, of course, make this more official but I'm sure you don't want to go down that route.'

The solicitor stared back at Croft, trying and failing to take control of the situation. 'Sit down, Connor,' he said to Linklater.

Linklater shook his head, heat spreading across his face. 'This is ridiculous. Caroline and I used to argue, yes. But that was it. We couldn't live together. Now we don't. We have resolved our differences.'

Croft picked up her papers and leant towards Linklater. 'On one occasion, our officers had to separate a fight at your house. The same house which has now burnt down.'

Lambert sensed Linklater's frustration. His face was flooded with colour, his breathing rapid. He stared at Croft with unmasked hostility.

'That's quite enough, officer,' said Linklater's solicitor, his face mirroring the reddening shade of his client's. 'Mr Linklater has never received anything as much as a caution in his lifetime. It is frankly outrageous to make these unfounded accusations.' The solicitor made a big show of shaking his head. 'Really, DS Croft, I'm surprised at you. This meeting is over unless you want to charge my client with anything.'

Croft turned her attention to Linklater. 'Anything you want to tell us about this?' she said.

Linklater's early antagonism had vanished. 'We used to fight all the time, it was that sort of relationship, and things occasionally got out of hand,' he said, his voice thin and weak. 'But we both gave as good as we got. We had a combative relationship but it wasn't an abusive one.'

'Where were you yesterday evening between the hours of nine pm and four am?' asked Lambert.

'Oh, come on,' said the solicitor.

'Answer the question,' said Lambert.

'I was at home, watching television until about eleven pm, then in bed,' said Linklater.

'You live alone?' said Croft.

'Yes.'

'So no one can corroborate your whereabouts?'

'No, but…' Linklater's face contorted into a patchwork of wrinkles. 'You can't think I had anything to do with her murder? She was my wife.'

'Ex-wife,' said Lambert.

'She was once my wife. I would never hurt her.'

Croft juggled the papers on her desk once more. Lambert was impressed by the pacing of the interview, the way Croft was asking the bare minimum, allowing Linklater to fill in the spaces. 'You and Mrs Jardine didn't have children?' she asked.

'No.'

'How did you feel when she had Teresa?'

Linklater sighed, an air of belligerence returning. 'It meant nothing to me, why would it?'

'She was your ex-wife. She'd had a child with another man. You wouldn't be human if that didn't affect you in some way.'

'Maybe I'm not human then,' said Linklater, sounding like a child arguing in a playground.

'Did you and Mrs Jardine ever try for children?' asked Croft.

'DS Croft, this is sounding more and more like an interrogation,' said the solicitor. 'May I remind you, once again, that my client is here voluntarily?'

Croft held her hands up. 'Of course, my apologies. Before you go, Mr Linklater, can you think of anyone who would want to hurt Ms Jardine in any way?'

'You think she was deliberately targeted?' said Linklater.

'We can't rule anything out at the moment.'

'I don't know anything about that. Her husband, on the other hand – I can imagine quite a few people wanted him dead.'

–

Croft escorted Linklater and his solicitor out of the station whilst Lambert made his way to the video room to see Bickland. 'What do we know about Marcus Jardine?' he said, before Bickland had opened his mouth.

'Not much more than we did this morning. Our focus has been on DI Jardine,' said Bickland.

'Drop everything and work on that. Usual stuff. Enemies. Who wanted him dead.'

'He was a banker, everyone wanted him dead,' said Bickland.

'Go to his place of work first, start with his most senior colleagues and work your way down.'

'Great. Fun day at the bank,' said Bickland, full of sarcasm as he left the room.

Another man entered. Better dressed than Bickland, the man held himself with a confidence that suggested he was a high-ranking officer. 'Lambert?' said the man, confirming Lambert's theory. Only someone on or above Lambert's pay scale would call him by his surname.

'You have me at a disadvantage,' said Lambert.

The man rubbed his right hand across his face before offering it to Lambert. 'DCI Thomas Mills, pleased to meet you.'

Lambert placed Mills' accent as Mancunian. From his tone, it was clear that his fellow DCI was anything but pleased to see him. 'You're Croft's governor?' asked Lambert.

'Yep.'

'I was told you'd signed off on her working on this case?' Lambert doubted this was what was bothering the man, but he wanted to avert any potential confrontation as early as possible.

Mills turned towards him, his hand rubbing his face once more. 'You know it has nothing to do with that. I don't care about losing Croft.'

Lambert took a deep breath. 'I realise this isn't an ideal situation, Mills; the decision was made above both of us.' Lambert understood his colleague's frustration. The Jardine case was potentially the case of a lifetime, a high profile murder which would have national press coverage. The murder had taken place on Mills' patch, and here was Lambert strolling in from the NCA, taking everything over. If the roles had been reversed, he would have probably been less cordial than his fellow officer.

Mills nodded his head and rubbed his face. Lambert sighed, and gave him one more chance. 'I don't want to patronise you, Mills. I've been in your position before and it's bloody annoying. But the truth is, I need your cooperation on this. I'm happy to call it a joint operation and to work fully with your team. Technically I'll still be SIO, that's not going to change, but I'm happy to share the credit equally with you and your team.' It was the most he could offer.

'That's big of you,' said Mills, his northern accent guttural.

Lambert turned his palms up. 'I don't want to sound like a wanker, Mills, but it's take it or leave it. I would rather do this with your support, but I will work without you if I have to.'

It was Mills' turn to sigh. 'I'll supply you a few more bodies,' he said, meeting Lambert's gaze.

Lambert offered his hand, which Mills accepted. 'Persistent, isn't she?' said Lambert.

'Croft? You could say that,' said Mills, a grimace forming on his face, replaced swiftly by a smile.

# Chapter Six

Tillman was nowhere to be found by the time Lambert reached HQ. It had taken Lambert two hours to drive from Chislehurst. He'd spent the time stuck in traffic, the image of Teresa Jardine lost and scared in her room, calling for help as the heat crept towards her, replaying over and over in his head. Would she have had any idea what danger she was in?

Lambert went to his desk and uploaded the System. The System was an amalgamation of various police databases, with access to the majority of social media back ends. The legality of the System was clouded – to say the least – and only members of Tillman's section currently had access to it. Once in, he began a search on recent arson attacks in Greater London. As he searched the incidents, which were numerous, his mind kept wandering: back to Teresa, and then on to his own daughter, Chloe. Chloe had died during a road accident – Lambert had been driving. Although he'd been told she'd died instantly, it had always troubled him that she'd suffered; that her final moments had been all alone, pleading for his help whilst he ignored her.

'You made it, then,' said Tillman, waking him from his reverie.

'I made it?' said Lambert, the full weight of the day's events hitting him.

Tillman fidgeted with his tie. 'They've arrived. Waiting in the conference room.'

Lambert wiped his eyes. 'Who have arrived, Glenn?'

'Everyone. Follow me.'

—

No one stood as Lambert followed Tillman into the conference room. Lambert recognised two of the four men in the room: the Chief Constable, Alexander Mitchell, and the Assistant Chief Constable Thomas Daly. One of the others – a tall, sullen-looking man – he presumed was DCI Barnes, Caroline Jardine's boss. A fourth man sat at the head of the table. Round of face, he had a full head of silver-grey hair. Lambert recognised the face but couldn't place him. 'DCI Lambert, please take a seat,' said the man, staring straight ahead.

Lambert took a seat towards the centre, Tillman sitting next to him.

'My name is John Weaver,' said the silver-haired man. 'I'm sure you're aware that I am the Minister of State for Policing, Fire and Criminal Justice.' Weaver paused, gauging Lambert's response. It was all Lambert could do not to shrug his shoulders.

'Anyway,' continued Weaver, pursing his lips. 'I believe you know the Chief and Assistant Chief Constable.'

Lambert nodded to the two senior officers. 'Sir. Sir.'

'This is DCI William Barnes,' said Weaver, pointing to the other man in the room, who nodded. 'Obviously, we are to discuss the Jardine case. As you can imagine, the case is highly sensitive.'

'Of course,' said Lambert.

Weaver pursed his lips once more as if he had something stuck between his teeth. 'Terrible business, naturally. As you can appreciate, the death of such a prominent member of the police force, in such a horrendous manner, can have many repercussions.'

'Such as?' said Lambert, turning to Tillman, who was uncharacteristically silent.

'Imagine the panic when word spreads that a high-ranking officer was murdered in her own house. "If it can happen to DI Caroline Jardine, then surely it could happen to anyone," will be the general consensus.'

'It is of concern, but I'm not sure it would cause an out-and-out panic?'

'Semantics, DCI Lambert.' Weaver paused, exchanging looks with the Chief and Assistant Chief. 'I was emailed this earlier,' he said, pushing some paper towards Lambert. 'I think you know the journalist,' said Weaver, as Lambert saw Mia Helmer's name.

The newspaper had the following day's date on it. The headline read, 'Senior Policewoman Dead in Arson Attack.'

'I see,' said Lambert.

'Do read further,' said Weaver.

Lambert saw his name in the text of the article. At one point he was referred to as the man who'd solved the Soul-jacker and Watcher serial killer cases. Later, he was referred to as being "constantly at odds" with his superiors. His relationship with the journalist had been destroyed during the Watcher case. He'd come close to arresting her when he'd found her snooping at a victim's house, and following his dismissal of her earlier that day it seemed clear that she was not the forgiving sort.

Lambert pushed the papers back towards the MP. 'I don't see the problem, I'm afraid.'

Weaver's face contorted as if in shock. 'Don't you, DCI Lambert?' he said, looking at the two most senior officers in the room for reassurance.

The Assistant Chief, Daly, leant forward. 'I think what Mr Weaver is getting at is that this is a bit of a PR disaster for the government,' he said.

'Not quite,' interjected Weaver, his tone borderline angry. 'What I'm saying is that sometimes it is worth keeping on the right side of the press. Miss Helmer's paper does have a certain impact and it can affect public confidence, rightly so, when they think a senior police officer can be a victim of such an atrocity.'

'Can you talk to her, Lambert?' asked the Assistant Chief.

Lambert held his tongue.

'Good, good,' said Weaver, taking Lambert's silence as an agreement. 'We realise this is a very awkward situation. The three of us,' said Weaver – again looking at the Chief and Assistant Chief – 'feel it's best that we find those responsible as quickly as possible. Put the public's mind at rest, as it were.'

Even the Chief Constable frowned at this last statement.

Lambert was staggered that he'd been called in to hear such platitudes. He had no intention of speaking to Helmer, but to be told he should solve the case as quickly as possible was offensive. He wanted to ask what the hell else Weaver thought he would be doing, but again held his tongue. 'I presume there is some sort of reporting structure you want me to adhere to,' he said, turning his attention to the Chief Constable.

It was the Assistant Chief, Daly, who answered. 'Yes, everything must go directly through me, as well as through Chief Superintendent Tillman.'

Lambert shook his head. 'That is practically the process anyway. You would have access to everything anyway, sir,' he said to Daly.

'I mean everything, Lambert. You were assigned this role because of your expertise, but we can't miss anything on this. Every step you make must be accounted for. *Every* step. Do I make myself clear?' Weaver pursed his lips again as they waited for Lambert to answer.

Lambert made eye contact with each man in the room, desperate to leave and to find who was responsible for making an orphan of Teresa Jardine. He understood what he was being told. He was trusted, but only so far. He sighed, the sound louder than necessary. 'I understand,' he said, and walked out of the room.

—

'Would you like to tell me what the hell that was about?' he asked Tillman, back in the Chief Superintendent's office.

'Ignore it,' said Tillman, tearing his tie off and throwing it onto his desk. 'You know they are simply protecting their own interests.'

'Find those responsible as quickly as possible? What do they think I planned to do?'

'Ignore it,' said Tillman, more forcefully this time. 'Tell me where we're at.'

Lambert told him about the interview with Linklater. 'Autopsies are going to be first thing tomorrow.'

'The arsonist is responsible for the murder?'

'It would seem likely. It's possible there was more than one person. We lifted a number of fingerprints, but none from the remains of the incendiary devices.'

Tillman leant against the wall as Lambert took a seat. Sweat dripped from his forehead, which he wiped away with an angry swipe of his hand. 'You think the killer was working alone?'

'No inkling either way at the moment. Individual or not, it's a professional job. Getting in there in the first place would not have been easy, then the actual killing, followed by the explosions. Whoever it was must have planned this for some time.'

Tillman grunted as he took a seat behind his desk. 'The child. Oversight?'

Lambert had been considering that possibility ever since he'd set foot on the grounds. It was doubtful that the killer could have overlooked a sleeping child. Everything about the case so far suggested he was too professional. He must have known that there was a child. And that she was in the house. However, a true professional would have eliminated the child whatever her age. 'Either the killer has a conscience,' he said 'or he was convinced that the child would be unable to survive the explosions.'

'I would imagine the latter.'

'Maybe.'

Tillman drummed his fingers on the desk, rubbing his chin with his other hand. 'CCTV?'

'We're going through all traffic in the twenty-four hours preceding the incident and naturally anything during the incident itself. There is gated security, so if the killer was using a vehicle it should show up.'

'How easily could he have gained access without a vehicle?'

'Not that easily, but someone with experience wouldn't have had any trouble.'

'OK, get on top of that. That must be a priority,' said Tillman, drumming his fingers again.

'Something you want to tell me, sir?' said Lambert, who couldn't remember the last time he'd seen his boss so agitated.

'What?' said Tillman, as if only half listening. 'No, why do you ask?'

'You're like a caged animal.'

'You know they're expecting an immediate result.'

Lambert glanced at Tillman in surprise. In all the years he'd known Tillman, Lambert had never heard the man show any consideration for his superiors' desires.

'And that changes something?'

'No. Just get the job done.'

Lambert nodded, and rocked in his chair. 'You know what's likely to happen next?'

'I know only too well. Let's make sure we catch him before he starts getting a taste for it.'

—

Lambert was about to get into the lift when DCI Barnes stopped him. 'I thought we should touch base,' said Barnes.

Lambert couldn't remember coming across him before. He towered over Lambert. Straight-backed, Barnes stood with a rigid awkwardness, as if his body had outgrown him.

'Of course,' said Lambert. 'There's a conference room through here.'

They walked side by side through the open plan office, neither speaking. 'Through here,' said Lambert, opening the door.

'Get you anything?' said Lambert, taking a seat. The conference room looked out on the Thames, which had a layer of fog hovering above it.

'You're OK,' said Barnes. 'Nice place you got here.'

'It's got its perks. You're out of Hackney, right?'

'Yes, not quite the same views.'

'How are your team taking things with Caroline? Stupid question, I know.'

Barnes frowned. 'Yeah, not great. Everyone is in shock, as you can imagine.' He paused. 'Listen, I wanted to say that I had nothing to do with that little get-together back there. I have no idea why that Weaver guy has stuck his nose in.'

'Don't sweat it. Main thing is we find out who's responsible for that fire.'

Barnes nodded, frowning again. 'I've been told I can't get directly involved in the case but I wanted to offer any help I can. I can spare manpower – whether we go through the proper channels or not.'

'I appreciate that and I'll definitely keep that in mind. What can you tell me about DI Jardine?'

Barnes considered the question. He'd remained stoic ever since Lambert had first seen him in the room with Weaver and the two senior police officers, with the occasional glimpse of emotion when Caroline was mentioned. He was hard to read, but Lambert saw the inner strength in the man, could understand how he'd reached a senior position in the Met.

'DI Jardine was an exceptional officer, and I don't say that lightly. She had a steely determination which I've rarely seen before.'

'How did she get on with the rest of the team?'

'She was well respected, though she wasn't shy about confrontation. She was promoted ahead of some of her colleagues, so that brought with it the usual challenges, but she adjusted. You need only experience the atmosphere in the office to tell how much she'll be missed.' Barnes placed his hands on the conference table, tapping the index finger of his left hand three times before stopping himself.

'What was she working on?'

'She's been heading a case on organised crime in the Hackney area. Mainly out of the estates. We have people down there cracking skulls, as it were.'

'Any threats?'

'Nothing beyond the usual empty taunts. We've made a couple of arrests and we'll be talking to them as well.'

'Informants?'

'She had a couple on the books, some off it. We'll be speaking to them too, I can promise you that.'

Lambert sensed that Barnes was holding something back and wondered if his behaviour was a façade to protect his emotions. He was reminded of Tillman and Matilda. It wasn't unusual for officers to have affairs and Barnes' reticence implied there was more to his relationship with Jardine then he was letting on.

'If there's anything else you can think of,' said Lambert, getting to his feet.

Barnes got up, unfolding himself until he was standing in that rigid manner again. 'Good luck,' he said, shaking hands with Lambert. 'I can see myself out.'

# Chapter Seven

Lambert called Sarah as he made his way back to Chisle-hurst. He hadn't spoken to her since their awkward meeting the previous day at the restaurant, and he wanted to make contact before a lengthy silence developed between them. He hung up as he went through to her voicemail.

They'd been seeing less of each other lately, both preoccupied with their respective caseloads. Their living arrangements were still complicated. They lived in separate places, and though he hadn't admitted as much to Sarah, Lambert was grateful for the fact. He was used to living alone. Even during the last couple of years with his estranged wife, Sophie, he'd slept in a different room. He'd come to enjoy the solitude of his own company, and was unsure if he could adjust once more to the daily rhythm of a shared life.

His relationship with Sarah had developed in unusual circumstances. They'd shared the trauma of being kidnapped, and sometimes Lambert wondered if it was this experience which kept them together. He still enjoyed her company, thought about her in idle moments, but something had changed since she'd moved to London. He'd put it down to the first rush of infatuation fading, but more and more he was convinced their time together was close to an end.

As he edged through the rush hour traffic, it occurred to Lambert that the thought should have saddened him. He promised himself that he would broach the subject with Sarah at some point, for her benefit if nothing else.

He reached Chislehurst ninety minutes later. Croft and Bickland were in the incident room, both on the phone. Bickland hung up as Lambert took a seat at the desk next to him.

'We have a lead on the CCTV footage, though I'm not sure how strong it is,' said Bickland, turning his laptop so Lambert could see the screen. It showed the blurred image of a small, dark goods van entering the main gate. 'One-thirty am,' said Bickland.

'How did he gain entry?'

'The security system uses a sensor system. A device is fixed on the vehicle's windscreen which links with the main gate.'

'OK,' said Lambert, impatient for Bickland to get to the point.

'Only, the van's not registered.'

'No surprise there. Could the driver have swiped someone's sensor?'

'That's what I thought. I contacted the security firm. They have a register of all the coming and goings through the gate. List of number plates and times. Sounds like a great system,' said Bickland.

'But?'

'Nothing for the van entering and leaving. The gate is recorded as opening at one-thirty, and then again at three-ten when the van left, but the security firm have no idea how the van bypassed their system.'

'Did they give you their best idea?'

'The guy I talked to suggested the driver either had some master copy, or had manufactured some sort of device to bypass it.'

'So not a great system after all?'

Bickland shook his head. 'I spoke to one of our tech guys who looked into it. He said that overall it's pretty sound, but someone with strong technical knowledge could manufacture something.'

'Without access to the security firm's system?'

'Apparently so.'

'Great,' said Lambert.

'Next issue is the monitoring of the CCTV images,' said Croft, who had left her desk and stood behind Lambert, staring at Bickland's screen.

Lambert stifled a smile as Bickland glared at Croft. 'Yes,' he said, returning to the laptop and accessing another file which showed the van drive along the main road and disappear around the corner.

'Blind spot in the monitoring, one of many,' said Croft. 'We've pinpointed where we think the van would have parked and have interviewed the residents for sightings, but no joy.'

'Here,' said Bickland, pointing to the screen. 'We believe the suspect would have crossed this line,' he said, dragging his finger across the screen. 'A hundred yard blind spot from the road to the Jardine house. The house itself is not monitored, remarkably enough. Residents have the option but the family wanted their privacy. We think the suspect would have made his entrance through the back garden.

The back door was still intact and it looks as if the lock was picked.'

Lambert leant back in his chair. 'Someone knew the system top to bottom,' he said.

'Possibly someone who used to live there?' said Croft.

The thought had occurred to Lambert. Linklater, Caroline Jardine's ex-husband, was an obvious fit – and in Lambert's experience the obvious fit was usually the correct one. 'Do we have any close-ups on the van driver?' he asked.

Bickland grimaced. 'We do,' he said, showing Lambert a blurred image of a face covered by a balaclava.

'Shit.'

'Indeed,' said Bickland.

Lambert glanced over at the whiteboard where pictures of Jardine and her husband had been posted. A number of names were scrawled beneath the images, including Linklater's. 'Let's get Linklater in again. See if he still has access to the gate. Bickland, did you manage to get to Marcus Jardine's office?'

'I popped in. Not the most talkative lot. General consensus was that he was very hard-working and extremely good at his job. I've got some more of his colleagues to see but no one had a bad word to say about him.'

'Let's keep looking at him. See if there are any jealous ex-girlfriends on the scene. Extra-marital affairs, that sort of thing.'

Bickland nodded.

'Where's the girl?' asked Lambert.

'Teresa? She's with her grandparents on Caroline's side. A Family Liaison Officer is situated on site with them,' said Croft.

Lambert sighed. 'I'm going to need to speak to her first thing.'

'Sir,' said Croft.

'Right, don't work too late,' said Lambert, getting to his feet. 'Better to be fresh for tomorrow.'

Both officers stayed silent as he left the incident room.

–

Lambert was almost at the main entrance when the duty sergeant called over to him. 'DCI Lambert, someone here for you.'

Lambert walked over. 'We haven't been introduced,' he said to the man.

The sergeant raised his eyebrows a centimetre, a hint of humour in his eyes. 'Sergeant Carberry.' Carberry had the withered look of many in his position.

'How long have they been here?'

'Oh, about an hour and a half,' the sergeant told him.

'Carberry,' said Lambert, fixing the sergeant with a stare of his own. 'Any reason you waited until I was walking out the door before you decided to share this information?'

Carberry returned the stare with the same elevation of the eyebrows, the weary humour in the eyes. 'Must have slipped my mind. Room three. Lovely chap. DS Duggan.'

'Right,' said Lambert.

'You know Duggan?' asked Carberry, his words laced with distaste.

'I know him,' said Lambert with a sigh, as he made his way to the interview rooms.

Duggan was sitting with his back to the door. Lambert entered without knocking. 'What are you doing here, Duggan?'

'DCI Lambert,' said Duggan, turning to face him. 'Please take a seat.'

'No need, I won't be staying.'

Duggan ran his hand through his hair, sweeping it to the side. He worked for AC-Six, one of the Met's Anti-Corruption units. He'd been pestering Lambert on and off for the last six months. From what Lambert could ascertain, AC-Six were putting together a case against Tillman. 'We can do this somewhere else?' said Duggan.

'No. I realise this hasn't crossed your mind but you are a subordinate officer. I have the right...'

'Yes, yes, to be questioned by an officer at least one rank higher,' said Duggan, interrupting. 'You're not under caution, DCI Lambert, we're simply having a friendly chat. We can make it a bit more formal if you prefer.'

Lambert took a seat. 'Chat away.'

'I wanted to give you some friendly encouragement more than anything.' Despite the lateness of the hour, Duggan was dressed impeccably. His suit was creaseless, his tie pushed tight against the top button of his crisp shirt. Even his hair was immaculate, the brown mop styled to perfection. Only his right eye betrayed the look. It was half-closed, a legacy from a violent incident when Duggan had first joined the force.

'I've told you before, Duggan, I won't be testifying.'

Duggan ran his hand through his hair, a subconscious gesture which Lambert took to signify his nervousness. 'You may prove superfluous.'

'So why are you here?'

'Some things have come to light.'

Lambert sucked in a deep breath, exhausted from the day. 'I'm not playing games, Duggan. Tell me what you want or let me be.'

'Some new evidence has come to light. From the Watcher case.'

Lambert tensed. The climax to the Watcher case had been a catastrophe. Lambert had been with Tillman when they'd captured the man responsible. The Watcher had been fleeing the building, his body consumed by the explosion. Lambert knew what was coming.

Tillman had been in a relationship with Matilda. He still was, as far as Lambert could ascertain. Tillman had pulled a gun on the Watcher and only Lambert's intervention had prevented him from shooting the suspect dead. 'Tell me, Duggan, whilst we're both young.'

'We have two witnesses,' said Duggan, unable to disguise his satisfaction.

Two paramedics were present at the time Tillman had pulled the gun, but Lambert thought they had been occupied elsewhere. He didn't reply.

Duggan shuffled in his chair, his hand moving through his hair once more. 'Two witnesses who saw Tillman reach for his gun.'

Lambert nodded, trying to control his increasing heartbeat.

'Two witnesses who saw you spray Tillman with pepper spray before he had the chance to shoot.'

Lambert stared at Duggan, waiting until the officer broke eye contact. 'What is it you want, Duggan? Do you have any idea what we went through that night? Not just that night, but the whole wretched case?'

Duggan tilted his head. 'I appreciate it was a difficult case, DCI Lambert, but we're here to uphold the law. That law applies to all of us. No exceptions.'

It had to happen sooner or later, thought Lambert. Tillman's behaviour was always borderline when it came to his investigations. The Watcher case was not the only one where Lambert had seen him push the boundaries of what was acceptable. Despite this, Lambert was convinced Tillman was committed to the law. 'I'm afraid your witnesses are mistaken,' said Lambert.

Duggan shook his head. 'Why do you protect him? He has a complete disregard for his position.'

Lambert shrugged his shoulders. 'If there's nothing else, it's late.'

Duggan stood and smoothed out the crinkles in his suit. 'Failure to report is a crime as well, DCI Lambert. I would suggest you decide which side you're on.'

# Chapter Eight

Lambert was still brooding over Duggan's visit when he eventually reached his flat. Sarah hadn't called, and he considered pouring himself a drink, before deciding he needed to keep his mind clear. He opened his laptop instead and logged into the System.

Whether out of spite, or to prove a point, Lambert typed Duggan's name into the database. The Anti-Corruption cases were the few files not available to him, for obvious reasons, but Lambert was able to access Duggan's personnel file. He skimmed through the pages, not finding much of interest. Duggan had a solid educational background. He moved straight into CID after his probation, and had spent five years on various teams before moving to Anti-Corruption, where he'd spent the last four years.

Lambert flicked through some of the officer's cases prior to him joining AC. He often worked this way, accumulating what at first seemed to be useless information. He would examine case files over and over, searching for a word or visual clue which would unravel everything. Duggan's last case before joining AC made for gruesome reading. A man, recently divorced, had turned a gun on his ex-wife and eighteen-year-old son. He'd then attempted to commit suicide but had somehow failed, shooting off most of his jawbone but surviving the gun blast. Lambert knew some of the names on the case file, officers and support staff he'd worked with before. Out of curiosity, Lambert clicked on the file of the gunman, Ross Wiseman. The man was still alive, currently under supervision at Broadmoor Hospital. He'd undergone reconstructive surgery, but his face was grotesquely misshapen. Lambert tried to imagine Wiseman's life, having to relive what he'd done every time he looked in the mirror. Such incidents were usually the result of moments of uncontrollable rage, the archetypal crime of passion.

He clicked off and returned to Duggan's file, before saving it for later study. He called Sarah again, annoyed when it went to answerphone. He didn't sleep well at the best of times, even less so when working on an important case. He could survive with two to five hours sleep a night, but such sleep deprivation sooner or later resulted in a blackout. He slumped onto the sofa and switched on the television. Restless, he flicked though various channels, unable to concentrate for more than a few minutes on any one show.

Giving in, he brewed a pot of decaf coffee and returned to his laptop. Minimising Duggan's file, he searched for arson cases in the last six months. The Chislehurst case was already showing. Chapman, the fire chief, had entered a preliminary report and Lambert was surprised to see that DS Croft had already written up her notes from the day.

He scanned Chapman's entry first, gaining little additional information from their chat earlier in the day. Chapman was noncommittal, stating a need for further examination of the building. However, he alluded to five separate detonation sites, and repeated the similarities between the one incendiary device which didn't detonate, and those of the infamous arsonist, John Orr.

Lambert looked Orr up and discovered he had worked as an arson investigator in the USA. It was believed he'd been responsible for over two thousand fires before being discovered.

The recovered incendiary device found in Chislehurst was almost identical to the type favoured by Orr. It had contained a box of matches wrapped in paper, cotton and what appeared to be bedding, held together by an elastic band. Instead of a lit cigarette, the device had been connected to an electronic timer, which had not been set. Chapman was doubtful they would be able to discover if the other detonations – which were activated – had used the same incendiary device. The only hope of uncovering further details would be when the arson investigators examined the place tomorrow.

Lambert ran nationwide searches on arson cases, attempting to uncover similarities with John Orr's MO, but nothing promising appeared. The closest he found were a couple of home fires, where cigarettes were dropped onto bedding.

He read some more on Orr, fascinated by how the man had gone undiscovered for so long. At midnight he stopped reading. He considered calling Sarah but decided she would call when she was ready. Still fidgety, he lay on his bed hoping for a quick and easy sleep.

He must have dozed off at some point, as the next time he looked at his clock alarm it was three-thirty am. Knowing he wouldn't get back to sleep again, he showered and changed and headed to the one place where his restless mind could do some good. The crime scene.

# Chapter Nine

The security guard at the entrance to the estate took only a peripheral glance at Lambert's warrant card.

Lambert glared at the man, who looked to be in his early twenties. 'Were you working here last night?' he said.

'Nah, mate, agency,' said the guard.

'You're from the agency?'

'Yeah. Bloke from last night has had some sort of breakdown apparently.'

'Have you worked here before?' asked Lambert.

'Once, ages ago.'

'Out of interest, what security checks do they put you through to work here?

'The agency?'

Lambert stared hard at the guard, ascertaining if he was purposely being obstructive. 'Yes, what checks do the agency run on you?'

The guard stepped back a step. 'Work reference, DBS check. Why?'

Lambert nodded and drove off. Aside from the haphazardly placed cameras, the security in the gated community was worthless. Lambert wondered what premium residents paid for the illusion of security, and how many of the residents would be negotiating a reduction following last night's incidents. He made a mental note to check out the guard who was off sick.

He parked in the blind spot that Bickland had highlighted on the video earlier that day. Noting the static camera to his left, he crept through the darkness to the back entrance of the Jardine household. The air was still heavy with the smell of burning, despite the cold wind which gusted through the building. Lambert edged through the debris to the room where the two bodies had been discovered.

The image of the pair would forever be imprinted on his mind. Lambert had seen burn victims before, both alive and dead, but nothing which matched that particular image. It still troubled him, the pair lying next to each other on the sofa as if they'd given in. He knew they had been killed before the fire started, but the way they had been placed together haunted him. The image had a sense of theatre to it, as if the arsonist were making a statement.

He couldn't sit on the remains of the sofa, so he perched in front of it, scanning the room, picturing the waves of flame which would have decorated the walls and rolled towards the already deceased victims.

A theory came to mind. It was probably too implausible, but he wanted to discuss the matter with the pathologist, Harrington, as soon as possible.

–

Lambert stopped at a newsagent on his way to the station and picked up a copy of Mia Helmer's paper. He was relieved not to have made the front page, the story pushed back to page eleven. The text was similar to what he'd read at the meeting with John Weaver, and his pulse quickened as he read his own name before screwing up the paper and placing it into the nearest dustbin.

Bickland and Croft looked surprised to see him as they arrived at the station early that morning. Both carried coffee cups from the same high street chain, and it was clear they'd met up prior to entering the incident room.

'Where's mine?' Lambert asked Croft, who grimaced as she took her seat.

'The Family Liaison Officer is bringing Teresa here at nine-thirty,' said Croft, trying to change the subject as she took her seat and switched on her PC.

'I'm well aware of that, Sergeant. I would like you to interview the girl,' said Lambert, receiving a glare from Bickland.

Croft stopped what she was doing and turned to face him. 'What exactly to you want to get from her, sir? The girl is only three.'

'Three-year-olds can be perceptive, Croft,' said Lambert, remembering Chloe at that age. His daughter had been insightful, joining in conversations with opinions he'd often thought no three-year-old could hold.

'I'm sure the FLO will stop you if your questioning gets too difficult. Try to find out what she remembers, but not just the fire. Anything out of the ordinary in the last week. Her parents' behaviour, any conflict, you know the sort of thing. I'm sending you in as I imagine I could possibly scare her, and I know for a fact Bickland would,' he said, with a smile aimed at Bickland, who shook his head, his eyes still glued to the screen.

–

Teresa Jardine was a sweet little girl with two bunches of raven-coloured hair. She walked hand in hand with the FLO into the station. Lambert shook hands with the woman who introduced herself as Geraldine Herbert. Lambert went down on his haunches so he was eye level with the girl. 'Hello Teresa, my name is Michael,' he said, smiling.

Teresa turned her head away, pushing it into the thighs of the FLO. Lambert stood back up, stifling a groan, his thighs burning, and offered a smile to the woman. 'My colleague DS Croft will be speaking to Teresa. She's waiting in interview room eight. Can we get you anything?'

'Would you like some juice, Teresa?' Lambert asked.

The girl nodded, never once letting go of the woman's leg.

Lambert and Bickland observed from the video room as Croft won the girl over with the gift of a small teddy bear. The Family Liaison Officer watched with grim determination as Croft gently sought answers from the girl. The FLO had the power to cut the interview off at any time, and whilst Lambert accepted it was right that the child's interests were a priority, he resented having to be on best behaviour for the woman.

He could see Croft was avoiding asking questions which were too direct. He accepted that as well. Teresa would not have been told her parents were dead yet, not until there was a formal identification, and Croft would have to be careful not to make any such suggestions.

Croft slipped the incident into conversation when she saw the opportunity. She was playing a game with Teresa, the girl's new teddy bear making an imaginary journey across the wild lands of interview room eight's carpet.

'This is so much fun, Teresa,' said Croft. 'It's so nice making new friends, isn't it?'

Teresa moved the bear across the floor one stuffed leg at a time, a hint of a smile forming on her sullen face. 'Do your Mummy and Daddy like new friends?' she continued.

Teresa stopped, looking for reassurance from her carer. Geraldine smiled and nodded her head.

'They have lots of friends,' said Teresa.

'That's nice,' said Croft, holding her own toy and bouncing along to Teresa's rhythm. 'Have any nice new friends been to your house recently?'

'Abigail did,' said Teresa.

'Abigail, that's a nice name,' said Croft.

'She goes to my preschool.'

'Oh, OK. How about friends of your parents'?

Teresa sat the teddy down and glanced at the ceiling in contemplation. 'There was a man who came around tomorrow.'

Croft hesitated before saying, 'You mean yesterday.'

Teresa smacked her forehand gently with the palm of her hand. 'Yes, yesterday, I meant.'

'Did you know him?'

'Yes.'

'Great, do you know what his name is?'

'Of course. The postman.'

Croft laughed and glanced at the two-way mirror as she wrapped up the meeting with Teresa. The young girl's face twitched as she asked if she could keep the teddy bear Croft had supplied. It was such a simple gesture, an innocent request born out of politeness, but Lambert was deeply moved by it. He saw something of Chloe in the girl's movements and he closed his eyes to shut out the comparison.

'You OK, boss?' asked Bickland.

'Yeah, just a bit tired,' said Lambert, leaving the room.

Rushing through the waiting area, receiving quizzical looks from the duty sergeant, Lambert barged through the station's doors into the cold morning and dragged in a deep breath. It wasn't very professional, but seeing that look on Teresa's face brought back too many memories. He didn't like to think about what lay ahead for the little girl, he couldn't imagine how she could ever fully recover from the events of the last two days.

Without a coat, the air stung his skin as if he'd been slapped.

Lambert leant against the wall for a moment, watching the people walking down the street, oblivious to what was happening within the station and the lives that were slowly being damaged beyond repair. An approaching uniformed officer stopped by the entrance and stared at him.

'What?' said Lambert, not looking at the young woman.

'I think your phone's ringing, sir,' said the PC.

Lambert reached into his suit jacket. Retrieving his phone, he frowned at the flashing number as if examining some foreign object. He shook his head, dragging himself back into the reality of the situation. 'Lambert.'

'Ah, Michael. Lindsey Harrington.'

It was the pathologist. 'A pleasant surprise, Ms Harrington. What can I do for you?'

'It's more what I can do for you, Michael.'

'You could get to the point, Lindsey, I'm rather busy.'

'Feisty,' said Harrington, a hint of amusement in her voice. 'I couldn't sleep last night – something troubling me about those two human bonfires. Decided to start the autopsy early.'

If it had been anyone else, Lambert would have surprised, but Harrington seemed to be a force unto herself.

'Didn't take me long to confirm my suspicions. You need to get down here, Lambert, pronto.'

'Care to elaborate?'

'I would love to,' said Harrington. 'I'll go through the details with you when you arrive.'

'The point being?' said Lambert, growing impatient.

'I can share one possibly telling point.' She paused, clearly savouring the moment.

'Stop pissing about, Lindsey, and tell me.'

'Wait for it, Michael. OK, here goes. How best to say this? I know. I'm not sure who the two bodies found at the Jardine house belong to, but I can tell for a fact that they are not Caroline Jardine and her husband.'

White noise rang in Lambert's ears. 'Come again?'

Lindsey chuckled down the line. 'Come visit me, Mikey. Whoever those poor folk are, they've been dead for some time longer than twenty-four hours.'

# Chapter Ten

Lambert went back into the station to collect his belongings. He was about to leave when Croft entered the main area of the station, hand in hand with Teresa Jardine. Geraldine Herbert, the Family Liaison Officer, stood behind the pair. The fact that her face was formed into something resembling a smile suggested that she was not too unhappy about the situation. Lambert stood frozen. The news from Harrington had thrown him. He needed to speak face to face with her before informing the others.

Now he saw the child he had an overwhelming urge to tell her. But what could he say? *There's a chance your parents are alive after all?* The thought that they were dead had probably not even entered the young girl's mind.

'Do you want to say goodbye to DCI Lambert?' said Croft, crouching down on her haunches as Lambert had done earlier. 'He's very nice. He bought that teddy.'

Instead of clinging to Croft's leg like she had to the FLO earlier, Teresa stood her ground and smiled at Lambert.

Lambert was surprised at the effect the girl had on him. Each time he looked at Teresa, he felt like Chloe was looking back at him. He crouched down and offered his hand.

'It was an honour meeting you, Teresa,' he said.

The girl laughed and looked at Croft before grabbing his hand and shaking it.

He stood quickly, dismayed at the twisted emotions he felt.

'I'm off to the pathologist's office,' he told Croft without looking back.

He caught his breath outside and headed towards the car. Teresa was not Chloe, and seeing his daughter in that little girl was indulgent and unhelpful.

As he drove he turned his focus back on to the case. If what Harrington said was true, then the case had become something far more complex than even a double homicide. Now there were four bodies, two unaccounted for. It appeared Lambert now had to solve the riddle of two missing people and two unidentified victims, as well as determining how the arsonist had somehow placed two corpses in the Jardine household whilst managing to subdue and kidnap two adults.

If nothing else, it was a sure sign that the security systems at the gated community were not very effective.

–

Dr. Lindsey Harrington's office was situated in the basement of St. Matthew's hospital. Lambert shuddered, the temperature dropping as he took the steps down into Harrington's department, a faint hint of damp coming from the walls of the building. One of Harrington's assistants, an obese bearded man Lambert thought was called Stowage, didn't look up from his sandwich and newspaper as Lambert asked after her.

'In there,' said Stowage, still eating.

Lambert put on a clean surgical gown and mask before making his way through to Harrington's lab.

'You should have waited for me,' he said, pulling down his mask for a split second.

The remains of the two bodies were laid out on separate gurneys.

'Really?' said Harrington, smiling as she examined the burnt tissue on a corpse's neck. 'Even if I didn't know you, I could tell you hate being here.'

'What?' said Lambert, pulling off his mask in mock outrage as he edged closer to the tables. 'I thought I was just following protocol,' he said. 'What can you tell me?'

'Very interesting,' said Harrington. 'Like I said on the phone, these are not the remains of Mr and Mrs Jardine – unless they've been missing for the last few days. Despite the fire, I was able to run a number of tests. There was no sign of rigor in the bodies at all, which suggests they died a minimum of thirty-six to forty-eight hours ago. There are also signs of decomposition in the internal organs. I would estimate the time of death to be at least seven to eight days. It could possibly be longer if the killer was keeping them somewhere cold.'

Lambert frowned. 'Any means of identification?' he said, sensing the case slipping away.

Harrington placed her right hand on his shoulder. 'As long as they had a dentist at some point, we could be OK. Mr Stowage is checking the dental records. Both bodies have well maintained dentistry so we should be in luck.'

'In luck?'

'Think of that little, girl, Michael,' said Harrington. 'Her parents are only missing now and you have the opportunity to find them.'

Lambert nodded. 'I hope it's that easy. Is the method of death still the blow to the back of the head?'

'I believe so, but we'll be going through chemical analysis. Because of the fire, its difficult to give an exact time of death.'

'You'll let me know as soon as you have an identification for me?' he said, taking off his gown.

'You'll be one of the first.'

'Thanks, Lindsey.'

'No problem, Michael. I hope you find them.'

## Chapter Eleven

Tillman had agreed to meet Lambert at a bar near the Chislehurst Caves. The Chief Super was already halfway through his first drink by the time Lambert arrived.

'You're starting early,' said Lambert, glancing at the tumbler of gold liquid in Tillman's hands.

'It's five o'clock somewhere. Now tell me, what's so important that you had to drag me out of the comfort of my office to this god-forsaken part of town?'

Lambert zipped up his jacket, nursing a black coffee he'd ordered from the barmaid inside.

'Two things. First, Duggan came to see me last night,' he said, taking a seat on the hard wooden bench opposite Tillman.

If his superior was bothered, it didn't show on his face. He remained inscrutable, staring at Lambert as if he'd told him something he already knew.

'You didn't get me here for that, did you?' he asked.

'You know they effectively want me to keep tabs on you? To report your every movement,' said Lambert.

Tillman shrugged. 'When's the last time you saw Matilda? She's been asking after you.'

It pained Lambert every time he saw his former partner – however much she protested, he couldn't help but feel responsible for her injuries.

'Tell her I'll see her as soon as possible' said Lambert. 'Though it hasn't got past me that you're changing the subject.'

'I've told you before she doesn't blame you for it,' said Tillman.

Lambert shook his head to stop his boss from talking further.

'Why would she?' continued Tillman undeterred. 'She was just doing her job like we all were that day.'

'I know, Glenn. Can we get back to the subject at hand, Duggan's investigation into you?'

Tillman's lip curled as he took a short sip of his whisky. Rubbing his hands together, he said, 'What's his latest?'

'I think the paramedics have been turned. Duggan claims to have two witnesses that you withdrew your gun.'

'And what did you see?'

Lambert remembered the desperation in Tillman's eyes, the pain which had made him draw the gun, and his own quick movement with the pepper spray. 'I'm not going to change my statement, you know that, but I don't like it.'

'Let me worry about it. Duggan is all bluster. He'll soon blow himself out.'

Lambert doubted this particular wisdom but didn't push further. They had greater concerns at the moment.

'So, what's the real reason why you called me here?' said Tillman.

'I came straight from the pathologist's, Glenn. You're not going to like what I have to say.'

He relayed Harrington's findings as Tillman stared at him as if he'd lost his mind.

'You're telling me neither of those bodies belongs to Caroline Jardine?'

'Those are the facts, Glenn,' he said, leaning back in his seat.

'Christ, what the hell does this mean?'

'It means DI Jardine and her husband may still be alive,' said Lambert.

'But why this?'

'I think it was either a distraction to put us off the trail for a few days before we knew we were dealing with a missing person's case...'

'Or?' said Tillman.

'Or, the killer thought that he would get away with it. The way those bodies were burnt, my guess is that if the fire service had arrived ten or twenty minutes later there'd have been nothing left but bone.'

Tillman brushed away a bead of sweat as it dribbled down his cheek. 'Even so, if the killer knew anything about his job he would have realised that wouldn't prove much of a deterrent to solving the victims' identities.'

'Maybe he's not that clued up on forensics,' said Lambert. 'But I agree. I think he's taken the Jardines and left these other two in their place.'

'Practice run?' asked Tillman.

'Could be. We're matching dental records as we speak. All the burns are post-mortem but we knew that already.'

Tillman shook his head and downed the rest of his whisky in one gulp. 'I knew something like this would happen,' he said.

Lambert scowled. 'You knew something like this was going to happen?' he repeated, not hiding the incredulity in his voice.

'Every time I put you in charge of a case, Lambert – every single time – something out of the ordinary occurs.'

It was Lambert's turn to shake his head. Tillman was being purposely facetious, but it was clear part of him believed what he was saying. They'd come to blows on many cases before and Lambert understood that only a thin sense of allegiance kept Tillman loyal to him.

Tillman stood up and went to the bar, returning a minute later with a second large order of whiskey and a glass for Lambert.

'Drink it,' said Tillman.

The cold air of the beer garden bit into Lambert's skin as he sipped at the drink.

'So let me get this straight,' said Tillman. 'We've gone from a simple arson stroke murder to a possible arson stroke murder stroke missing person stroke kidnapping case?'

'Looks that way,' said Lambert. He took a second sip of the drink, the heat of the alcohol filling his throat and spreading across his chest. 'I'm going to need to speak to DCI Barnes again.'

'That's going to be a fun conversation, but leave it to me for the time being.'

'I want to speak to him in person, Glenn. I need full access to DI Jardine's cases. Not just the recent ones.'

Tillman leant into his chair and propped his shoulders backwards, his chest darting outwards until the buttons on his shirt reached breaking point. He exhaled loudly, sounding anything but healthy. Reaching down for the double measure of whisky he surveyed the amber liquid, swirling it in his glass before downing its contents.

'This is a new one to me,' he said sighing. 'Is your pathologist friend confident she'll be able to identify the bodies?'

'They have dental records,' said Lambert.

'Well, I'll look forward to hearing those names,' said Tillman, groaning once again as he pushed himself to his feet. 'I'll speak to Barnes now. I'll get those files to you by the end of the day.'

'And Duggan?' said Lambert.

'They've got nothing on me, Michael, and they never will.'

Lambert sighed as an unspoken thought passed between the two men. Tillman knew as well as Lambert did that he had the power to bring Tillman down. What Duggan had said was true. Clearly, Tillman was not concerned about his loyalty. 'You worry too much, Michael. I'll be in touch once I've spoken to Barnes. I presume Harrington is under orders not to speak about this?'

'Of course.'

'Just keep it that way for the time being. There's a chance the Jardines are alive and any advantage is a bonus at this stage. We continue to act like it's the Jardines' murders we're investigating. Let's lull this bastard into some vague sense of security. You'll tell Croft and Bickland at this stage only.'

Lambert finished the last of his drink as Tillman headed for the exit.

As he left the bar, he felt a lightness in his body. At first he mistook it for a side effect of the alcohol he'd drunk, but then he realised that he'd been thinking about Teresa Jardine – and that the faint possibility that she'd see her parents again, however unlikely, was responsible.

# Chapter Twelve

By the time Lambert returned to the station the joyous effect of the alcohol had rubbed off. His throat was dry and the beginnings of a headache sprouted from the left side of his forehead. Croft and Bickland sat in accidental imitation of Tillman as he shared the news. At one point, Lambert nearly told Bickland to close his mouth, the DS sitting mouth agape like a schoolboy learning the facts of life.

'At this point the news goes no further than this office. The only other people who know that the bodies don't belong to Caroline Jardine and her husband are Chief Superintendent Tillman, the pathologist Lindsey Harrington and Caroline's boss, DCI Barnes.'

'How does this change things going forward?' asked Bickland.

'Our main responsibility now is locating Mr and Mrs Jardine, at least until we find out whose bodies those were in the house.'

'Why kidnap with no ransom note?' asked Croft.

'At the moment we're working on the presumption that the arsonists wanted us to think the bodies belonged to Mr and Mrs Jardine, at least initially.'

'It's been over forty-eight hours now,' said Bickland.

Lambert's body tensed. 'Exactly. It's to our great disadvantage. For nearly forty-eight hours we've been investigating a murder case when we should, at least partly, have been working on a missing persons case.' He knew, as he was sure the others did, how crucial this time period was. Unless they were lucky, or unless whoever was responsible wanted them to, it was highly unlikely they would ever see Mr and Mrs Jardine again.

'We need to extend our work on the CCTV footage,' he informed them. 'Get as many bodies in as necessary, but I want to see where that van entered from and, more importantly, where it left.'

'I've been tracing some routes, sir,' said Croft. 'Possible exits from the crime scene where the van could have avoided detection.'

Lambert had feared there would have been such routes. 'Find the first camera on each route and search for the van. If they've travelled beyond London there must be a point where we spot them. Bickland, I want you to go to the pathologists. Stick with Lindsey Harrington and her colleague until they've made an ID. Please remind Ms Harrington this information is not to become public knowledge.'

–

Later that evening, Lambert found himself back on his old street in Beckenham. He sat in his car, the radio tuned to 6 Music, watching with absent interest as his former neighbours went about their business.

He'd lived on the street for over fifteen years with his then-wife, Sophie, and his daughter, Chloe. The visits were an unhealthy habit which had started shortly after the Watcher case. Officially, the house was still his — at least a percentage of it — and it was surreal viewing the building from this abstract position knowing he couldn't enter without causing something of a disruption. Days never passed without him thinking about Chloe. He was resigned to the fact, even welcomed it. It was an honour to carry her memory, however painful. Occasionally minutes would pass where thoughts of her would leave his mind, only for the memory to rush at him, making the wounds of her departure as raw as they were on that first day.

He tried to turn his thoughts to the arson case in Chislehurst. By tomorrow morning they would have to go public. He was waiting to hear back from Tillman about Barnes' response to the situation. He wanted to speak to Caroline Jardine's direct superior. If she had been kidnapped, then chances were it was related to her work. Barnes had mentioned an organised gang case she'd been working on in Hackney, and Lambert was keen to get more information about her involvement.

The case was finely balanced. Hopefully the identification of the two bodies would be made soon and this would change things. Until then, everything was focused on finding the van, or at least those responsible for allowing the van access to the gated community.

Lambert was wasting his time in the street, but sometimes a case was best viewed from a distance. Maybe he was kidding himself but it felt like justification enough for him to sit there and watch for a glimpse of his wife.

The shrill tone of his phone dragged him back to reality.

'Glenn,' he said, answering the call.

'I just met with Barnes,' said Tillman, avoiding pleasantries. 'Naturally he blames us for not discovering the bodies didn't belong to Mr and Mrs Jardine earlier. Even more naturally, I told him where he could shove his accusation.'

Lambert was not surprised by either comment.

'The files from DI Jardine's last cases, the last five years of her work, are uploaded to the secure section on the System.'

Lambert doubted there was anything on the System that was secure from Tillman's prying eyes, but he held his tongue.

'How did Barnes react when you told him that Jardine was potentially still alive?'

'Hard to read – he has a better poker face than you. It's possible he was surprised. His eyes twitched. Whether it was surprise at the news that Jardine had been kidnapped, or that we'd only just found out, is still unclear.'

'What about going public?' asked Lambert.

'Barnes is in agreement with you for the time being. Best we let the kidnappers believe we think she's the victim of arson, though I believe Barnes' motivation is more selfish. This all has the smell of one enormous cock-up and I imagine he is busying away behind the scenes trying to divert blame.'

Lambert hung up. For an absurd second, he almost opened the car door and walked over to his former house. He wanted to examine Jardine's files on the system from the comfort of his old office and instinct almost guided him across the street. Instead, he started the car and was about to set off when he noticed movement at the front door opposite.

Seconds later, Sophie walked out into the front garden carrying some items for recycling. Lambert's chest trembled as he watched her bend from the knees to place the items in the recycle bin. She was dressed for indoors, in light-coloured jeans and a vest, but still she stopped in the coldness of the early evening and glanced both ways down the street as if she knew someone was spying on her. Lambert crouched down in his seat, feeling ludicrous. It wasn't fair on Sophie and it wasn't fair on Sarah. He needed to get out of the habit of coming here at times of turmoil. He peered outwards from his crouched position, uncomfortable in the role of voyeur. What would Sophie think of him if she could see him now? He imagined she would pity him, would be saddened that his life had come to this. Somehow that was worse than her being angry.

Eventually Sophie gave in. With a last glance in his direction, she retreated inside.

Lambert started the car again, vowing never to return, and set off back towards Chislehurst.

# Chapter Thirteen

Lambert met Chapman outside the ruins of the Jardine house. In the fading light, the house had taken on a ghostly appearance, as if haunted by its former occupants. A swirling wind attacked Lambert as he stepped out of the car. It whistled through the remains of the house, rustling the tarpaulin which had been stretched to cover the numerous holes in the structure.

A second man stood with the fire chief. 'William Finch,' said the man, offering his hand to Lambert. 'Crime Fire Officer with the Met.'

'Right, gentleman. If the pleasantries are over, let's find whatever shelter there is in the house,' said Chapman.

Chapman led them through each room, talking mainly to Finch who was taking copious notes. He repeated what he'd told Lambert about the American arsonist, Orr, and showed them the area in the loft where the final device had been left inactivated.

Finch bent over and examined the area as if the empty space of carpet could tell him something. 'No signs of accelerants anywhere?' he asked.

'Not up here. The living room was drenched in petrol.'

'Maybe he ran out of time,' said Lambert.

'I don't think so,' said Finch. 'If he'd wanted to light the loft, he would have started there.'

'I agree,' said Chapman. 'I think he wanted the fire to be contained to the first two floors.'

'Why do you say that?' asked Lambert.

'All the activated devices were downstairs. Naturally the fire would spread, but we're stationed two minutes away. Even if the fire had reached the loft there was always a good chance the device would be recoverable.'

Lambert made a mental note to listen to the emergency call tapes. 'You're saying he wanted the device discovered?'

'You're the detective,' said Chapman. 'I've seen this before, though. For some of them it's not enough to burn things. They need to show how clever they are too.'

'And the wing where Teresa was found?'

'Nothing in that area at all. It was furthest from the epicentre of the fire.'

Lambert wondered again if the arsonist knew Teresa Jardine had been in her room.

'Either way,' continued Chapman, 'it was merciful we got there when we did. One or two minutes later and that girl wouldn't have been so lucky.'

Downstairs, Chapman pointed out the scorch marks on the floor of the living room where the two bodies were discovered.

'A literal ring of fire,' said Finch. 'He didn't want the Jardines escaping.'

Or he wanted us to think that, thought Lambert.

–

Back at the station, Lambert and Finch worked through the case in detail. The officer was not easy company. Finch struggled to maintain eye contact, his gaze wandering around the room as if he could see things not visible to Lambert.

'Have you seen anything like this before?' asked Lambert.

'Orr has a lot to answer for,' said Finch, animated. 'I see copycats all the time, though rarely as well executed as this. This guy knew what he was doing.'

'Tell me about it,' said Lambert, thinking about how in addition to setting fire to the place, the arsonist had managed to kidnap the Jardines whilst replacing them with two other bodies.

'Yeah, it's more than that,' said Finch, rubbing his ear. A glow had spread across the man's face.

'You sound quite excited by this.'

Finch blushed. 'Don't get me wrong. What he did was horrendous, but the execution was second to none. Some of these arsonists...' He faltered, lost in some reverie.

'Some of these arsonists,' repeated Lambert.

Finch shook his head. 'It goes beyond a simple attraction to fire.'

'I guessed that much.'

Finch blushed again, the reddening of his face a stark contrast to his pale complexion. 'I guess it goes beyond my words as well, I suppose. You should speak to a psychologist who specialises in the field. What I've learnt, at least from the most serious cases, is that these guys have an affinity with the fire. It usually stems from some childhood incident, like most things you deal with, I guess. Sometimes they experienced a fire in their homes, sometimes it can be a memory of a bonfire at a time of happiness. That's what I find most terrifying, that a happy memory can do this to you.'

From Lambert's experience, such a happy memory would usually be counteracted by something tragic later down the road. 'But what is getting you so excited about this guy?'

Finch resumed glancing around the room. 'That ring of fire confirmed it for me. Look at the way he lay out the incendiary devices, the placement of the accelerants.'

'You've lost me.'

'He thinks he can control the fire,' said Finch, folding his arms.

'Is that unusual?'

'You can't control fire. Not really. You can have safe explosions. Contained areas where the fire is unable to spread. But this guy thinks he can control a fire in an open area, where there is oxygen and flammable materials.'

'And this is obviously impossible.'

'It is, but he's made a bloody good attempt.'

# Chapter Fourteen

As Lambert drove home, he thought through what Finch had said about the arsonist believing he could control the fire. He had found Finch's romanticism tiring by the end. There was nothing special about delusion, it just made the arsonist more dangerous.

On the System, Lambert requested a full report of arson incidents from the last five years with similar MOs. One point on which he agreed with Finch: this was definitely not the arsonist's first attempt.

Lambert parked outside his building, surprised to see a light on in his flat. He skipped up the stairs, wondering if Sarah had let herself in. 'Hello?' he called, as he opened the front door.

'Hello yourself,' said Sarah, who was sitting on his couch, a glass of red wine in her hand.

'Sarah? Sarah May?' said Lambert, in mock surprise, pouring himself a glass from the open wine bottle.

'Very funny. Some of us have jobs, you know – can't spend every waking minute with our boyfriends.' She said it with a smile but Lambert sensed something beneath the words. They hadn't seen each other since the awkward lunch, and though it felt good to see her the situation felt awkward. He poured some wine and sat next to her.

She held his eyes in the same unnerving way as always. Her mouth curled into a smile as she assessed him. 'You look tired,' she said.

'You look great,' he replied.

'Liar.'

'How's the case going?'

She'd been working on a number of cases recently, including a stalker case involving an officer worker and an enamoured ex-colleague. As she talked, he found his eyes drooping.

She offered him another smile, maintaining eye contact as she sipped her wine. 'What about you? Any news on the arsonist?'

Lambert told her about the bodies.

'So the Jardines have been kidnapped?' she said, pulling her legs up to her chest.

'Either that, or they've staged an elaborate disappearing act.'

'They wouldn't leave their little girl behind like that.'

'You would hope not,' said Lambert. As Sarah edged closer, he had an absurd notion to tell her about his visit to Sophie's house earlier that evening. In the end, he half-heartedly convinced himself that it wouldn't benefit anyone.

'Can I stay tonight, Michael?' she whispered. 'I'm shattered.'

'Well, if you're shattered,' said Lambert. It was an innocent request, but it troubled him. She'd never asked permission to stay before, and again it suggested a growing distance between them. He thought that maybe she wanted him to follow her into the bedroom, but he was too restless.

He kissed her goodnight before moving to the dining table, where he began work on his laptop.

His first step was checking Finch's file on the System. The fire officer was an awkward character, and Lambert wanted to make sure there was nothing in the man's background which would later cause a problem. John Orr had allegedly been responsible for over two thousand cases of arson during his time as fire officer. It was too much to hope that something in Finch's background would alert Lambert to such a link, but he still wanted him checked out. It came as no surprise to discover that Finch had transferred from the fire service to the police force. He was technically a civilian, working as a contractor for the NCA. Lambert studied the man's file, assessing his background from his time in University to the present. Lambert didn't quite have a photographic memory, but words, once read, stuck with him and sometimes it could come down to just that: one word or phrase, a connection which made everything clearer.

It would take some time to read each of Finch's cases, so Lambert narrowed each to a summary. Next, he tried various searches, including 'Orr' and 'box of matches'. Surprised by the multitude of results, he began trawling through the information, unsure as to what he hoped to find.

He wasn't even halfway through when tiredness overcame him. He hadn't thought about his time beneath the MRI machine since the case began. Now, he reminded himself that the tests had proved negative. He stood up and made his way as quickly as possible to the bedroom, his hands pressed against the walls in case he blanked out.

Sarah sat up in bed as he stumbled into the room. 'Michael?' she said, her figure a blurred silhouette.

'I'm OK,' said Lambert, collapsing on the bed. Sarah's hand touched his forehead as his eyesight became clouded. He closed his eyes, but the pattern of fiery colours remained in focus. 'I'm OK,' he repeated.

–

He woke with a shudder four hours later. Sarah stood at the end of the bed, pulling on her clothes.

'I've woken up to worse views,' he said.

Sarah murmured 'I'll take that as a compliment. You remember last night?'

'You didn't take advantage of me, did you?'

'Hardly.'

'I conked out?' said Lambert, rubbing his eyes.

'You certainly did. Conked completely out.'

Lambert looked down and realised he was still wearing last night's clothes.

Catching his look, Sarah said, 'I took your shoes off.'

'Thanks. Sorry you had to witness that.'

She shook her head, compassion in her eyes. 'Don't be so bloody ridiculous. You can be so frustrating at times, Michael. Do you know that?'

'What?' He understood what she was getting at, but was loath to admit it.

'When are you going to see someone about this? It's obviously not doing you any good.'

He hadn't told her about the MRI scan, and didn't want to burden her with the knowledge now. 'I will, but I have to be careful, Sarah, I've told you that.' He could hear the slight whine in his voice and hated himself for it.

'What would you prefer, being dead, or retired with no health issues?' she said, leaving the bedroom.

She'd never been this angry with him before. He didn't blame her. She obviously cared about him, and his inaction could be seen as a reflection on his feelings towards her. He considered calling out to her but it was too early for a fight.

A couple of minutes later, he heard the front door slam.

After showering, he read through Caroline Jardine's file on the System whilst eating breakfast. He reacquainted himself with her most recent cases, the latest of which was the ongoing investigation into a number of organised groups in the Hackney area. Most of the information was readily available to him on the System, only the occasional passage blanked out. He wouldn't rule anything out at this stage but he doubted anyone from these groups were responsible for her disappearance and the fire. For one, it was unlikely they knew they were under surveillance, and even if they did, it was even more unlikely that they knew Jardine was one of the operatives. He could be wrong; some form of ransom note or hostage video could arrive any minute, but at the moment it didn't ring true to him. Why leave two bodies in place of the Jardines?

He began working backwards through Jardine's cases, trying to ignore the nagging sense that he should call Sarah and apologise. He gleaned little from the files. She'd investigated and successfully prosecuted a number of high profile individuals, but again he couldn't see anything in the files which suggested a revenge attack was likely.

Shutting his laptop, he sipped at his coffee and tried to ascertain what he was missing. The two major anomalies in the case were the missing ransom note and the two replacement bodies. He struggled to make a coherent argument for why the arsonist was working this way. The killer had clearly exchanged the two dead victims for two new victims. Harrington hadn't uncovered any signs of torture on the two bodies, though that didn't mean it hadn't occurred. Lambert had learnt from experience that torture could take many forms. More would be evident when they discovered the identities of the two bodies, which he hoped would happen that day.

# Chapter Fifteen

Lambert swore as he approached his car. He felt an unwelcome sense of déjà vu as he saw Mia Helmer sheltering beneath an umbrella. She was the last person he wanted to see first thing in the morning. Lambert was struck by the slightness of the woman, her lack of physical presence standing in stark contrast to her fierce and combative personality.

'Are we dating now?' he said, unlocking the car.

The mask on Helmer's face didn't crack. 'Would you care to report on recent developments in the Jardine fire case?' she asked.

Lambert leant against his car door. 'I've told you before, Mia. If you want anything from me you need to go through our press department.'

'I don't need anything from you, DCI Lambert. If anything, I'm trying to help you.'

Lambert yawned. 'You can help me by not bothering me any more,' he said, climbing into the car.

'I know it wasn't the Jardines in the house,' said Helmer, as he was closing the door.

Drops of rain fell into the car as he sat behind the wheel, his eyes closed. He wanted to shut the door, start the engine, and drive off, but knew he had to question the journalist.

Helmer's face was smooth and unreadable. 'What do you know?' asked Lambert.

'As I said, the bodies at the scene do not belong to Caroline and Marcus Jardine.'

'I'm not confirming that, Helmer, but where the hell did you get that information from?'

Helmer's lips moved. Lambert wouldn't quite call it a smile, but it was as close as he'd seen from the woman. 'I can't share my resources, DCI Lambert, surely you know that?'

'That information is confidential and is not for public consumption. If you publish that you will jeopardise the investigation. That means risking the lives of Caroline and Marcus Jardine. If that happens, Mia, you'll have me to answer to. Do you understand me?'

'Is that a threat, Michael,' said Helmer, unfazed.

'Yes,' said Lambert, returning to the car seat and slamming the door.

–

Lambert arrived at the station to find Jardine's boss, DCI Barnes, waiting for him. The man sat in the main reception area, a thick three-quarter-length coat buttoned to his neck.

'You could have gone through to our back offices,' said Lambert, approaching him.

'I wanted to speak to you alone,' said Barnes, standing up. His face had the same indifferent quality Lambert had seen on it the other day, but now there was also a hint of anger. 'Where can we go?'

Lambert guided him outside and they walked to a small coffee shop off the high street. Lambert ordered as Barnes took a seat at the back of the shop.

Lambert rubbed his face as he waited for the barista to make the drinks. His skin was dry from the cold weather, his cheeks decorated with a day's worth of stubble.

'Thank you,' said Barnes, as Lambert placed the coffees on the table.

'I'm glad you came in to see me,' said Lambert.

'Are you now?' said Barnes. The DCI looked uncomfortable, his long limbs cramped beneath the low table. 'I've heard a lot of good things about you, Lambert. And some not so good. I need to know you are the right person to find Caroline.'

'A fair summary,' said Lambert. He was being assessed and he couldn't blame Barnes for that.

Barnes chuckled. 'You just manage to stay on the right side of the fence, don't you? Though you have a habit of going, shall we say, off grid.'

Lambert took a drink, not answering, allowing his fellow DCI to vent his displeasure.

'And now you're leading a missing persons case. A case involving one of my team.'

'I appreciate this is important to you, but is there a point to all this?'

'You think she's alive?' asked Barnes.

It was the only logical working proposition. 'Do you?'

'I've lost officers before. You're probably aware of that?'

Lambert hadn't read about it in any of the files but made a note to check the details. 'I think this is different,' said Lambert.

'So do I. That's why I wanted to make sure I had the right team working on this.'

'I'm not going to give you the normal platitudes on this, Barnes. The Jardines have been missing for over forty-eight hours now. You know as well as I do that this significantly decreases the chances of us finding them. Add to this that we've had no contact from a kidnapper, and the complication with the fire and the two bodies, and I have to confess the prognosis is not good. However, you know my work, and Tillman's for that matter. We will not stop until everything that can be done has been done. And then, we will go one step further.'

Barnes stared hard at him. 'All my resources are at your disposal.'

'Thank you. I've read Caroline's file. Is there anything I'm missing? Some aspect I should be focusing on? You mentioned her investigation into the organised crime racket in Hackney.'

Barnes shook his head. 'I've spent every waking minute looking into her work since that fire. Our team have been out speaking to every informant. We've drawn a blank. As I said, you are free to access all our resources.'

Tillman was correct about the man's poker face. The hint of anger displayed at the beginning of their meeting was the only readable sign of emotion he'd revealed. 'OK, thank you. I'll keep you updated as well.'

Lambert remained sitting as Barnes left the coffee shop, walking with that fixed, robotic gait. Meeting the man again had told Lambert two things. First, Barnes was clearly running his own internal investigation into Jardine's disappearance. Secondly, he knew something he wasn't willing to share with Lambert at this juncture. He wondered if

Barnes, or someone in his team, had shared the information with Mia Helmer, and if so, to what end.

Outside, he was about to return to the station when someone placed a hand on his shoulder.

'Sorry, sir, you were miles away.'

Lambert turned to face DS Bickland. He was wearing his suit but no coat. Despite the cold he was sweating profusely. 'We think we've got a hit. I wanted to catch you before you left.'

'Get your breath back, Bickland,' said Lambert. 'What's the problem?'

'Sir, it's the two bodies at the Jardine house. The Doc has made an identification.'

# Chapter Sixteen

At the station, Lambert went through the dental records sent over by Harrington. The corpses belonged to Jonathan Turner, aged thirty-two, and Maxine Berry, aged twenty-eight. Electoral records showed that Turner was from a harbour town in Cornwall, Berry from Peterborough.

After giving the team some time to process the information, Lambert gathered them into the incident room. 'What do we know about these two?' he asked the assembled group.

'Berry worked as a dental hygienist. She was reported missing four weeks ago,' said Croft.

'Turner was reported missing as well,' said Bickland. 'But only two weeks ago.'

'We need to find some link between these two people. Anything, however tenuous. Croft, I want you to speak to the respective CID teams in their hometowns. See what they have on the pair. Bickland, I want you to lead the tech team on the search of their digital footprint. A connection is our major goal. We need access to the pair's computers, and their online activity.'

After dismissing the team, Lambert spent the rest of the morning in his new office, searching the System. The randomness of the two bodies was troubling him. How did the two victims, from different parts of the UK, end up in the living room of Caroline and Marcus Jardine? And why?

From what he could gather Jonathan Turner had little of a social media presence apart from a rarely used Twitter handle. Maxine Berry appeared to be more active, with a Facebook and Instagram account in addition to her Twitter handle. Nothing seemed to link them online, so he decided to try another tack.

Again he returned to how the bodies were arranged on the sofa. Although he now understood they were already dead at this stage, the image still troubled him. It was as if they were welcoming their fate, linked together waiting for the embrace of death. It made him think of them as suicide victims. He began accessing websites which dealt with the issue of suicide.

Lambert had come across such sites before, working on other cases. In Lambert's experience, people visited them for many reasons. Some users had terminal illnesses, others were manic-depressives or suffered from uncontrollable grief. Amongst such tragedy, Lambert had discovered great compassion. People reached out for one another, understood the extent of despair which led to thoughts of suicide. On the sites he'd visited, Lambert rarely encountered people being judgmental. Visitors were neither encouraged nor discouraged from their wishes, only prompted to fully explore every possible remedy to their circumstances.

Lambert had briefly considered ending his life following his daughter's death. He'd been in a bad way both physically and mentally. Grief could do terrible things to the mind, especially when coupled with guilt. For months following Chloe's death, he'd struggled with the idea that he could live his life without her in it. Too many nights he'd sat alone on the top floor of his house, a loaded gun by his side. Even now, those same thoughts occasionally returned to haunt him. He would never recover from what had happened to his little girl, and at times like that he had to remind himself why he had never pulled the trigger. Sometimes, a dark part of him would tell him he was a coward and that was the only reason he was alive. Whilst he accepted the truth of that, he realised the only way to fully honour Chloe, to accept his part in her death, was to carry the burden for the rest of his life.

He was onto his third site when he got the hit he was searching for. Maxine Berry's Twitter handle was Miss-Maisy, and sure enough it appeared on the site in the main forums. Lambert called in Croft and Bickland and told them about his discovery.

'We need full access to that website. Our arsonist friend either knew Berry or Turner, possibly both, or found their details on this website. I'm hoping there is some kind of forum where they started talking. Trawl everything you can. I have an appointment.'

# Chapter Seventeen

The car park was full so Lambert manoeuvred the car into a corner space, ignoring the double yellow lines and the no parking sign. He gazed out of the windscreen as rain descended onto the glass, the water fierce and incessant. The building was a thirty-second dash across the tarmac.

He jumped from the car and opened the boot of the estate car, swearing when he realised there was no umbrella within. He sheltered beneath the boot, rain splashing onto his trousers, contemplating the damage thirty seconds of falling water could cause.

Thirty seconds later he found out. He stood in the reception area of the building, his hair matted to his scalp. He'd managed to run through numerous puddles on the short journey. His trousers clung to him like skin and even his shirt was damp, his wool overcoat proving little defence from the torrential downfall.

Lambert could see the receptionist was trying not to laugh as she asked him how she could help. 'I'm here to see Dr Samantha Beresford,' said Lambert, dragging a hand through his hair which released droplets of water onto his back.

'Second room on the right,' said the receptionist, pointing up the stairs.

A woman was waiting outside the room. 'DCI Lambert?'

'A wetter than normal version, yes,' said Lambert.

'Sam Beresford, do come in. Can I get you a towel?'

'I'll survive.'

'OK, try not to drip anywhere,' said the woman, pointing to a seat.

Lambert smirked and took off his coat. 'Thanks for taking the time to see me.'

Beresford was a consultant psychiatrist whose specialities included pyromania. 'My pleasure. The case made for fascinating reading,' she said. As she spoke, her face lit up. Lambert had seen the look many times before, a person consumed by their passion.

'You must have seen this sort of thing before?'

Beresford leant forward on her desk, and stared intently at Lambert. 'Nothing quite like this. From the fire report, it seems whoever was responsible was obsessed with John Orr. I've seen mimics before but from what I can ascertain, this was extremely methodical and well planned. As for the victims, and that poor girl, well…'

Lambert held his hand up. Beresford talked as if she only had seconds to explain everything, one sentence running into the other with no pause for breath. 'Let's start at the beginning. You say you've seen mimics before?'

Beresford sat back in her chair. 'Sorry, I get ahead of myself sometimes. I imagine you've read about Orr before. His mode of setting fires was quite a simple one. One that can be readily copied, unfortunately with some success.'

'So there has been a copycat incident before.'

'I wouldn't quite call it copycat. Orr doesn't really have copyright on his mode of arson. It existed long before he did it. I guess it worked for him as he could set the fire before escaping. Nothing original in that. What made Orr so infamous was the number of fires he set, and the length of time he got away with it. Not to mention his job title.'

Lambert pictured Finch, the awkward fire investigator from the NCA, and wondered if he harboured any such fantasies. 'So you think our arsonist has some obsession with Orr?'

'Hard to tell, Mr Lambert. He's probably aware of him, and obviously knows his work, but it may simply be that Orr's method was best suited to the job in hand.'

'Can you offer any insight into the placement of the bodies in the living room? Or the girl being left in the burning building?'

Beresford sighed, as if reliving the memory of the fire. 'I'm afraid I can only hypothesise at this juncture. People start fires for many reasons. I'm sure you are as aware of people's motives as I am. My experience is more related to why people commit arson – why they kill people is more your line.'

'Then why would this man choose to set a fire in this way?'

'You're presuming it's a man?'

'Not necessarily, though it usually is, and some extra information we have suggests the arsonist would have been particularly strong – so that's a starting point.'

'OK. So why would he set a fire? The million-dollar question, Mr Lambert. I presume in your line of work you've come across murderers and rapists?'

'Of course.'

'And what percentage of those do you think were inherently...' Beresford sighed, 'for want of a better word, evil. In other words, inherently prone to committing murder or rape.'

'Not my line really, Mrs Beresford. When you're confronted with such people, the murderers, rapists, paedophiles of this world, it's hard to dwell on the reasons for the way they are. When you see what these people are capable of, giving them a reason for behaving the way they do is like giving them an excuse. That said, I get the point you're trying to make. People are shaped into behaviours. The majority at least.'

'Yes. I'm not trying to excuse anyone's behaviour. I simply want to make it clear that an interest in setting fires is rarely something one is born with. In my experience, I would go so far as to say that it never is. True pyromania, if there is such a thing, is an impulse control disorder.'

For all her talk, the psychiatrist wasn't telling him anything he didn't already know. 'So what would trigger such behaviour?'

'If we don't consider the other psychotic behaviours in this particular case, perhaps the desire for power, the need to control, then there could be numerous reasons why he chose to set the fire. It could be something as simple as being excited by the sight of fire, though this sounds a little different. It's possible this particular arsonist may have a more complex relationship with fire. I'm sorry I can't be more certain, but there is a chance that you are looking at someone who is psychotic and/or paranoid, and obsessed with the sensory aspects of fire setting.'

'Is this common?'

'Not really, no. Research suggests that like most things, such obsessions are often related to childhood. Often a serial arsonist would have shown other conduct disorders as a child.'

'Such as?'

'The usual. General aggression, cruelty to animals, a disregard for authority, that sort of thing. There are, of course, other pathological reasons for continued pyromania. It's often a cry for help, especially in younger adults and children. Occasionally it can be the result of something more innocuous. It can be triggered by the experience of a fire during a time of high grief such as a death in the family or divorce, perhaps even abuse. For example, the memory of a parent burning waste at the end of the garden during a divorce can lead to a fixation on fire. Or perhaps, the memory of a shared bonfire night with a parent is the last happy memory of the child. Perhaps the parent dies, or becomes abusive. This can become the trigger for the desire to return to happier times. The child, or child within, identifies fire – the sight, the sound, and the smell – with happier times. They set fires to recapture that feeling.'

'There must be more to it than that.'

'Of course, that's just a starting point. Picture a child surviving a fire, particularly where a loved one has perished. Like the poor girl in your case. Such experience can drive an obsession with fire, unsurprisingly an unhealthy one. I've dealt with patients whose behaviour has been triggered from witnessing an accident at a firework display. I have one case where a boy saw his father stub out a cigarette on his sister. He self-harms, and has tried on numerous occasions to set fire to himself.'

Lambert considered what he was being told. 'Anything in your files more specific to this type of thing?'

'Plenty. Retribution by fire? Have you read the Bible?'

'Let's narrow it down, shall we?'

'I'm afraid that's impossible, and obviously I have client confidentiality issues. From what I've read about this case, this was obviously not the arsonist's first attempt. He would most likely have started on a much smaller scale. Chances are he's faced prosecution at one time or another.'

Lambert stood. 'Thank you, Dr Beresford.'

'I'm sorry I couldn't be more helpful. I'll let you know if I can think of anything more specific, and please send me any more details as they become apparent.'

–

Tillman met him close to Beresford's office. The rain had relented and Lambert was able to make his way without receiving a second soaking.

'You're sharp today, sir,' said Lambert, noticing his superior's new suit.

'Yes, and everyone's a fucking comedian,' said Tillman, obviously having heard the remark more than once that day.

Lambert updated him on the identity of the two bodies.

'Suicides? Did they have some kind of fire fetish?'

'Not that we can ascertain.'

'Good luck with that one, Lambert. You met Barnes again this morning?'

'Yep.'

'How was that?'

'Interesting. I think he's running his own investigation.'

Tillman drew in breath. 'Of course he is, so?'

'He's withholding something.'

'I repeat. Of course he is. This is a bloody travesty for him, could lose him his job. He will try and pass the buck – and that buck will probably be passed to us. Or more specifically, you.'

Lambert couldn't help but laugh. 'We've a missing officer. Shouldn't we be more concerned with that than assigning blame?'

'We should be, yes, but you need to be forewarned.'

'I truly couldn't care less, Glenn. There was no presumption beyond what was logical. No way we could tell those bodies weren't the Jardines until the post-mortem.'

'Like that matters,' said Tillman. 'We find Caroline and it's no longer a problem.'

'You coming back to the station?' he asked, as Tillman struggled into his car.

'Things to do, keep me posted. We're going to have to go public on this soon. Better we release it than it leaks.'

Lambert imagined the journalist, Mia Helmer, was probably already on the case. 'I'll speak to Barnes again and get it processed.'

# Chapter Eighteen

The incident room at the station had expanded, DCI Barnes having pulled in a number of additional recruits to the team. Lambert passed through them, noticing a few of the new additions. The extra bodies created a wave of heat, and he removed his coat as he entered the room. Croft and Bickland barely looked up as he sat down.

One of the phones rang, and Bickland pressed a button forwarding it the outer office. 'The press know it's a missing persons case,' he said, almost accusatory.

'That doesn't need to distract us,' said Lambert.

Bickland hesitated. 'Maybe not. Anyway, an update on the site. I've only speed read so far, but I think we have a link between Berry and Turner. We believe they first made contact a couple of years ago on the main forum. After a few months they began private messaging one another.'

'I want a transcript of everything, of everyone they ever talked to, basically of everyone who has ever used that site.'

'That leads onto our major problem,' said Bickland.

'Tell me,' said Lambert.

'It's that bloody website. It was taken down thirty minutes ago. We cached the pages we needed but now we can't access it.'

'Have you located the owner of the site, or the webmaster?'

'Emails and phone calls. No response yet.'

'Shit. OK, where were we up until that point?'

'Tough site to penetrate. We have some tech guys out there,' said Bickland, pointing to the outer office. 'Even they struggled to get past the public pages. The site used a self-designed chat room which the tech guys were most impressed with. So impressed, in fact, that they failed to penetrate it.'

'How much do we have on Turner and Berry?'

'Some, on the members' forum which had little encryption. Very mundane conversations; I've read more exciting exchanges on Netmums.'

'Do we have an address for the owner?'

'Sir,' said Croft, getting off the phone. 'Just managed to get this off the hosting company.'

Lambert took the address from her. The site was owned by Peter Boxall. 'Cornwall?' he said, noting the address as Bickland and Croft both took a sudden interest in their screens. 'It's North Cornwall, not that far,' he continued, into the silence, knowing at this time of day it would take a good four or five hours to reach the location.

'Talk amongst yourselves,' he said, spotting Tillman in the outer office.

'I thought you were going back to head office,' said Lambert, opening the door to a rush of stale, hot air.

'DCI Lambert, a word,' said Tillman.

'Let's go through here,' said Lambert, pointing to an interview room.

Once the door was shut, he told Tillman about the website.

'You realise the press know that the Jardines have been kidnapped. A leak from within,' said Tillman.

'It was only a matter of time, and we were about to go public, so I can't see what the big deal is.'

'Can't you? Well, I've just had that wanker MP, Weaver, on my case for the last thirty minutes. I had to pull the car over so I could fully listen to his wrath.'

'I'm sorry about that, Glenn, but there's not much else I can do about it now.' Lambert knew that Tillman has something else on his mind and was using the potential leak as a diversion. It was Tillman's method of working. 'What do you really want to tell me?' he finally asked, tired of the game.

'I'm getting tired of this bullshit, Michael. This case is now big news, and I don't just mean in the press. A missing officer, and the two burnt bodies... it has every fucker talking.' He sat, as if a dead weight pushed heavy on his shoulders. 'Everyone is getting involved, and I mean everyone.'

'You just told me the Secretary for the Police was bollocking you, so I kind of gathered,' said Lambert.

'If you only knew. Some advice, Michael: do not move beyond your current pay grade. If this was ever fun, it stopped being so a long time ago.'

'Jesus, Glenn, I never took you for the melodramatic type before. It can't be that bad. Are they taking me off the case?'

Tillman shook his head. 'No, but they clearly don't trust either of us. That's why there's a room full of new officers in the revamped incident room.'

'I can live with that,' said Lambert.

'Good. One more thing, though.'

Lambert smiled, thankful they were finally getting to the point.

'They don't want you working on your own.'

'Right,' said Lambert.

'I don't actually blame them, considering your past,' said Tillman, his tone lightening. 'You can be a troublesome little prick at times.'

Lambert couldn't help but laugh. 'I'm not relinquishing the case now, Glenn. I don't care what those fuckers say.'

'No one's asking you to relinquish it, but I had to think fast about a partner for you. They wanted a more senior officer but I said that wouldn't work.'

'Of course not.' A sinking feeling spread over Lambert. 'Oh God, they haven't assigned *you* to work with me?'

Tillman pretended to be wounded, clutching his chest in a convincing parody of a heart attack. 'Of course not,' he said, snapping back to reality. 'What do you take me for, Lambert? I don't do the grunt work.'

'I've noticed. Who then?'

Tillman paused, gauging Lambert for a reaction before he'd even said a name. 'Matilda.'

Lambert took a seat. 'I see.'

Although he'd seen DS Matilda Kennedy on a couple of occasions since the last time he'd worked with her, the suggestion of seeing her again knocked the wind out of him. He still carried around the guilt of what had happened at the mansion in Hampstead. His complicity in sending her into a situation where she risked being injured.

'She was signed back to work a few weeks back. I decided not to tell you.'

Lambert tilted his head, unwilling to be provoked by Tillman's attempt at humour. 'You think this is the case to get her back working?' he said, incredulous.

'We need someone we can trust, Michael.'

'But what about…?'

'No one knows about my relationship with her,' said Tillman.

'I do,' said Lambert, getting to his feet, his body tensing with anger.

Tillman's face reddened, his hand reaching for the thick knot of his tie. 'Sit down, Lambert. You'd rather work with someone new? One of their lot, for instance, who would be taking notes on your every move? If anyone is going to find Caroline, it's you, but not with one of Barnes' team up your arse.'

Lambert sighed, then started laughing at Tillman's outburst. 'What?' he said.

Tillman stared hard at him, then did something Lambert couldn't ever remember him doing before: he joined in with the laughter.

–

After Tillman left, Lambert called Sarah. She sounded annoyed when she answered and he went to end the call. 'It's not important,' he said.

'Sorry, Michael, bit chaotic today. What is it? It's a pleasant surprise to hear from you during the day.'

He hesitated, hearing impatience in her tone. They were caught in a conversation neither of them now wanted to be involved in. 'Matilda's coming back to work,' he said.

'Oh that's great,' said Sarah, this time with a lightness of voice which made her sound genuine.

'Tillman's put her on the Jardine case with me.'

'I see, that's not a problem is it?'

'I don't know,' said Lambert, no longer interested in talking the matter through.

'We've gone through this before, Michael. You can't blame yourself for what happened to her. She doesn't blame you, and neither does anyone else.'

Part of him wanted Matilda to blame him, to at least question him over his decision to send her into danger. Another part was desperate to put it all behind him. 'I know, it will be a little strange but I'm sure it will work out.'

Sarah sighed and he knew he'd somehow annoyed her. 'Is that it then?'

'I guess so.'

'Fine. I'll speak to you later,' said Sarah, hanging up.

Lambert threw his mobile phone on the desk, heat spreading across his face. More and more of their conversations seemed to be ending this way recently. He couldn't quite determine why they had so little patience for one another. His natural instinct was to blame himself. He could close himself off at times, and sometimes it took only the slightest thing to make him retreat from communication. It needed resolving, but neither of them had time at present. He vowed he would make more of an effort when the Jardine case was closed, whilst trying to ignore the nagging doubt that he'd made the same vow many times before.

–

DS Matilda Kennedy arrived an hour later. Lambert was working on the System, accessing files on the suicide website, when the duty sergeant called him. 'I've put her in interview room three for the time being,' he said.

Lambert snapped shut his laptop and held his head in his hands. It was ludicrous to feel nervous about seeing Matilda again. He'd seen her since the incident, first by her hospital bed, and later as she'd been convalescing, but never alone. During those months of recovery, he'd always hoped she would return to work but never thought it would happen. He admired her bravery, though he wasn't surprised by it. In the short period of time they'd worked together she'd proved to be tenacious and relentless in her work ethic. Despite her time away, Lambert was convinced she was perfect for the role Tillman assigned her. Yet he still remained sitting at his desk.

The decision to send her undercover in Hampstead had been a joint one between Lambert, Tillman, and Matilda herself. It was possibly a failure on Lambert's part, a sense of self-importance, that made him blame himself for what had happened. She wasn't a child that needed protecting. Like everyone else on the force, she knew the risks at every stage, and if Tillman didn't blame himself, then why should he? But it was something he couldn't shake. He should have articulated his concerns better to Tillman. Should have explained that his guilt would possibly make him over-protective, that the uneasy relationship could jeopardise the case, but Tillman didn't work that way. Such a response would sound weak to his ears, and he would no doubt point out, correctly, that Matilda didn't need his protection or pity.

Lambert punched his fists onto the desk and used his knuckles to push himself up. He opened his office door and made the short walk through the incident room, blood ringing in his ears. Taking a deep breath, he opened the door to interview room three.

DS Matilda Kennedy sat behind a desk like a suspect, staring intently at the screen of her mobile phone. She paused before turning to face him, a stern look on her face. 'You keep everyone waiting this long?' she said.

Lambert held her gaze and tried not to look at the scar tissue on the left side of her face, the legacy of the explosion at the Hampstead mansion. 'Some of us are busy you know, Kennedy.'

She smiled and Lambert felt his pulse drop. 'It's good to see you again, sir.'

He would have hugged her, had they not been at work. 'Enough of the pleasantries, Kennedy, work to do. You cleared for driving?' he asked.

'I need to wear glasses now, but yes,' said Matilda.

'Good, I need a lift.'

'Where we going?'

'Cornwall.'

# Chapter Nineteen

Lambert would have liked to sleep but was too uncomfortable in the small confines of the car. He sat in companionable silence next to Matilda, who studied the road with an intentness he didn't remember, leaning towards the windscreen, her new spectacles pushed tight against the bridge of her nose.

After failing to make contact with Peter Boxall, the owner of the suicide support website, Lambert had obtained the man's last known address. It would have been easier to have sent over the local CID, especially considering how far south Boxall lived, but it was too much of a chance to take. Lambert was convinced that the arsonist would have had some contact with Turner and Berry. How else to explain their appearance at the Jardine house?

The suicide website was the most obvious starting point and the fact that the owner had recently withdrawn the site from the web was suspicious. It could have been taken down for simple maintenance, but that sounded too much of a coincidence. Lambert's guess was the owner had seen the added traffic from the police searches and had taken it down to protect himself. In turn, this suggested he had something to hide. It was possible that closer inspection of the site would reveal that Boxall was aiding people in their suicide attempts and he'd been spooked by the attention.

A second possibility – and more of a long shot – was that Boxall knew the arsonist in some way.

It took over an hour to reach the M25 and nearly the same time again to reach the M3. 'Are we staying the night?' asked Kennedy.

'Haven't packed my overnight bag, but we may have to catch a few hours at some point,' said Lambert. If things continued like this they wouldn't reach their destination until mid-evening, and he already felt too tired to contemplate a six-hour journey home.

Fortunately, the traffic thinned as they got further south and Matilda made good time on the A30. Lambert was glad to be working with her again, whatever his misgivings about his role in her injuries.

At eight pm they reached the area where Boxall lived, a remote area on the North coast of Cornwall. The night was cloudless, the sprinkling of stars that mapped the sky a stark contrast to the grey London skyline they'd left behind. They drove up a hill towards a single-track road, covered on each side by unkempt bushes and trees which scraped the sides of the car.

Boxall lived in a gated area which was a polar opposite to the one in Chislehurst. It appeared to be a single dwelling, a ramshackle bungalow with just one front window and what appeared to be a metal-plated door. The house was fenced in by a makeshift perimeter created by piecemeal material on top of which hung loose reels of barbed wire.

The faint sounds of the sea greeted them as they opened their car doors. 'Welcoming looking place,' said Lambert, stretching his arms towards the sky.

Matilda peered through the fence towards the building. 'The front window looks as if it's frosted over. I can't tell if there's a light on.'

'I'll try the back,' said Lambert, his footing slipping as he scampered up the small hill to the side of the building.

Bending down, he picked up a handful of sand. The fence stretched on further than he'd expected, enclosing a compound which held several vehicles, including a derelict school bus. A number of lights decorated the fence, illuminating the rusting vehicles within.

A sense of isolation rushed over Lambert as he reached the back gate. Behind him, the land stretched into the distance towards the sea. Being there made him miss the hustle of the city. He couldn't imagine spending prolonged periods of time in such seclusion, the distant sound of lapping waves his only companion.

From nowhere, a scrambling noise destroyed the tranquillity. Lambert glanced up in time to see an animal rushing him, gums pulled back to reveal a set of large white teeth. The dog – a Rottweiler cross, Lambert guessed – rammed into the other side of the fence, snarling and barking. Lambert tried to control the stream of adrenaline in his system as the dog continued running at the fence, biting at the metallic barrier as if it could snap its way to freedom.

Lambert twitched as Matilda put her hand on his shoulder. 'Jesus Christ, Kennedy,' he said, through gritted teeth.

Matilda pulled him back into the darkness, far enough away that the dog stopped barking. 'No movement from within,' she said.

'Probably used to that thing going off at local wildlife.'

Matilda chuckled. 'That thing? You're not keen on your new friend then?'

'I'm just glad that fence was there,' said Lambert.

They crouched down, surveying the house, waiting for a non-canine sign of life.

'It's a long way to come for nothing,' said Matilda.

Lambert sensed the sand shifting beneath him. It reminded him of torturous summer holidays as a child, the sand a constant enemy invading every part of him. 'You realise one of us is going in,' said Lambert.

'May I remind you, sir, this is my first day back after a long convalescence,' said Matilda, a familiar tone of mischievousness in her voice.

'You're going to play that card, are you?'

'Afraid so.'

They retreated back to the car, mapping out the full extent of the building.

'We could always wait till morning, get the local plod involved,' said Matilda.

'We're not on holiday, Kennedy. You got spray?'

Matilda produced her can of pepper spray for his inspection. 'Keep hold of it. I've got mine. Don't be afraid to use it on that mongrel.'

'That dog is probably fine – he's doing what dogs do, protecting his territory.'

'I'll be protecting my territory if he comes anywhere near me,' said Lambert, searching for a safe place to attempt climbing the fence. He found a small area, half his body width, which had the least amount of barbed wire. From the boot of his car he retrieved a roll of canvas which he threw over the fence. 'Ready,' he said.

Matilda nodded and headed to the back of the compound.

Lambert waited for the signal, the sound of blood drumming in his ears a backbeat to the crashing of the waves which sounded nearer than before.

Seconds later the dog started barking and Lambert made his ascent. He leant his hand against the material, the barbs beneath close to the surface, and managed to swing himself over the fence. His left knee gave way as he landed and he struggled to contain a groan of anguish.

He pushed himself up, grateful he could still hear the dog being entertained by Matilda in the distance. He peered through the small window at the front of the house, unable to see any light through the minuscule slits of the shutter. He tried the door and was surprised when it creaked open.

He was surprised further by the man who stood behind the door, staring at him with a manic grin, holding a shotgun pointed directly at Lambert's chest.

# Chapter Twenty

'You really are stupid,' said the man, holding the gun steady.

Lambert had been on the other end of a gun on enough occasions not to panic. 'DCI Lambert. If you would like to reach into my inside left pocket, you'll be able to see my warrant card.'

'I wasn't born yesterday.' The man holding the shotgun had a deep Cornish accent. Lambert estimated he was in excess of six feet four. 'And your friend teasing my dog? I've been watching your antics for the last hour on my security system.'

'Impressive. What's so important that you need such security?' asked Lambert.

'I ask the questions. What's so important that you have to breach my perimeter?'

'You're Peter Boxall?' asked Lambert, noticing a slight reaction from the man.

'I'll ask you again, what is it you want?'

'We came to talk to you about your website.'

Boxall moved out of the shadows towards him. 'Step back,' he said to Lambert, who retreated back to the fence. Boxall was dressed in combat gear, camouflage trousers and shirt and what looked like army-issued boots. He kept the gun pointed at Lambert and whistled.

Lambert's pulse quickened as the dog approached, appearing within seconds at his master's side. Lambert dropped his left hand, ready to reach for his spray as the dog sat down, its gaze as steady as Boxall's arm which still held the shotgun.

'Call your colleague,' said Boxall.

Lambert paused, assessing the best course of action.

The man lowered the gun and aimed it at Lambert's knee. 'Call her or walk with a limp for the rest of your life.'

The dog tilted his head as the man spoke, as if querying the instruction. Despite the situation, Lambert had to stifle a laugh. He was sure the man was bluffing, and wasn't about to jeopardise Matilda.

The man flicked off the safety on the shotgun. 'Last chance,' he said.

'I'm here,' came a voice from the front gate.

Lambert kept his gaze on the man he believed to be Peter Boxall, and the dog sitting obediently by his side.

Boxall didn't move. He kept the gun pointed at Lambert's chest. 'And you are?'

'DS Matilda Kennedy.'

Boxall sighed, as if the fight had left him and he realised the trouble he was in. 'You better come in, then. Catch,' he said, throwing a set of keys at Lambert.

Lambert caught the keys and thought about throwing them back at Boxall and attacking the man, the dog and shotgun convincing him otherwise for the time being. He unlocked the padlock on the steel gate, noticing the pepper spray in Matilda's left hand. 'Welcome back to work,' he whispered to her, as she made her way through the entrance.

To Lambert's surprise, the dog wandered over to her, his tail wagging.

'Lock it,' said Boxall, pointing to Lambert. 'You have ID?' he asked Matilda.

Matilda withdrew her warrant card and showed it to the man. It was unlikely he could see the details in the relative darkness but he seemed satisfied with the glint of metal from Matilda's shield.

'And his?'

'Inside pocket,' said Lambert.

Matilda reached in and displayed the warrant card to Boxall.

'I guess I'm in a whole shit-heap of trouble,' said Boxall, lowering and opening the barrel of the gun. He turned it around, showing that the two barrels were filled in. 'Decommissioned. I keep it for protection. It's a remote place for a man alone.'

Lambert felt himself relax. 'Can we come in and talk?' he said.

The man nodded. 'I'm Peter Boxall, by the way, though you obviously know that. This is Stevie,' he said, stroking the dog on the head.

Stevie wagged his tail, his ears pushing back as the man scratched his head. 'You don't have to worry about him. Once you're in, you're fine. You coming in?'

Lambert nodded and followed the man into the house, keeping his distance. The dog ran between the three of them, seemingly excited to have guests. Inside, Boxall switched on a light, revealing an area which looked like a makeshift garage. The floor was tarmacked, the air heavy with the smell of petrol and oil.

'You live here?' said Lambert.

'Living quarters out back. I do some part time work as a mechanic. Not a great call for it around here. Get you anything?' said Boxall, opening a decrepit fridge, and pulling out a bottle of lager.

'Not for us,' said Lambert, noticing the man's hand was shaking. 'Take a seat, Mr Boxall,' he continued, pointing to a small desk and chair.

Boxall sat behind the desk, every inch of which was covered with papers and various car-parts. Boxall was older than Lambert had first thought, his face sprinkled with numerous liver spots, his tired eyes sunk deep into his face. 'This is about the site, you say?'

Lambert took a seat opposite Boxall, as Matilda made a tour of the garage accompanied by an excited Stevie. 'Yes, you took it down earlier today. Why?'

'I noticed a lot of external attention. Hackers.'

Lambert nodded. 'Did you read the emails we sent you, or check the numerous messages left by phone?'

Boxall's shoulders drooped. It was clear the man was defeated.

'Just tell the truth, Mr Boxall.'

'The truth is, I was going to sleep on it. It was a bit overwhelming thinking the site was hacked, and then the calls. Why do you think I was sitting in the dark?'

'With a gun.'

'A replica,' said Boxall, almost hopefully.

'We'll come to that later.' Lambert told him about Turner and Berry, how their bodies were found in Jardine's house.

Boxall nodded. 'And what has this to do with me?'

'I think you know that,' said Lambert. 'We had just discovered that Turner and Berry were chatting on your site when you pulled the plug, as it were.'

'Even if that was the case, there's no reason for me to divulge details to you. This is a private site. The users have a right to privacy as well as anonymity.'

'That maybe so, but I'm working a murder and missing persons enquiry and you and your site might may have a direct link to both cases. There's a chance you're technically an accessory to both.'

'Bullshit,' said Boxall, for a second regaining some of his earlier bravado.

'You'll find the English legal system works in mysterious ways. You cooperate now, you're going to save yourself a lot of heartache.'

'IT equipment is in the back,' said Matilda, returning with the Rottweiler cross running between her legs and threatening to trip her up.

'Shall we?' said Lambert, leaving Boxall in no doubt it was an order and not a request.

–

The IT room was little more than a mismatched set of laptops and antique freestanding PC machines. 'This is where the magic occurs?' said Lambert.

'It did,' said Boxall.

'How long has the site been running?' asked Matilda.

'Three years,' said Boxall, folding his arms.

'What made you start it?' said Matilda, her voice soft, almost soothing.

'Does it matter?'

'No, I'm just interested. I imagine there must be a story behind it?'

Lambert wanted to get down to work, wanted to push the man until he gave them all the information Lambert required, but he was happy to be patient whilst Matilda took a more gentle tack.

Boxall shrugged. 'I wanted to create a community where others like me could share their experiences. That was all.'

'Others like you?'

Boxall spoke to Matilda as if Lambert wasn't present. 'I suffer from depression. Sometimes I have suicidal thoughts. Look where I live, I'm not going to find much support around here.'

'And the other stuff?' said Matilda.

'Other stuff?'

'The arranged suicides?'

'All of sudden I feel I need a solicitor with me,' said Boxall.

'We don't care about your site, Mr Boxall. We're trying to locate someone and some background information would be welcome.'

Lambert was impressed by Matilda's approach; the way she empathised with Boxall, searching for answers whilst remaining unthreatening.

'Whatever users do on the site is their affair. If they decide to make agreements, it's no concern of mine.'

Lambert thought that Boxall would soon discover how much it did concern him. From the few glimpses he'd had of the site, there were links to the illegal purchase of narcotics which would assist in the process of taking one's life.

'Do you have any personal connections with the users?'

'Occasionally. I moderate the main chat rooms. Sometimes I speak personally to some of the users.'

'What about?' asked Lambert.

Boxall took a seat. Whatever fight there had been in him at the beginning had evaporated. It was almost as if he welcomed the company, the opportunity to unburden himself. 'Believe it or not, the goal of the site is not to help people commit suicide. Never. Each user is made aware this is a last measure. The community exists to help one another, to offer advice or point to places where more advice is available. Sometimes…' Boxall faltered, his eyes watering. 'Sometimes no amount of words can suffice. There's so much suffering out there, you can only guess. I suppose you encounter it at times in your line of work, but things like grief, long-term illness, we never talk about these things. That was all I was trying to do.'

'You can help us now,' said Lambert. 'Two people are missing and you might be able to help.'

'How?' said Boxall.

'We believe Mr and Mrs Jardine are still alive, and that their kidnapper used your site to contact Ms Berry and Mr Turner. That was why we hacked your site. We need to access every conversation involving Berry and Turner. Is this something you can help us with?'

'Theoretically,' said Boxall.

Lambert gripped the back of the chair where Boxall sat. 'Can you do it or not?'

Boxall was close to tears. 'I can do it but I'm not sure I should.'

'You're not sure you should? Berry and Turner were found in the living room of the Jardine house, burnt beyond recognition.'

'Maybe it was what they wanted.'

'And what about Caroline Jardine and her husband. Do you think they want to die?'

'You need a warrant,' said Boxall.

Lambert looked at Matilda. He didn't have time for this. 'I could get a warrant within the next hour. If I apply for one you'll be arrested as a murder accomplice.'

'Bullshit,' said Boxall, echoing his earlier statement.

Lambert swung the man round in his chair, and bent to his haunches so he was eye level. There would be no warrant. Boxall would either agree to share the information with him now or Lambert would be forced to take a different, less pleasant approach. 'A colleague of mine has been missing for three days and the only lead I have is you and your website. I am asking you politely, Mr Boxall, please, for Mr and Mrs Jardine's sake, help us with our investigation.'

Boxall matched Lambert's stare, but Lambert could see in the man's eyes that it was bravado. 'OK, for them, I'll help.'

–

Lambert kept a close eye on Boxall as he began tapping away at the battered keyboard of his PC. He acted compliant, but for all Lambert knew a single keystroke could delete everything.

'I believe these are their accounts,' said Boxall, producing a split screen displaying two files. One file was labelled RedStarBelgrade, the other MissMaisy. 'Those were their usernames. At least those were the two files your teams were interested in this morning. Both accounts were anonymous, but Turner's IP address was local to Devon and Berry's IP address was situated in Peterborough.' Boxall pressed a button on the file marked RedStarBelgrade. 'I guess your team ran a search on their names.' He pointed to one of the entries on the main chat room. 'I presume Jonathan was RedStar's first name?'

Lambert nodded.

'And MissMaisy, Maxine?'

'Yes.'

'Let's be thankful they used their first names,' said Boxall.

'Can you narrow the search to where they appear in the same conversation?' asked Matilda.

Boxall clicked a few buttons. 'A hundred pages of results,' he said.

Lambert shut his eyes. 'Is this all in the main chat room?'

'Yes.'

'Could they private message one another?'

'Yes, but we don't keep those records.'

'Private message boards?' asked Matilda.

Boxall looked away. 'We don't keep those either. The site was designed to respect the users' privacy.'

'You're fucking kidding me?' said Lambert.

Boxall let out a low whistling sound. 'Hang on,' he said, tapping his keyboard so fast that Lambert struggled to keep up. 'This might help,' he said.

Matilda leant towards the screen, squinting through her glasses. The backlight of the screen illuminated her face and Lambert saw up close for the first time the damage the fire had inflicted on her. The tissue on her face looked so damaged and inflamed that he wondered if she was still in pain. 'What is this?' she asked Boxall.

'A list of the private chat rooms where either or both of them were involved in the chats.'

Again, the list ran through many pages. 'Can you display the usernames of the other participants?' asked Lambert.

Boxall made a few more keystrokes. 'There,' he said.

Sixty-two entries appeared on the screen. Lambert stopped scrolling halfway down. 'It can't be that easy,' he said, highlighting one of the usernames.

Lambert clicked on the name.

'Press there,' said Boxall.

Lambert clicked again.

'That shows a private group used by three people. It was accessed two hundred and fifty times over in the last four months. That means they were all using it on a daily basis more than once.'

'When was the last time it was accessed?'

'Five weeks ago,' said Boxall.

Lambert exchanged a look with Matilda. Berry had officially gone missing just over four weeks previously and it was possible Turner had been missing for that time as well.

'I think we may have found our man,' said Lambert, pointing to the third member of the group. The username couldn't have been more obvious if it tried.

TheFireman1973.

# Chapter Twenty-One

After the local CID secured the area, Lambert and Matilda packed a squad car with all the tech from Boxall's home which Matilda drove back to London.

'You're coming with me,' Lambert said to Boxall.

'Am I under arrest?' said Boxall, looking at a local uniformed officer for support.

'Do you want to be?'

'I want to know my rights,' said Boxall.

Lambert glared at the uniformed officer, who suddenly found something more interesting to do. Without a word, Lambert cuffed Boxall and guided him to the back of his car. 'You realise one of my colleagues is missing?'

'So?' said Boxall, grunting as Lambert threw him into the back seat.

'Let's get back to you London, so you can meet Caroline Jardine's team. See if you want to repeat what you just said to me.'

Lambert called Bickland as he drove, telling the DS to get all bodies together within the next couple of hours. Lambert had considered going through the files in Boxall's home, but it wasn't feasible to have two teams working so far apart.

'What do you know of this Fireman?' said Lambert, an hour into the journey.

'I told you, I never accessed the private conversations,' said Boxall.

'Did you chat to him in the public rooms?'

'Not that I remember.'

'Your site can't be that busy,' said Lambert.

'You'd be surprised. People from all over the world use it. The majority don't contribute. They use it for advice, or until they're ready to join in.'

'Are we going to be able to access the conversations between those three?'

Lambert saw Boxall shrug in his rear-view mirror. The look of utter disinterest on Boxall's face made Lambert want to pull the car over and teach him the meaning of police brutality. Instead, he wound down his window, placed a siren on the roof and began accelerating for home.

–

The team were already working by the time Lambert got to the station. Some of the officers were setting up Boxall's equipment, whilst others were analysing the files Matilda had emailed earlier.

Croft bypassed any pleasantries as Lambert led Boxall into the incident room. 'We've been searching for the handle, TheFireman1973, on social media. No direct match apart from a Yahoo account which was accessed once in 2006. However, you'd be surprised at how many people use a handle with 'fireman' in it. Runs into the thousands. Don't you think this is one hell of a coincidence, sir?'

'Depends who we're dealing with. If it is our arsonist friend he might deliberately be looking for attention, or he just might be so computer illiterate that it doesn't matter. Find a room for Mr Boxall, would you?'

As Croft led Boxall away, Lambert poured himself a large cup of coffee and retreated to his office. He pulled the blinds before drinking it in a number of uneasy gulps. After locking the office door, he leant back in his chair and went to sleep. Thirty minutes later he sprung awake, the coffee and brief sleep having vitalised him.

He rubbed his eyes and opened the shutters, looking out at the activity in the incident room as if viewing a new day.

A nervous looking tech guy Lambert had never met before knocked on the door. He swayed from foot to foot as he stood at the end of Lambert's desk. 'DC Robson, sir,' said the man.

'What you got for me, Robson?'

Robson placed a sheaf of papers on the desk, smiling as nervousness made way for smugness. 'We're printing the rest, sir. There's quite a few.'

Lambert picked up the first page, sitting straighter in his chair as he realised what he was reading.

'It's the transcripts between the two victims and the Fireman,' said Robson.

'Thanks, Robson. I can see that.'

Robson hovered at the edge of Lambert's desk as Lambert scanned the transcripts. 'Is there anything else, Robson?' said Lambert, not looking up.

'No, sir.'

'OK then.' Lambert reread the first page as Robson tiptoed out of the room. Neither of the three addressed each other by first name, though they were familiar with one another.

'You've read this?' said Matilda, walking into the office uninvited. She was still wearing her glasses and it was this, rather than the burn tissue on her face, which caused him to do a double take.

'I'm trying to.'

'It gets good. They made a pact, the three of them, to meet this year in November.'

'A pact?'

Sitting down, Matilda removed her glasses and pinched her nose. 'To kill themselves.'

'I see. What page?'

Matilda flicked through the pages. 'First mention is page eighty-eight.'

'You've been busy,' said Lambert, flicking through his transcript to the relevant page. He scanned the next ten pages, trying to make sense of the words. Try as he might, he couldn't see any signs of coercion from the person using the Fireman handle. 'What else do we have?'

'We're looking at all messages involving the Fireman. And the other two as well. We've lots of reading ahead.'

'Any way we're going to trace this guy?'

'He was using an IP proxy as far as we can tell. We're checking each time he logged in.'

'I need you to read this for me, Kennedy, all of it.'

'I'll get a summary to you in the next couple of hours,' said Matilda. 'It's great to be back,' she added, waving the pages of the transcript at him as she left his office.

It was nine-thirty am before Lambert left the office. He'd read as much of the transcript as possible since instructing Matilda to summarise it for him. The majority could have been skimmed, featuring as it did the mundane everyday conversation of three online friends, but Lambert studied each page in detail, searching for a hint that the two victims were somehow being manipulated by the Fireman.

'Robson, where are we on finding the Fireman's location?' he shouted across the incident room before leaving.

The nervous IT guy almost fell off his seat at the question. 'Nothing yet, sir,' he replied, confused.

Lambert ignored him and walked over to Matilda to tell her where he was going.

'You want company?' she asked, the long night showing in the darkness beneath her eyes.

'I'll go alone on this one. You can continue on the transcript. Anything else I should know? I reached page one twenty.'

'It's heartbreaking stuff. If the Fireman's faking it, he's one hell of a writer.'

—

Lambert decided to make the short walk to the school rather than driving, hoping the frost would reinvigorate him. He passed the high street, surprised by the volume of traffic on the roads. He stopped at a newsagent, remembering his last meeting with Mia Helmer. The little shop was illuminated by bright neon lights, regurgitated air filling the sterile atmosphere. Lambert peered down at Helmer's newspaper, thankful not to see any mention of the case on the front page. He supposed he would have heard about it already if Helmer had published the story, but he decided to purchase the newspaper anyway.

He tucked it under his arm as he walked up the hill, his thoughts focused on Caroline Jardine and her husband. He wondered if they were subject to the elements at the moment or if such human concerns were no longer relevant.

A high-pitched buzzing sound assaulted his ears as he pressed the button at the school gates. 'DCI Lambert for Mr Linklater,' he said to the enquiring voice, which buzzed him in without a reply.

A frizzy haired woman greeted him at the reception desk. 'I'm afraid Mr Linklater can't see you at the moment. He's involved in a senior management meeting. You really should have made an appointment,' she said, taking only a cursory glance at his ID.

Lambert was in no mood for such a jobsworth, but was too tired to rant at the woman. 'Tell Mr Linklater I will see him in the next five minutes, one way or another.'

The woman was a parody of indignation, shaking her head as if Lambert had just insulted her mother. Lambert watched for a second in amusement before taking a seat. Two minutes later, Linklater appeared.

'Could you not have phoned ahead at least?' said the man, who looked as tired as Lambert felt.

'Sorry to drag you from your meeting, Mr Linklater,' said Lambert, getting to his feet. 'We've had some developments you should be made aware of.'

'Fine, follow me,' said the headmaster.

Linklater's office was more impressive than Lambert had envisaged. Recently decorated, it was sparse and minimalist. Linklater sat behind a wide glass topped desk, on top of which was a widescreen monitor with the Apple logo stencilled in grey on it. 'Take a seat,' said Linklater.

'Thank you. There's no easy way to tell you this, Mr Linklater,' said Lambert, deciding not to wait, to see if he could ascertain anything in Linklater's response. 'It seems that the two bodies recovered from Mrs Jardine's house did not belong to her or her husband.'

It was the subtlest of movements, but Linklater reached for his wedding finger. 'I don't understand,' he said.

'After post-mortems, it was discovered that the two bodies belonged to another pair of individuals.'

Linklater grimaced, his eyes narrowing. 'Sorry, I'm lost here. Are you saying Caroline is alive?'

'Possibly.'

'Possibly?' said Linklater, raising his voice as if speaking to an unruly pupil.

'We believe Mr and Mrs Jardine have been kidnapped. That the two bodies were placed as decoys.'

Linklater glanced sideways as if imagining the scene. 'Come on,' he said, refusing to believe what he was being told. 'Why? This doesn't make any sense.'

Lambert studied the man, analysing his reaction.

'Do you think she's alive?' said Linklater.

'I honestly don't know. We've had no notification from a would-be kidnapper, no hostage note or similar.'

'Isn't that unusual?'

'Not necessarily. Kidnapping for ransom is not that common. I'm afraid even nowadays people disappear for no apparent reason. Sometimes never to be seen again.'

'I don't believe this. Somehow, this is…' Linklater hesitated. 'This is worse.'

Lambert nodded. 'The not knowing is hard but there is still hope – and you can help.'

Lambert told him about the suicide site, about the two victims found at Jardine's house, and the Fireman.

'You think the guy who befriended these people was the arsonist? Christ, did he murder them?'

'We're not sure about that. They were already dead before the fire. He could have assisted them with their suicide and used them as replacement bodies.'

'What sort of sick individual would do that?'

'That's what we're trying to ascertain. I'm sorry to ask you this, but did Caroline ever suffer from depression or ever mention feeling suicidal to you?' said Lambert.

'Caroline?' Linklater chortled as if such a thought was unthinkable. 'She got fed up with her job, was depressed sometimes in the general way we all get depressed about work and some of the things she had to endure, but there was nothing clinical about it. She wasn't on medication and despite our differences and the arguments, I wouldn't say her moods were particularly changeable. By the end, she just didn't like me.'

Lambert was surprised by the last admission, admired Linklater's honesty. It highlighted a sense of vulnerability in the man. 'There's nothing you can think of, anything from her work perhaps.'

Linklater stood up and walked to a small window at the corner of his office. 'Sorry, this is all hard to take in. Until a few minutes ago I thought she was dead. I'm relieved that's not the case but still. Caroline didn't share much about her work. It was one of the reasons why...' Linklater faltered, and Lambert thought of the secrets he'd kept from Sophie during their marriage.

'Anyway, she didn't tell me much. She was like two different people, if you can believe that. There was the policewoman, and there was Caroline. My Caroline. At least for a time.'

'So there's a chance she could have kept things like this from you?' asked Lambert.

'Like what?'

'Being involved with whatever this is, this suicide thing.'

'No, no, no,' said Linklater, shaking his head as if to convince himself. 'She wasn't like that. Are you married, Mr Lambert?'

'Yes,' said Lambert, lacking the strength to explain his situation with Sophie.

'You'll know what it's like, then. There are some things you just know. She wasn't suicidal, I would have known it.'

Lambert didn't share his conviction. 'You've been separated for some time now. How close have you been in the last few years?'

Linklater returned to his seat. 'I hadn't thought about that. I forget sometimes, it feels like yesterday we were still together. To be honest, I've only seen her once or twice since the divorce. I heard about the child but I haven't seen her. Could she be suffering from some form of depression? It's possible I guess, but as I said, it wasn't like the Caroline I knew.'

Linklater played the hurt ex-husband very well, possibly too well. 'What do you know about Marcus Jardine?'

'Nothing. She sent me an email about their marriage. I deleted it. I'm not sure I would have remembered his name if your fellow officer hadn't mentioned it to me.'

Lambert watched the man's hand rub his ring finger once more and knew he was lying.

'I'm not sure if it's of use, but I do remember one thing she told me when we were together,' said Linklater, interlocking his hands as if he knew Lambert had spotted his deceit. 'One of her colleagues, don't remember the name, sorry. She committed suicide. Caroline was pretty cut up about it. I guess you know about that already, though?'

Lambert stood up, not offering a reaction to the surprising news. 'Thanks for your time, and apologies for interrupting your meeting,' he said, placing his card on Linklater's table. 'If you think of anything else, please let me know.'

# Chapter Twenty-Two

Matilda had finished the full transcript by the time Lambert returned to the station. 'The last time they'd talked was the night before they planned to meet. Central London of all places, at the Fireman's suggestion. They planned to do it at his flat,' she said.

'Jesus, that's convenient. I presume there's no mention of an address?'

'No, but we have arrival times for the trains so we're searching CCTV as we speak.'

'Let me know as soon as you get a hit. I need to check something.'

Lambert rushed to his office and switched on his laptop. It was probably nothing, but Linklater's revelation about Jardine's former colleague had thrown him. He hadn't read anything about it in her file and it was troubling to think he'd missed something so relevant. He spent thirty minutes scanning her file with no results so instead he called Tillman and asked him what he knew.

'I heard about it at the time. Let me think. Alistair Newlyn. It was about four years ago. Didn't take any notice of it then,' said Tillman, who was back at head office.

'You didn't think it was relevant to mention?'

'Christ, Lambert, he wasn't the first and he won't be the last.'

'It would have been useful to have been notified.'

'Why? It would be one hell of a leap if Newlyn's suicide has any bearing on this.'

'Why don't you let me decide that, sir.'

Tillman went silent. Lambert pictured him fuming on the other end of the receiver, his face reddening. 'I'll put Newlyn's file on the System for you. Get back to me when you've tied up both cases,' said Tillman, hanging up.

Not for the first time in a case, Lambert had a sense something was just out of reach. Tillman was correct in stating Newlyn's suicide was not the first or last time an officer took their own life, but whilst Lambert accepted coincidences in his line of work, he couldn't help but feel the various strands of the case were moving in the same direction.

The file appeared on the screen a few minutes later. Alistair Newlyn had committed suicide four years ago. DI Caroline Jardine and her colleague, DS Florence Colville, had discovered his body. Newlyn had hung himself from a high beam in the living room of his flat. From the autopsy report, Jardine and her colleague had arrived three hours too late.

Lambert scratched the stubble on his face. He was missing something. Newlyn's file stated he'd been investigating an organised crime ring at the time. Along with Jardine and Colville, he'd been part of a large interdepartmental team looking at people trafficking from certain Baltic states. It was the type of larger project Lambert had been used to during his time in The Group and latterly in the NCA – the investigation into the serial killer dubbed The Watcher, and the present case, being the exceptions.

It was at times like this, midway through a case, where Lambert doubted he was suited to either type of investigation. He accepted such self-doubt as a necessary part of the job and convinced himself that things would soon unravel, and that he should trust his experience. He clicked on the third member of the team, DS Florence Colville. Colville was five years Jardine's junior. Flicking through the people trafficking case, Lambert noted Colville's successful participation in the arrest of four foreign nationals. After which, her file was virtually blank until the mention that she had officially left the force three and half years ago. He was about to study her file further when there was a knock on his office door.

Matilda didn't bother waiting for a reply before entering the office. 'Sir, we've had a hit from the CCTV imaging at Waterloo station on the date where Turner and Berry were due to meet the Fireman,' she said.

'Show me,' said Lambert, shutting off the System with one click and turning the laptop to Matilda.

Matilda adjusted her glasses, a gesture which still seemed alien to Lambert, and tapped at the keyboard until Lambert's screen mirrored her own. 'Here,' she said, pointing to a freeze frame of three people greeting one another. 'Facial recognition software is starting to pay for itself. That's Berry and Turner,' she said, pointing to a frail looking woman wrapped in a coat two sizes too big, and a heavyset man with a greying beard.

'And that's the Fireman?' said Lambert, pointing to the third of the trio.

'Better than that,' said Matilda, pushing her glasses up the bridge of her nose. 'We have a name. Trevor Hodge.'

'That was a quick,' said Lambert, studying the image. In the freeze-framed image, Hodge held his hand out towards Turner in greeting. He looked as if he was holding his chest back as if pulling away from something, his face looking away from Turner.

As if reading his thoughts, Matilda played the video. As Lambert had thought, the exchange was an awkward one. Hodge didn't look comfortable either shaking hands with Turner, his hand limp in Turner's grip, or exchanging kisses with Berry. 'This man is not used to social situations. How did we discover his name?' asked Lambert.

'That's the wonderful thing. He's on our database. You'll never guess what for?' said Matilda, a triumphant smile spreading across her face.

'You're kidding me?'

'Nope. Three separate cases of arson. And we have an address for him.'

'What the hell are we doing here, then?'

# Chapter Twenty-Three

'We already have back-up from the local CID outside the building,' said Matilda, as she drove to Hodge's last known address in Romford, Essex. 'I've told them to maintain an eye on all exit points, but not approach.'

'I'd expect nothing less,' said Lambert, with a smile, opening the System on his laptop and the file on Hodge.

Trevor Hodge was forty-five. His file picture showed someone who looked much older. In colour, Lambert made out the pronounced lines which cut into the man's face, the tiredness in his eyes. Hodge was taken into care aged thirteen when his father died and family life became too much for his mother. As was often the case, this was when he turned to crime. He was cautioned on three separate occasions for theft, each time from large department stores. Then, aged seventeen, he was convicted for his first foray into arson and sentenced to a year in a young offenders' institution.

In Lambert's opinion, and despite Hodge's relative youth at the time, the sentence was lenient. Hodge had snuck into a local allotment site where he managed to burn down five huts used by the local gardeners. Fortunately, it being the middle of the night, no one had been hurt, which would explain to some extent the leniency of the sentence. The most interesting aspect of the file was that

Hodge had waited at the allotments. He'd been sitting near the burning sheds watching the fire with an uncanny intensity, according to the arresting officer, and hadn't put up a struggle whilst being arrested.

Hodge had spent time with a therapist during his incarceration. The report suggested he had an unhealthy obsession with fire, which made Lambert snort.

Hodge was briefly monitored on his release, and it wasn't until age twenty-eight that he had struck again. This time he was caught before he'd managed to carry out his plan, which was a repeat of his first crime. Hodge had been arrested at a second set of allotments following a call from a local gardener who had been working late at his patch. On arrest, the team discovered a number of undetonated matchboxes which reflected Orr's work.

Lambert shared the information with Matilda. 'I did a search on this on the System,' he said.

'On what?'

'Arson cases which matched Orr's MO – but this case was not mentioned.'

'Is Orr mentioned in the report?' asked Matilda, who was weaving the squad car expertly through the lunchtime traffic.

Lambert scanned the report. 'Doesn't look like it. You would think someone would have made a link.'

'Would you?' said Matilda.

Lambert sighed, conceding there was no real reason someone would have made such a leap.

'What was the third case?' asked Matilda, narrowly missing the back of a white van as she manoeuvred through the lanes.

'He set a fire at a campsite which got somewhat out of hand. He'd set it near a scattering of trees and, unsurprisingly, it spread. He only received a deferred sentence.'

'How long ago was that?'

'Eight years ago,' said Lambert, shutting his laptop. 'It's not these cases we need to be concerned with. It's the ones we don't know about.'

'He sounds a bit sloppy,' said Matilda, blasting her horn and flashing her headlights at a car in front of her.

'I'm not so sure. He may have got away in the first instance if he hadn't hung around to admire his handiwork. Even the second time sounded like bad luck.'

'And his forest fire?' said Matilda, turning to face Lambert.

'Jesus, keep your eyes on the road, Kennedy,' said Lambert, prompting laughter from Matilda. 'Who knows. Cry for help maybe?'

'He doesn't fit the profile I had in my mind for the Jardine job. He sounds like a fire obsessive, but switching bodies like that?'

Lambert agreed but they didn't know enough about Hodge at the moment to dismiss him so easily.

Matilda switched off the lights as they approached the house. Lambert spotted the two squad cars in the street and instructed Matilda to park next to the nearest one. As they left the car, the driver of the patrol car did the same. 'DCI Lambert, DS Kennedy,' said Lambert.

'DS Belton,' said the officer.

Lambert shook hands with the man, who had a vice-like grip. Belton obviously worked out. Even beneath his three-quarter-length coat, Lambert could see the shape of his muscled torso.

'We have two officers to the rear of the property,' said Belton. 'This is to do with that missing officer, isn't it? I'll help in any way I can. Do you want me to accompany you?'

In all the drama of discovering Hodge, it was easy to forget Caroline Jardine was missing, that her and her husband could be in a perilous situation somewhere; that they could even be in the property in front of them. 'No. Just keep an eye on the front door,' said Lambert, nodding to Matilda for her to follow.

Their desired property was the central one of seven terraced bungalows. The curtains on the two front windows were pulled shut, each set a fading shade of brown. Chipped paint flaked on the windowsills and door panels giving the place the look of somewhere either not cared for or derelict. Lambert nodded as Matilda reached for the doorbell which emitted no sound. Lambert rapped his knuckles against the battered paintwork, pressing his ear to the door when no one answered. He peered into the downstairs window but the drawn curtains obstructed his view. He knocked on the window a few times but if anyone was in they weren't coming to the door.

'No sign of movement since you arrived?' Lambert asked Belton, who stood attentively on the pavement.

'No, sir.'

Lambert rubbed his chin and made a decision. 'Tell your team we're going in,' he said.

# Chapter Twenty-Four

Lambert pushed the door a few times, confirming it was secured only by the Yale lock. 'You doing the honours?' he said to Matilda, who looked down at her Converse trainers. 'You do dress casual, Kennedy, you know that?'

Matilda shrugged. 'Maybe DS Belton has an enforcer.'

'You questioning my ability to get this door open, Sergeant?'

'Go on then,' said Matilda.

Lambert considered ramming the door with his shoulder but decided injury was less likely to occur if he used his feet. His first kick managed to shatter the side panel so he aimed his second kick a bit higher. This was enough to shatter the lock. Lambert barged the door open and was immediately hit by a wave of putrid air. 'Police,' he shouted.

'Police, is anybody in the building?' he repeated, breathing through his mouth as he made his way down the confines of a narrow hallway.

Behind him, Matilda flicked a light switch but they were left in semi-darkness. Lambert tried a doorway to his left, sending out a warning before opening the door which led to a self-contained kitchen area. Lambert winced, discovering the source of the smell which overran the flat. The kitchen was being used partly as a makeshift garbage dump, and partly as a toilet. Bin bags were strewn across the tattered linoleum flooring, ripped and overflowing with moulded food. The top of one of the bags appeared to be moving. Lambert leant forward to be rewarded by the sight of hundreds of maggots feasting on the contents. 'Open a window, Kennedy,' he said, retreating to the hallway.

The first of two bedrooms was directly opposite the kitchen and was being used as an overspill for the bin bags which had been placed on a stained mattress. Matilda tried the bathroom, as Lambert made his way to the larger bedroom. Lambert turned away as he spotted a mound of what appeared to be faeces in the corner.

'Police,' he called, once more entering the living room, which in comparison to the rest of the house was well presented. At the far end of the room, a glass door led to a patio area.

Lambert tried the door, sidestepping a two-seater bed settee which faced an old box-shaped television. As Matilda entered, Lambert noticed a wooden school desk which had been hidden by the door Matilda had pulled shut. On top of the desk was a laptop which was switched on. 'Stop,' said Lambert, trying to hide the panic in his voice.

'What is it?'

'Did you try the light switches in the other room?'

'Yes, I think it's been a while since the electricity has been on in this place.'

Lambert beckoned her forward a step. 'How do you explain that, then?' he said, pointing to the laptop.

'Sir, it's connected to something.'

Lambert tiptoed across the room. The laptop was attached to a small device housed in an aluminium box.

He peered closer. Attached to the box was a second wire which led to a second device.

'Sir,' said Matilda, who was staring intently at the laptop. 'Something's changed on the screen.'

Lambert was tempted to rip the wires from the laptop. One look at Matilda dissuaded him. Was she thinking back to the explosion in Hampstead? 'Maybe we should call in someone who knows what they are doing?' she said.

Lambert hesitated. 'Look at the door,' he said, pointing to a set of three silver tabs adjoined to the hinge of the door. At that second, the laptop beeped. 'Let's get out of here.'

They both retreated from the house, the cold rain a welcome sensation. 'I want this whole block of houses evacuated immediately,' shouted Lambert to the confused DS Belton. 'And get your men away from the house.'

Matilda called base and instructed them to send the fire service and the Bomb Disposal Unit. She seemed to be in control of the situation but Lambert kept close, studying her actions in as unobtrusive a manner as possible.

'We've cleared the row,' said Belton. 'What are we looking at?'

'Possible explosive device. Make sure everyone is the required distance away. No one is to approach the house.'

In the distance, Lambert heard the wail of sirens approaching. He tried to rationalise why the device had been placed at the house whilst regretting not tearing the wires from the laptop when he had the chance. Did the Fireman know they were coming? The set-up with the explosive device was certainly elaborate but why hadn't it gone off when they were in the house? Surely the point had been to guide them into the house to trigger the device.

So why were they sitting safe on the roadside waiting for the bomb disposal squad to arrive?

As if in answer to Lambert's thoughts, an explosion ripped through the house.

Everyone cowered, Lambert instinctively protecting his eyes. He was taken back to the mansion in Hampstead, the explosions which had permanently disfigured the woman crouched next to him. He'd been further away from the epicentre than he was now. The wave of energy from that blast had felt inconsequential compared to what he'd just experienced. It was as if the space had evaporated before his very eyes. He glanced up to see a hole where the Fireman's bungalow had once been. Flecks of debris swarmed through the air as if suspended, pieces of the house falling around him as he sheltered beneath his arms. To his right, Matilda mirrored his pose, protecting her head from the impact of falling fragments.

Convinced the last of the debris had fallen, Lambert stood up. A ringing sound permeated his ears, adding to the unreal feeling of the situation. 'You OK?' he said to Matilda, his words muffled as if his ears were filled with water.

Matilda got to her feet, a look of defiance on her face. 'Jesus, there's nothing left,' she said, They turned their backs in unison as a second, smaller, detonation rang out, releasing a torrent of flames into the sky.

Despite the brightness of the day, and the sprinkling of rain still falling from the sky, the flames burnt with a startling clarity. It was like a staged bonfire display, Hodge's bungalow the only building affected.

'It was lucky we got out in time,' said Matilda, as the fire service screeched into view, followed closely by the flashing lights of the bomb disposal unit.

Lambert glanced around him, scrutinising the onlookers with phones in their hands filming the rising flames. He'd had this feeling before, the sense of being watched.

'I don't think it was lucky,' he said.

# Chapter Twenty-Five

Lambert spent the afternoon back at Chislehurst station researching Hodge further. He'd left Matilda at the scene liaising with the fire and bomb disposal teams. He'd meant what he'd said to her: in his opinion they hadn't been lucky, and their miraculous escape was no accident. He waited for the specialist team to confirm, but his best guess was that the metal tape in the door held sensors which had alerted Hodge to their presence. The incendiary device had then been detonated by Hodge remotely when they were safe and in the open.

If this was true – and Lambert conceded it was simply a hypothesis at this point – it meant many things. First, Hodge was watching them; at least to begin with. Secondly, Hodge had spared them but decided to set off the device anyway. For what reason? Lambert considered that Hodge might have wanted to protect his invention from prying eyes. Maybe something in the set up would have given them a lead to the man's whereabouts, but Lambert doubted he would be so careless. Lambert believed Hodge set off the detonation because he wanted to see the explosion. The fire chief had alluded to the staged nature of the fire at Jardine's house, and having witnessed the devastation firsthand Lambert understood the terrible beauty to the staged explosions; how someone with Hodge's predilection would see something artistic in his endeavours.

The most important consideration for Lambert at this juncture was the fact that Hodge had let them escape. If he was the psychopathic killer they suspected, capable of kidnapping two people and replacing them with two corpses, then why hadn't he killed him and Matilda when he had the chance? It could be a vanity thing, a sign of power, demonstrating he was in control.

It could also mean one more thing: the fire had not been meant for them.

After an hour of struggle, Lambert eventually discovered what he was looking for: a living relative for Hodge.

Gladys Hodge was aged eighty-two and lived in a care home in Dartford, Kent. Lambert called the home and made an appointment to see her. Noting that Bickland wasn't in the incident room, he summoned the local detective. 'Croft, we're off to Dartford,' he said.

'Sir,' said Croft, grabbing her coat off her chair as Lambert headed out of the room.

—

'You drive,' said Lambert, throwing his keys to Croft. They were on the main road outside the station. The sky was already dark, the crisp air close to freezing point.

'How long have you been working at Chislehurst?' asked Lambert, as Croft pulled out into the stationary traffic of the high street.

'Five years now.'

'You made DS four years ago?'

'Sir.'

Lambert nodded but didn't ask any more questions. He wanted to know if Croft had more ambition beyond her current role but wasn't going to ask her outright. From what he'd seen of her so far, she was competent and had shown a certain backbone with her determination to remain on the case. He didn't like knowing so little about someone on his team.

He'd only briefly perused Croft's file. He could relate to her situation even though his tenure as a detective sergeant had been short lived. He'd been part of the accelerated program and bumped up to Inspector when he'd joined Tillman in his now defunct Group.

Croft kept her eyes on the road, the traffic thinning. 'I'm finding it very exhilarating,' she said, unprompted. 'This is the most high-profile case I've worked on. I only hope we can get a result.'

Lambert nodded, his thoughts returning to the Jardines. He wouldn't share his thoughts with Croft, or anyone else for that matter, but he was convinced the Jardines were still alive. It was more than a mere hunch. To Lambert, it was a logical conclusion to the situation. If the Fireman, Hodge, had wanted the pair dead, he could have killed them in the fire. Since he'd replaced the bodies with those of Turner and Berry, it was a logical step to presume the pair were still alive. To what end remained to be seen.

At the care home, a harried-looking woman dressed in a floral print dress and heavy cardigan greeted them at the reception. Like most of these places, an aroma hung in the air which to Lambert was reminiscent of school buildings – a mixture of cleaning products and cooked food.

'Glenda Parsons, duty manager,' said the woman, offering a limp handshake first to Croft, then Lambert.

Croft made the introductions, Lambert choosing to remain silent as he studied the interior of the home: the thick pile carpets which led from the hallway to a communal living area, the comfortable armchairs occupied by people in various states of old age. Some of the residents were alert, reading or watching the old style television screen off to one corner. Others were asleep, or permanently comatose.

'I must say, I was surprised you wanted to see Gladys. She doesn't get many visitors,' said Parsons.

'Would you have a list of who has visited her in the last year, Mrs Parsons?' asked Croft, not wasting any time.

'I'll check, but I'm pretty sure there will be no results. I'm not sure she has any living relatives. A son maybe, I'll have to check. As this is a government facility, there are no families to chase for payment. I can't remember anyone visiting Gladys before, I'm afraid.'

'May we see her?' asked Croft.

'Of course, follow me.'

No doubt it was a familiar refrain in such places, but Lambert couldn't help but wonder if this was all there was to look forward to. It was difficult not to become despondent as they made their way to Gladys's room, past small cubicles where the half-dead endured their last days unloved and abandoned. A tight smile formed on his lips as he considered there would be no one to visit him when he reached this stage. No children to make the occasional guilt-ridden visit, no one to watch his humiliating decline. His own parents had died when Lambert was in his early thirties, and at times like this it almost seemed a blessing.

The Duty Manager stopped outside one of the rooms and knocked. 'Gladys, you have some visitors,' she said, opening the door.

A resolute woman was sitting on a bedside chair, staring at them with a look of unconcealed distaste. 'Visitors?' said the woman, as if the word was alien to her.

'Mrs Hodge, my name is Gemma Croft. Detective Sergeant Gemma Croft. This is my colleague, Detective Chief Inspector Michael Lambert.' Croft approached the woman with short slow steps.

'Police?' said the woman, with the same uncertain voice.

The duty manager barged past Croft, and opened a small window to the rear of the room. 'They just want to ask you some questions, Gladys, isn't that nice,' she said, as if talking to a child.

Gladys placed the paperback she'd been reading on the bed. Lambert noticed the image of a woman with windswept hair in the arms of a bare-chested Lothario. 'Thank you, Mrs Parsons,' said Lambert, to the duty manager.

Parsons blinked, confused, before moving towards the door. 'OK, let me know if you need anything.'

'Well, sit then,' said Gladys, once Parsons had left. 'It will be nice to speak to someone who doesn't think I'm incapable.'

Lambert took in the bareness of the room as he sat, the mini bookcase perched on a desk the only sign of any personal possessions in the uncluttered room. He couldn't see any family photos and feared they'd approached the wrong woman.

'So, I guess you're here to speak to me about the mari-
juana,' said Gladys, stone-faced.

Lambert watched in amusement as Croft's mouth hung
open.

'I'm kidding,' said Gladys, maintaining the same unreadable expression. 'What do you want?'

Croft leant back in her chair, seemingly relieved.

'We're here to speak to you about your son, Mrs Hodge,'
said Lambert.

'You're the boss one?' said Gladys.

'I'm the more senior officer, yes,' said Lambert.

'Handsome one, aren't you?'

Lambert shrugged. 'That's neither here nor there. Tell
me about your son.'

Gladys gazed at Lambert. Her face was an incredible
map of lines and intersections, her dry skin decorated with
scabs and scar tissue. 'Trevor,' she said.

'Trevor,' said Lambert.

Gladys sighed, and Lambert sensed a world of meaning
in it. A sense of disappointment and regret. 'What's he
done now?' she said.

'When did you last see your son?' asked Lambert.

Gladys shook her head. 'Time is not the same nowadays.
I don't really function in this world any more. I live there,'
she said, pointing to the small library of books. 'They bring
me fresh ones each week, the only good thing about this
place.'

Lambert couldn't tell if she was purposefully sidestepping the question. 'Has he ever visited you here, Gladys?'

'He came when they first sent me here. Once more
since then. What's he set fire to now?'

'What can you tell us about his fires, Gladys?' asked Croft.

Gladys's resolve faded in a split second. A single tear fell from her right eye and made its slow journey down the dry wasteland of her wrinkled face. 'He had a baby sister.'

Lambert caught Croft's eye. He couldn't recall any mention of a sister in Hodge's file and from the look of it neither could Croft.

'What happened to her, Gladys?' asked Croft, who had softened her tone without sounding patronising.

The resolute look returned to her face as she dragged her hand across her eye in one quick movement. It was clear the woman had her wits about her and Lambert thought there should be a better place for her than here. 'She was stillborn. Trevor was eight at the time. He'd been desperate to have a baby sister.'

Lambert's body tensed as he sucked in his breath and tried not to think about Chloe.

Hodge looked away, lost in what must have been a horrendous memory. When she returned her gaze to Lambert it was unreadable. 'That was when the fires started,' she said.

'I'm sorry to hear about your loss, Gladys,' said Croft. 'Why do you think it started then?'

Gladys contorted her face, a sprinkling of further lines decorating her face. 'You have to be careful what you tell children. Or what they get to hear,' she said.

It was only then Lambert understood where Gladys's strength came from. It was the tone of her voice, measured, calm, and authoritative. If he wasn't sitting face to face with Gladys he would have said the voice belonged to a confident person in their fifties. Not some frail old lady, whittling away her last few days in a box-shaped, prison-like room, the lure of the next romantic doorstopper the only thing to look forward to.

'What did he hear?' asked Lambert, trying to mirror Croft's soft tone.

'I think it was his dad. Not sure he meant anything by it. He was a docile man, my Leonard, not the brightest.'

Lambert already had an idea of what Gladys was about to tell him, and wasn't sure he wanted to hear it.

'Trevor asked him what would happen to his little sister, and Leonard, bless him, told him.'

Lambert shut his eyes, blood thumping behind his eyelids. 'What exactly did he tell him, Gladys?'

Gladys' eyes widened. 'That her little body would be burnt,' she said.

# Chapter Twenty-Six

They sat in silence, Gladys Hodge staring at Lambert and Croft in turn, as if daring them to say something. From the research Lambert had gathered on arsonists, and his chats with Chapman and the fire expert, Finch, he knew what Gladys had said could have been enough to trigger something in the Fireman. It wasn't the words alone which would have prompted his behaviour: it was the combination of his sister's death and the spark of his imagination responding to his father's words. It would take someone with more psychological insight than him to decipher what Hodge had been trying to achieve by setting the fires. Could he see it as a way to somehow honour her, or in his delusion did he somehow believe he could resurrect her?

'It was about a year later that we first caught him,' said Gladys, ignoring the stunned silence at what she'd just said. 'He stole a bin from one of our neighbours. One of those metal ones. He filled it with paper and fallen wood. When we found him, he was sitting directly in front of it, staring into the flames like he was hypnotised, close enough to burn. His dad grabbed him away. He screamed when Leonard put out the fire.'

She shook her head. 'My God, he idolised his father. I think if Leonard had been there for him, then he would never have...'

'The other fires?' asked Lambert.

'Yes, I imagine you know about his arrests, his foolishness. It was too much for me at the time. I tried, but he would never listen.'

'What happened to Leonard, Gladys? I mean Mr Hodge?' asked Croft.

Gladys turned to the DS with a look which would have cowed a weaker officer. 'He was never the same after we lost our little girl. He tried, bless him, but something snapped within him, seeing our little baby like that. He wasn't a strong man, you see. One day he got lost in the darkness for a final time and never returned.'

–

Gladys's last words stayed with Lambert as he checked Leonard Hodge's file back in the station. Lost in the darkness. The words played in his head as he remembered the aftermath of Chloe's death. He too had been lost in the darkness then. He'd been driving when Chloe died, the accident sending him into a coma. When he'd awoken to the news of her death, he'd desperately wanted to retreat back to that nothingness.

Was it courage or cowardice which propelled Leonard to take the one final step Lambert had been unable to take? Leonard had committed suicide on the day of his fiftieth birthday, ten years after the stillbirth. He had suffered a decade of grief which had eventually proved too much for him.

The visit to Gladys Hodge had proven a success, in part. They now had an explanation for the Fireman's arson, and the information on his father's suicide hinted at a reason for Hodge approaching Berry and Turner. However, they were no closer to discovering why he had decided to kidnap the Jardines, and why he'd replaced their bodies with Berry and Turner.

A knock on the door tore him from his thoughts.

'Sir?' said Matilda, walking into the office.

Lambert had yet to adjust to the change in Matilda's appearance. He'd been at school with a girl who had a birthmark which covered over half of her face. He remembered the first time he'd seen her, the shock of what looked like a painful maroon patch on that smiling face. Within a few months, it had been like the mark wasn't there. He stopped noticing and recalled being surprised when a new boy at the school mentioned it to him. He wondered now if the same would ever be true when he looked at Matilda. If anything, the scar tissue looked more painful than ever. The affected skin spread from her eye down to her neck, the skin mottled and peppered with blotches of colour. The contrast of the unblemished skin on the other side of her face somehow made the effect worse.

'Some updates for you from the site,' said Matilda, moving her hand briefly to the scarred flesh as if he'd been staring too long.

'Sit,' said Lambert, shutting his laptop.

'From what they can tell the explosion was set remotely, as we thought. Little remains of the device we saw. Chapman believes the room was packed with PE-4, a plastic explosive, hence the ferocity of the blast.'

'I take it we're on to that.'

'Yes, checking who holds licenses, and obviously anywhere missing inventory.'

'Go through each name for a connection. Someone may have gotten hold of it for him. Let's find out if it was something he could make himself.'

'Sir.'

Lambert updated her on his meeting with Gladys Hodge.

'Bloody hell,' said Matilda. 'That explains a lot.'

Lambert thought again about Gladys, her fierce defiance despite all that had happened to her. 'I think we should put some uniforms at her home in case her son makes a visit.'

The care home had confirmed Gladys hadn't had any visitors in the last couple of years, but Lambert believed the Fireman was going through some form of crisis. Nothing about the fire at the Jardine house or today's explosion at the bungalow matched the profile Lambert had of the man from his file. It suggested something had snapped in Trevor Hodge. It was akin to a serial killer making his first kill. Those in custody always said the first kill was the hardest. Once that hurdle was overcome they were often released, whatever empathy they once had for potential victims fading into nothingness. The Fireman's actions were becoming more and more unstable and unpredictable. If he was ever going to resolve things with his mother it would be now.

'I'll get someone on it,' said Matilda. 'I coordinated interviews with Hodge's neighbours, and circulated the image from the CCTV cameras at Waterloo. Not one of the neighbours recalls seeing him. The bungalow has been derelict for at least a year, according to one of the locals.'

'It still had electricity. Get onto the utility companies, find out who's been paying the bills. We need to get hold of Hodge's bank details too, and apply to get his accounts shut.

If we're lucky, we'll get another address for him. What about Boxall?'

'He's been sent back to Cornwall pending further investigation of his website.'

Matilda left the room, a slight limp to her gait as if something was in her shoe. On the System, Lambert flicked through photos of the crater which had ripped through the line of bungalows. They'd searched all the rooms in the place, so he was sure the Jardines had not been held there. It suggested the Fireman had another address, or at least somewhere he was holding the pair. Presuming, that was, they were still alive.

He drove to Sophie's house before returning home. Once again, he'd driven there on instinct, muscle memory guiding him back to the place which had been his home for over ten years whilst his mind tried to unravel the mysteries of the case.

Did she know he was there, made these occasional visits? He was little better than a stalker. He should start the car and drive away but being there brought a sense of calm that was missing elsewhere in his life, especially given what was happening with Sarah. He knew it was a regression, a way of fooling himself that the past could be recaptured. He opened the door, and leant against the car gazing across to the house. Sophie would welcome him. She would be surprised but she would invite him in, would probably welcome the opportunity to show him Jane, Chloe's sister.

His hands began to go numb against the freezing metal of the car's roof. If only he could step forward, cross the road and knock on the door, but his legs wouldn't move. He took one final glance up at the pulled curtains of the room where Chloe had once slept in her cot, before returning to the safety of the car. 'Fuck,' he screamed, as the car roared into life and he drove away.

# Chapter Twenty-Seven

Struck with guilt, Lambert called Sarah as he left Sophie's house. She agreed to meet him in a bar in Blackheath, an area of south-east London where she'd rented a studio apartment. He parked up thirty minutes later, already regretting his suggestion to meet.

A fierce wind attacked as he dragged himself up the high street. At first he'd been surprised when Sarah had decided to move to the area. She'd been attacked and kidnapped in the village when working on the Souljacker case, and only when she'd explained she didn't want the place to have a hold on her did he understand. It said much about her that she would be willing to face such a traumatic memory on a daily basis, yet they'd never really discussed the matter.

A wave of heat rushed him as he made his way into the pub at the top of the hill. The small bar was bustling with patrons. Lambert made a circuit of the place, searching for Sarah. The bar had a faint underlying smell of spilt beer, which Lambert suspected no amount of scrubbing would ever mask. He ordered a pint of lager, taking a large initial gulp of the golden liquid, and thought how easy it would be to spend a few hours in such a place and to forget about the case and all it entailed.

He was on his second drink, a small bottle of ale, when Sarah arrived. He noticed immediately she was stressed, her face drawn and agitated as she made his way to him. 'You OK?' he said, as she kissed him on the cheek.

'Yeah, one of those days.'

'Drink?'

'Just some sparkling water please.'

Lambert attracted the attention of the barman and ordered two sparkling waters. 'Matilda's back in action,' he said, handing a glass to Sarah, who had taken off her coat and relaxed.

'Great. How is she?

'Same as ever,' said Lambert. He went to tell her about everything that happened in the short time since they'd last spoken but decided he could do with a bit of time away from the case. Even if it was only an hour or so, focusing on something different.

Sarah wasn't very talkative either. He could see the tiredness in her eyes, and after they finished their drinks they left the bar. They walked back to her flat, side by side but not touching. At the entrance to the flat, Sarah stopped. She offered him a tired smile. 'I need some rest,' she said.

'Of course. I've got to get back to the case anyway.'

Sarah nodded a couple of times, not speaking.

Lambert felt something slipping away. He wanted to suggest they go away together, get away from everything, but sensed desperation in the thought. Instead, he stood there like an awkward teenager on a date.

'Goodnight then,' said Sarah. She leant towards him, and kissed him on the cheek. She began to pull away but he held her for a second longer, noting a new perfume on her neck. As they disentangled she looked confused.

'Goodnight,' he said, overcome by a growing mood of melancholy as he retreated to the car.

–

Lambert headed back towards Dartford and the care home where Gladys Hodge resided. He hoped the drive would calm him, take his mind off both Sophie and Sarah, and he couldn't face going home at that moment.

Tillman called, demanding an update. 'I'm getting grief from all angles over this,' he said, once again surprising Lambert with his tone. Tillman knew as well as he did everything that could be done was being done.

'Something is off on this case, Glenn. You must see that.'

'All I see is a missing police officer and her husband, two corpses, and a second building burnt to the ground. How hard can it be to find this guy? I've read his file, he's not exactly brain trust material.'

'Kennedy has gone through the list of organisations licensed to use plastic explosives. We'll be conducting interviews tomorrow, trying to find a link between anyone on that list and Hodge. He must have got them from somewhere.'

'That's all you've got for me?'

Lambert was used to this approach from Tillman. Even after the years of working together, and the secrets they shared, he still felt the need to display his authority over him. Lambert usually ignored it, but Tillman's timing couldn't have been worse. 'Are you fucking kidding me, Glenn? I was almost blown up today, as was your girl-friend.'

The line went silent. Lambert pictured Tillman at the other end, gripping his phone so tight that it would come close to shattering in his hand. 'We agreed not to mention that, especially on the phone,' said Tillman, his voice lowered, rough and guttural.

'I'm hanging up now, sir,' said Lambert, doing so.

He should be used to such encounters by now, but Tillman always brought out the worst in him. Despite their years together, a distance had always existed in their relationship. Maybe it was because of their secrets, not despite them. Lambert knew things which could destroy Tillman's career, and sometimes he wondered if this had protected him from his superior. Tillman was not a man to cross, and even now Lambert wasn't sure he could be trusted.

He made slow time reaching Dartford, tailbacks stretching for miles on the approach to the tunnel. The case played in his head, from the time Tillman had first given him the case to the explosion this morning. There was a connection they were missing, something simple that would link Hodge, Berry, Turner and the Jardines.

It was nine pm by the time he reached the care home, time enough for Lambert to wonder what he was doing there. He was pleased to see a patrol car in the home's car-park as he drove past. The cost would be prohibitive but budget was not much of an issue when a missing officer was involved. He parked up further down the street, turning the car so he could face the entrance.

From his wallet, he took out the picture of the young Trevor Hodge which Gladys had given him. He'd been innocent then, and would have been treated as such. Now he'd reached adulthood, society no longer considered the events which had shaped the man. The thoughts which had twisted his mind towards arson, the suicide of his father which had possibly triggered something else in him: neither would suffice as a defence. It might provoke an ember of understanding, which could result in some form of mitigation, a sentence in a mental health detention centre, but the child in the photo no longer existed.

Lambert put the picture away, the photo prompting thoughts of Teresa Jardine. He'd felt the girl had been an oversight, not part of the arsonist's initial plans, but now he knew Hodge's history he wondered if she wasn't the target all along. It sounded perverse, but the mind was a curious thing. Hodge's stillborn sister had altered the young man forever, and it was impossible to conceive how such an obsession could manifest itself. Did Hodge somehow see his sister in Teresa?

Lambert's eyes began to feel heavy. He switched the A/C unit to cold and let the recycled air flood the car in an attempt to fight sleep but the first flicker of colour appeared to the left of his vision. He locked the doors from within, and turned off the ignition before reclining his chair as the colours swamped his eyes. He studied the patterns for as long as he could, the fire images more prominent than ever as if in honour of the real fires which blighted Lambert's waking life, before slumping to sleep.

He snapped awake, for a brief second confused by his surroundings. A check of the digital clock told him he'd been asleep for three hours. He groaned as he pulled his chair upright, a nerve trapped in his neck.

Rain bounced off the car, as he studied the thinning traffic and a lone couple walking the street. Things felt clearer for the sleep, and, noting the patrol car was still there, he started his car. His presence here was pointless. He pulled the car into the road, momentarily distracted by something he saw in the rear-view mirror. He drove back the way he came, past the care home and the silhouetted figures of the two uniformed officers in their car, noting the letters and numbers of the number plate he'd glimpsed in the mirror.

As he turned the corner, it came back to him. He'd seen that number plate before. He braked heavily, a car behind him blaring his horn. Lambert flicked on his hazard lights and pulled over. He studied his sat-nav, searching for a different route back to the care home. He swung the car back into the road, making his way back towards the building, his mind trying to quantify the reason for the car being there. He drove around the block and parked up a hundred yards away from the dark saloon.

He needed to see a face to confirm. From the boot of his car, he retrieved a raincoat which he pulled on, zipping it to this throat and pulling it over his head to hide his appearance. He was used to this sort of work, the kind of basic surveillance he'd been taught when moving to Tillman's Group, identifying a suspect without being spotted in return. As he made his way toward the car he practised his movements in his head. The line of cars was on his right, and he glanced at the interior of each car with a minimal turn of his eye.

He didn't stop as he approached the black saloon. Confirming the number plate he'd seen in his rear-view mirror, he walked straight past. The driver was in his seat on the roadside. Lambert glanced at him as he moved past, cursing himself for turning his head more than necessary.

He continued walking, not once looking back, hoping the figure hadn't recognised him. When he reached the end of the road, he took the slow way around the block on foot, the rain lashing at him, until he reached the car and peeled off the raincoat. Some of the water had soaked through to his suit and he switched on the heating as he started the engine.

He hadn't been mistaken. The car belonged to the Anti-Corruption officer, Duggan, who had questioned him the other evening about Tillman at the Chislehurst station. Lambert considered confronting him. There was no reason for him to be staking out the home. Even if Lambert was under investigation as well as Tillman, which was a possibility, Duggan shouldn't be interfering in an active case. The only positive Lambert could take from the situation was the knowledge that Duggan was up to something. A confrontation with the man now would negate that advantage. Instead, Lambert did a three-point turn and headed away from the AC officer.

Forty minutes later he stood outside the ruins of the bungalow in Romford. Mercifully, the rain had stopped. In its stead, a bitter wind whistled through the police tape and the fallen walls of the house.

Lambert stepped under the tape, walking through the gap where a door had been earlier that day. The interior of the bungalow was now rubble. Lambert clambered over a mound of bricks to the area which used to be the living room. Somehow, the skeletal remains of the sofa were still intact. He perched himself on the metal frame and looked skyward, glancing at the parade of stars above. There was something magical about sitting in the debris, glancing at the heavens. Maybe it was the sense of unreality, the juxtaposition of sitting in the open air with the memory of the claustrophobic tour he'd made of the house earlier.

He searched every inch of the house before returning to the car. Anything of value would have already been processed by the SOCOs, and not for the first time that night he wondered what he was doing in a location.

On the road, he scanned the area as he'd done earlier that day. Had the Fireman been watching, waiting for them to be clear of the house before setting off the detonation? Once again, Lambert couldn't help but think that the arsonist was desperate for attention. Furthermore, he couldn't shift the inkling that Hodge wasn't perhaps the cold-hearted killer they presumed he was.

It was past one am by the time he reached home. It was unlikely he would sleep now, after his three hours in the car, so he opened his laptop and went straight to work. His first call was the System, where he analysed Duggan's file once more.

Lambert had been in this type of situation before. Everything about the case, from his selection as SIO to the bizarre meeting with the senior police officers and the politician, Weaver, and now Duggan's surveillance, had the feeling of a conspiracy about it. He accepted he had the experience to lead the case, but an arson attack, even one featuring a fellow officer, was not normally the type of case with which the NCA would usually get involved. Lambert felt he was somehow being manipulated, and that was not something he could tolerate.

The file on Duggan was threadbare. Being in Anti-Corruption set the officer apart and even the intricacies of the System couldn't make inroads into his file. Lambert turned his attention to the fire at the bungalow today, distraught to find the list of contractors licensed to use plastic explosives was longer than he'd expected.

Frustrated, he snapped his laptop shut and made an early breakfast. An answer hovered just out of reach, a connection between everyone and everything involved in the case.

After breakfast, he was surprised by an onrush of tiredness. He lay on the sofa and closed his eyes, doubting he would sleep but hoping an explanation would come to mind. For the second time in the last few hours, his eyelids became heavy. This time, no lights flicked before him and he fell into an uneasy sleep.

Sometime later daylight flooded his flat. Lambert shielded his eyes as he grew accustomed to his surroundings. Somehow it was seven am: he'd slept for a further four hours, which was almost unheard of. He glanced at his phone, noticing a voicemail notification on the screen.

On first listen, he struggled to make out the caller. The woman's voice was laced with emotion. Her words were almost unintelligible, interspersed with sobs and guttural, animal-like noises.

Lambert played the message again. The voice belonged to Gladys Hodge. It was a confession, and one that made for difficult listening. It ended with a flash of clarity as Gladys composed herself, and shared with Lambert that she had a contact number for her son.

# Chapter Twenty-Eight

Lambert reclined on the sofa, sipping his coffee, and listened to the message again. Behind the high-pitched voice laden with tears, Gladys Hodge was rambling. She had been lying, but Lambert could forgive her that.

Lambert determined Gladys had spent the night unable to sleep, thinking about the horrible things Lambert had accused her son of doing. Contradicting what she'd said yesterday, she told Lambert her son had paid her a visit earlier in the month, for the first time in over a year. The rest of the message was indecipherable, but she ended it by telling Lambert she had the contact number.

Lambert showered, taking his coffee with him into the small cubicle. It was important not to get carried away but this felt like the breakthrough he'd been waiting for. He called Matilda before changing, instructing her to meet him at Hodge's care home along with the Tech team who would have a phone number they needed to trace.

Outside, ice blanketed his car. He switched on the ignition and the heaters, staring blankly ahead as the windscreen gradually cleared. It must have taken a lot for Gladys to have made the call. From their short time together, Lambert had noted the woman's sharp intelligence. He could only imagine what being trapped in the isolation of the care home must be like for her. With her husband dead and her son AWOL, it was remarkable she'd kept her wits about her. Her message on his phone had sounded genuine. It was clear she was in a quandary. She didn't wish to betray Trevor but deep down she knew what he was capable of.

Lambert stopped at a petrol station and grabbed a copy of Mia Helmer's newspaper. He was dismayed, though not surprised, to see the case was front page news. He skimmed the article back in his car before driving off. Helmer had kept her promise and had revealed that the two bodies found in Chislehurst didn't belong to Caroline and Marcus Jardine. It was a distraction he could do without, and he threw the paper onto the passenger seat and tried not to think about it.

At the care home, he made two circuits of the area, searching for the black saloon which belonged to the AC officer Duggan. Confident the car was not in sight, he pulled into the care home's car park, noting the patrol car was different from the one last night. He parked up and knocked on the passenger side window, receiving a confused, borderline angry, look from the uniformed officer within. Lambert waited for the female officer to wind down her window before displaying his warrant card.

'Sorry, sir, WPC Hoskins. This is PC Wynn,' she said, pointing to the male officer behind the wheel who looked at least twice her age.

'What time did you guys come on shift?' asked Lambert, buttoning up his jacket, the bitter air of the winter morning yet to abate.

'About forty minutes ago,' said Wynn, over his colleague.

Lambert noticed a flask of steaming coffee on the driver's side and regretted not making one himself.

'Did the night team have anything to report?'

'No, sir,' said the WPC.

Lambert explained the situation and instructed the officers to keep an eye on the perimeter of the care home. He didn't mention Duggan by name, but told the officers to be on the lookout for a black saloon car.

'Do you have a number plate, sir?' asked the WPC.

'No,' said Lambert, deciding not to share the information.

–

Lambert returned to his car and waited for Matilda and the team to arrive. He drummed his fingers on the dashboard, desperate to get going. Every minute they waited put Caroline and Marcus Jardine's lives at risk.

Impatient, he left the car again, receiving a curious look from the patrol team. He walked to the front of the care home glancing down the street for a sign of Matilda. 'Where are you?' he mouthed to himself, looking accusingly at each passing car.

In the end he gave in and entered the care home. The manager he'd met the other day, Parsons, was not on duty. In her stead was a male receptionist wearing jeans and a white T-shirt as if it was the height of summer. 'Can I help you?' said the man.

A bead of sweat trickled down Lambert's forehead, the interior of the care home stifling hot in comparison to outside.

'DCI Lambert. I'm here to see Gladys Hodge.'

'You're a bit early for visiting hours,' said the man, surprising Lambert with his high-pitched voice.

'It's a police matter. My colleagues will be here shortly,' said Lambert, taking a step towards the man who stood frozen on the spot as if guilty of some undeclared crime.

'I think Mrs Hodge is in the dining room eating breakfast. You wait here, I'll find out where she is for you.'

Lambert nodded and took a seat on one of the vinyl-backed chairs in the reception area. He'd been waiting five minutes when Matilda arrived flanked by three colleagues carrying heavy looking briefcases.

'Take a seat,' said Lambert, 'I believe we're waiting for Mrs Hodge to finish breakfast.'

# Chapter Twenty-Nine

The white-shirted receptionist returned a few minutes later, doing a double take at the sight of the officers. 'Mrs Hodge has finished her breakfast. Maybe you should use the office, as there are so many of you?'

Lambert nodded and instructed the Tech team to follow the receptionist into the office.

'I'd like to see Mrs Hodge in her room first,' he said to the man.

'OK, wait there. I'll get one of the nurses to take you up.'

'That's fine, we know the way.' Matilda accompanied him upstairs to the room and knocked on the door.

Mrs Hodge opened it within seconds, a look of accusation on her wrinkled face. 'It didn't take you long,' she said.

'May we come in?' said Lambert, introducing Matilda.

'It's fine,' said Gladys. 'Come through.'

They sat on the cloth-bound armchairs which were at least more comfortable than the plastic chairs in the waiting room.

'Thank you for the call this morning, Mrs Hodge. I know it must have taken a lot,' said Lambert.

'More than you'll ever know.'

Mrs Hodge eyes were bloodshot, as if she'd either been up all night or crying. She wore a thick woollen cardigan over a faded patterned dress. 'More than you'll ever know,' she repeated.

'Gladys, just for the benefit of my colleague, please can you repeat what you said on your voicemail message to me?'

Gladys sighed, a lifetime of regret in the sound. 'I told you Trevor had come to see me a few days ago now.'

'Can you remember which day exactly?' said Matilda.

Gladys looked heavenwards, as if an answer could be found above. 'Monday,' she said. 'Monday before last.'

'And how was he?' asked Lambert.

Gladys shook her head, suggesting the question was ridiculous. 'He was all over the place. Couldn't sit still. Of course, I hadn't seen him for two years. He looked slimmer than I remembered, malnourished, but his behaviour reminded me of something. He always used to behave this way before...'

'Before?' said Matilda, softly.

'You know what I'm on about. Before he'd set a fire.'

'You remember him behaving this way before?' said Lambert.

'It started after his father's death. He was like it for days on end. Something I'd never seen in him before. Permanently on edge, agitated. It took me some time to put two and two together. Of course, at the time I didn't know what he was up to. But after the third or fourth incident, I realised Leonard's death consumed him and the only way he could control it was by setting fire to something.'

The timing correlated with the incident at Chislehurst, being only a few days before the fire which had torn through the Jardines' house.

'And what did he say to you when he visited?' asked Lambert.

'He wasn't making much sense but he said he was in trouble.'

Lambert looked at Matilda. 'In trouble how?'

'He said he'd done something that he didn't want to do, that they'd changed the rules. He didn't elaborate but I had the sense...' said Gladys, her voice becoming trapped in her throat. 'Sorry,' she said, trying to fight the tears rolling from her eyes. 'I had a feeling this was the last time he was ever going to visit me.'

A knock on the door broke the atmosphere.

'We're ready now,' said one of the Tech team.

'OK, give us a few minutes,' said Lambert. 'Gladys, I need you to do something for us. I need you to call your son.'

Gladys rocked in her chair, not answering. 'What do you want me to say to him?'

'What would you normally talk to him about?' asked Matilda.

'I wouldn't normally talk to him about anything,' said Gladys, raising her voice and staring at Matilda as if she was stupid. 'When he came the other day, it was the first time I'd seen him in two years. We don't usually spend much time on the phone together.'

'Why do you think he gave you his number?' asked Lambert.

'I truly don't know. He said only to call in an emergency.'

'We just need you to keep him talking,' said Lambert. 'Tell him you've been thinking about what he said and that you want to speak to him. Tell him you have some things you need to tell him face to face.'

'This is my son we're talking about,' said Gladys, turning her accusatory tone to Lambert.

'I appreciate that, but people are in danger, Gladys. I think you understand that. I think that's why you called me.'

—

Matilda guided Gladys downstairs to the office which the receptionist had let them use.

'I'm not sure about this,' Gladys said to Matilda, sounding older and frailer than before.

Lambert didn't buy the act, but Matilda placated her. 'You don't have to do anything you don't want to, Gladys, but as we agreed upstairs I think you know this is for the best,' she said.

'What will you do to him if you find him?'

'We just want to talk to him,' said Matilda. 'He's a danger to himself as much as he is to anyone else.'

By the time they'd reached the office, one of the Tech team, Robertson, had already checked the mobile number Gladys had given them.

'It looks like a burner phone,' he said to Lambert. 'No registered name or address.'

'You'll be able to trace the location, though?' said Lambert, momentarily worried he'd been wasting his time.

'If we get an answer and get him talking long enough,' said Robertson, with a resigned look which suggested he'd experienced at least as many failures in his time as successes.

'Take a seat, Gladys,' said Matilda, ushering the woman to a leather armchair behind the desk. 'We're going to dial the number for you. When I nod my head I want you to speak.'

Gladys glanced around the room as if about to change her mind, but Matilda kept her hand on her shoulder, reassuring the woman.

Lambert nodded to Robertson and pressed the switch on the tracking device.

'It's ringing,' he said.

The dial tone of the Fireman's mobile played out in the quiet of the room. Lambert hugged himself, the overpowering heat of Gladys's bedroom having given way to the unheated confines of the office. His heart picked up in tempo, thundering in his chest.

The line clicked and a voice spoke. 'Hello?'

Trevor Hodge's voice was weaker than Lambert had imagined. Maybe he was reading too much into it, but the simple word 'hello' made the Fireman sound lost.

Gladys furrowed her forehead and stared at Matilda, confused by what was happening.

Matilda leant towards her and mouthed the word, 'Hello.'

Gladys mimicked the sound, sounding as confused and lost as her son.

'Mum, is that you? I told you only to call in an emergency.'

'It's good to hear you, Trevor,' said Gladys, authority returning to her voice.

'It's good to hear you as well, Mum, but now's not a good time.'

Nothing in the manner of the son's speech changed Lambert's impression of him. He sounded scared and out of control. It was difficult for Lambert to believe the man they were speaking to was responsible for the atrocities at the Jardine house.

Gladys shrugged her shoulders. 'This is important, son. I need to see you.'

'I saw you only the other week. You know I'm busy, Mum.'

'I know, son, but I have something important to tell you.'

'Can't you tell me now, over the phone?'

'It's not something I can say by phone.'

Matilda glanced at Lambert as the line went silent. Already Gladys had proved invaluable.

'Please, Mum, now is not a good time.'

Robertson glanced away from his equipment and gave Lambert a thumbs up. Gladys noticed the gesture. 'What have you done, Trevor?' she said, tears welling in her eyes.

Lambert swore to himself and tore the mobile phone off speakerphone.

'Trevor, this is DCI Lambert. We know about the fire at the Jardines' house and the explosion yesterday at your property. Trevor, I need your help. Do you know the whereabouts of Caroline and Marcus Jardine?'

Lambert wanted to scream into the phone, demand Hodge tell him but it wasn't the smart approach. 'I can help you, Trevor. I know you didn't want it to go this far but it's not too late. Tell us where they are and we can help you.'

Gladys began sobbing and Matilda guided her from the room.

'I can't,' said Trevor.

'Are they alive?' asked Lambert. Still talking to the Fireman, he left the office followed by Robertson and the other two tech guys. He summoned Matilda with a curl of his index finger.

'Who were you working for, Trevor? We know you didn't want to do this, Trevor. Tell us where they are and we can help. Where are they, Trevor?' he repeated, hoping the location on Robertson's iPad was not too far and that Hodge was speaking from wherever he was holding the Jardines captive.

'It wasn't my fault,' said Hodge, his voice rising to a crescendo.

'What wasn't your fault?' said Lambert.

'It wasn't my fault,' repeated the high-pitched voice.

'Calm down, Trevor. Just tell me, what wasn't your fault?'

Lambert heard sobbing; deep, uncontrollable sobs like an infant mid-tantrum.

'It wasn't my fault,' said Hodge for a third time. 'The man. The man slipped. He died,' he said, hanging up.

# Chapter Thirty

Matilda was reluctant to leave Gladys Hodge at the scene, but Lambert forced her hand. He nodded his head to one of the uniformed police officers, the WPC he'd spoken to earlier, and instructed her to stay with Gladys. Now was no time for sentiment. Like Matilda, he'd sensed the conflict in Gladys' exchange with her son but he had greater concerns than Gladys' feelings at the moment.

Lambert drove with Matilda navigating. Behind them the Tech guys followed, both cars with sirens blazing. Matilda called Bickland and told him to get the team to the site. As he drove, Lambert tried not to think of the time they'd wasted when the Fireman had been in Chislehurst all this time.

'What do we know about the building?' Lambert asked as he crawled through the stationary traffic.

'It appears to be a block of flats,' said Matilda, glancing at the picture she'd uploaded from Google Maps.

'Do we still have the signal?'

'At the moment. He either doesn't realise we've traced him or he's left the building and his phone behind.'

Lambert replayed the mother-and-son conversation as he drove towards the location the Fireman had called from. He was still surprised by the tone of Trevor Hodge's voice. Maybe it had been the shock of talking to his mother again, but the man he'd heard was far from the secure and focused individual Lambert had envisaged. An air of insecurity, even fear, had cloaked every word. Did he fear retribution? He'd told his mother he'd been told to do something he didn't want to. Had that been eliminating Caroline and Marcus Jardine? It would go some way towards explaining the switch of bodies at the scene. It would also explain his nervousness now, and the sound of genuine remorse at Marcus Jardine's supposed death.

The car in front refused to give way. Unlike the others which had pulled to the side, this vehicle, a decrepit red Mini, ambled along, blocking his path, seemingly unaware of the wailing sirens behind.

'What's this guy's problem?' said Lambert, blaring his horn as if the extra noise would make a difference.

'Looks like he's wearing earphones,' said Matilda, shaking her head.

'Right,' said Lambert, pulling out into the oncoming traffic.

Lambert ignored the startled faces of the other drivers as he pulled up beside the Mini. Behind him, Robertson and his colleagues made the same manoeuvre. Lambert didn't see the Mini driver's reaction as drove past, though he noticed Matilda's hand gesture to the teenager as they pulled directly in front of the car.

'Totally oblivious,' said Matilda.

Lambert sped on, knowing every wasted second was a chance for the Fireman to escape.

'Shit, the signal's dead,' said Matilda, as they headed into Chislehurst.

'Christ,' Lambert yelled, thrusting the gearbox into a lower gear as he sped by another idling car.

'Next left,' said Matilda.

As they rounded a corner Lambert skidded and applied the brakes, almost tipping the car onto two wheels as he screeched around the corner. All he could think of was Caroline Jardine. Was she alone somewhere? Did she know her husband was dead?

Lambert skidded to a stop outside the block of flats. 'Do we have a location for him?' he asked Matilda, rushing out of the car.

Robertson pulled up alongside. 'The signal's gone dead,' he said.

'Where was he when he spoke to us?' said Lambert.

The estate before them was monolithic in scale, an amalgamation of four high-rise buildings and various extensions which had been added on piecemeal over the years.

'I've been trying to break it down on the journey over,' said Robertson. 'The signals seem to be coming from floor five. That building there,' he said, pointing to the largest of the high-rise buildings.

'I had a look at the electoral register but the only Hodge on the estate is a Sidney and Eleanor and they don't appear to be any relation,' he added.

'Do you have an address for them?' said Lambert.

Robertson nodded.

'Right, you go over there,' said Lambert, to one of Robertson's colleagues.

'Robertson, you and your colleague here guard the stairwell. When the local plod honours us with their presence, tell them to cordon off the whole area. I want no one in or out. Do you understand?'

Robertson nodded.

Lambert turned and with Matilda made his way up the stairwell.

The journey was not a pleasant one. Lambert had visited such places many times before, especially during his period as a probation officer. Estates like this were tiny parcels of land forgotten by society. Only streets away, people were living in relative luxury, in semi-detached houses with two-car driveways. Here, the majority of people were struggling to make ends meet, living day to day off meagre benefits and whatever other forms of income they could scrounge together.

The stairwell was damp and had clearly been used as a makeshift lavatory. The bitter scent of ammonia stung Lambert's eyes as he made his way past the graffiti-laden walls. He was out of breath by the time he reached the fifth floor. An iron-plated door decorated with flecks of battered paintwork blocked their path.

'Is this to keep them in or us out?' said Lambert, as he pulled open the heavy piece of metal. 'Any signal now?'

'Nothing.'

From the gateway, they were able to head in two directions. 'You go left, I'll go right,' said Lambert.

Matilda nodded, her baton already in her hand. 'Let's meet in the middle.'

The local force arrived as Lambert made his way along the corridor. He glanced over the balcony, where he saw Robertson speaking to Bickland.

Lambert tried each door, peering through the windows into other people's lives. Many of the doors were chipped or even broken, boarded up with random planks of wood and plastic. From one door, he heard the loud thudding of house music, the first sign of life he'd encountered since arriving at the building.

The technology Robertson used was superior even to what they'd had a couple of years ago, but it still sometimes made mistakes. There was a chance the call had come from the fourth or sixth floor and Lambert was simply chasing shadows making his way along the dank corridors.

However, even if the Fireman had escaped, it was unlikely he would have taken the Jardines with him, or Caroline, if what Hodge had said about Marcus Jardine was to be believed. It would have been too much to move the body, willing or not, in the time it had taken Lambert to arrive. That was, of course, assuming he was holding Caroline captive in the estate.

Lambert was almost resigned to a doing a door-by-door search of the entire building when Matilda stuck her head around the corner and called to him. She waved her hand urgently, her baton held high in her other hand. Lambert sprinted along the corridor, skipping over an ornamental flowerpot a resident had left in the middle of the gangway.

'There are signs of a break-in,' said Matilda in hushed tones as he reached her. 'Just down here.'

Lambert followed her halfway down the landing. She stopped outside flat 516, the door of which had clearly been smashed open. The upper hinges of the door had been obliterated and the door dangled from the lower hinges at a diagonal angle across the threshold. Lambert pushed the door against the inside wall and made his way into the building.

The parallels with the derelict bungalow in Romford were obvious. The carpet was a patchwork of stains and litter, the smell just as repulsive. Lambert called out, his voice echoing from the bare walls. He pulled out his baton and tore through the living room door with a firm kick to the lock. The room was completely bare, save for one large object in the middle of the wooden floorboards.

The body of a man, surrounded by a growing pool of blood.

# Chapter Thirty-One

'Call it in,' said Lambert, as he moved towards the man he believed to be Trevor Hodge.

Despite the drama of the situation Lambert remained calm. His approach was slow as he tried to assess Hodge's injuries whilst keeping an eye out for explosives. The man's head was turned to the left, half his face submerged in a puddle of blood.

'Trevor, is that you?' said Lambert, leaning nearer so they were face to face. The man lowered his eyes and didn't speak.

'Trevor, my name is DCI Lambert. Can you tell me where you've been injured?'

Hodge was lying on his front, and blood pooled around his lower half. Lambert feared moving him before the paramedics arrived. He lifted up the back of Hodge's shirt revealing a deep laceration to his lower back.

'Paramedics are on their way, Trevor. You're going to have to hang on there. Who did this to you?'

Hodge began convulsing. Lambert stretched his hand out and placed it on the man's back, holding it in position.

'The same people who told you to kill the Jardines?'

Hodge nodded, the movement so slight Lambert wasn't sure if he'd imagined it or not.

'Where's Caroline Jardine, Trevor?' he said, his tone neutral. 'Come on, Trevor, you can do one more good thing. Just tell me where she is.'

The colour was fading from Hodge's face and the shaking had stopped. A pair of paramedics appeared and pushed Lambert out of the way.

'Do you think it's self-inflicted?' said Matilda, moving up next to him.

The paramedics couldn't get any sense from Hodge. They lay a stretcher on the floor, and when they turned the body over Lambert understood why. It was remarkable the man was alive at all. His abdomen and chest were punctured by what appeared to be tens of deep wounds. Blood flowed in a fierce torrent from one particular wound. One of the paramedics tried to stem the flow whilst the other placed an oxygen mask onto Hodge's mouth. They strapped him to the stretcher and were about to lift him out of the room when Hodge removed his mask.

'What is it, Trevor?' said Lambert, leaning towards him.

'Sir, you need to stay clear,' said one of the paramedics, but Lambert brushed him aside.

Hodge tried to speak as blood trickled from his mouth, but only air escaped.

'What was that, Trevor?' Lambert said softly, leaning closer to the man.

Hodge paused and took in a large breath before uttering one hushed word to Lambert and shutting his eyes.

The paramedic Lambert had brushed aside returned the favour.

'What did you say, Trevor?' said Lambert, raising his voice, but Hodge had uttered his last words.

Matilda followed the two paramedics out of the flat with Lambert close behind. As he crossed the threshold, he noticed something in the shadows of the flat. The second paramedic must have noticed the same thing, his face turning white with fear.

Lambert didn't waste any time. 'Run,' he shouted. He was less than twenty metres down the corridor when an explosion ripped through the building.

# Chapter Thirty-Two

Lambert lay on his side, clutching his chest.

The explosion had driven him across the passageway, the brick wall which separated the floor from the drop below breaking his fall. His eyes stung as he scanned the smoke-filled area. He must have been knocked unconscious. He checked his head for injuries, noticing flames dancing in the smoke by the doorway. His first thoughts were of Matilda. She'd been in front of him just before the explosion and he prayed she'd escaped unharmed. It was impossible to see from his prone position, and he was unable to make out the shapes of the two paramedics and Hodge. He opened his mouth to call for help, his lungs invaded by acrid smoke. The burning sensation spread through his body until it was too painful to move.

He recalled Hodge speaking to him seconds before the explosion. It had only been one word but in all the commotion, Lambert couldn't be sure if Hodge had spoken it or if it had been a trick of his imagination. Either way, he needed to remember it. He was sure he'd read it one time during the case, even if he couldn't quite place it now. He mouthed the word to himself over and over, a nonsense mantra he hoped would one day make sense should he escape his present situation.

He tried to push himself up, collapsing immediately. The procedure in such situations was to keep low, to search for pockets of oxygen and await rescue. He laid his head on the concrete floor and tried to stay awake. His eyelids were heavy and although he tried to fight it, he sensed he was seconds away from falling unconscious again.

From the gloom came a voice. Lambert couldn't make out the words. He realised his eyes were closed. As he opened them, acid-like tears streamed from his eyes and rubbing them with his grime-covered hands only intensified the burning sensation. He risked one more look, the heat even more intense. This time he glimpsed a break in the smoke as a hand reached for him and placed a mask over his face.

–

The next thing Lambert knew, he was lying on a stretcher at the top of the stairwell, the chilled air around him a relief. His eyes still burned but he managed to open them, relieved to see Matilda walking by the side of the stretcher. He went to speak, his throat burning from the fumes he'd inhaled, but the oxygen mask was still on him. He tried to pull it off, only for Matilda to hold it in place.

'Give it a few minutes, Michael,' she said.

It must have taken a lot for her to be there, so close to an explosion for a second day in a row, after what had happened to her. But Lambert didn't want to wait a couple of minutes. He pulled off the mask and instructed the paramedics to allow him off the stretcher.

'Let's wait till we get you back in the ambulance,' said one of the pair.

'Now,' said Lambert, a painful stabbing sensation hitting the back of his throat as he made the hoarse, garbled sound.

'Wait till we're in the back of the ambulance,' the man repeated, focusing his attention elsewhere.

The lift was out of order so they made slow progress down the flight of stairs. Matilda led the way, guiding the first paramedic as they carried Lambert as gently as possible to the bottom of the stairwell. Once placed in the back of the ambulance, Lambert tore at his constraints. An onrush of dizziness hit him as he sat up but he didn't let on.

'You need to go to hospital,' said one of the paramedics. 'You've taken in a lot of smoke.'

'I could do with some water,' Lambert said to Matilda, ignoring the man.

Matilda held a bottle to his lips.

'Just sip it,' said the paramedic.

Each drop of water pained him and he tried not to wince as Matilda studied his reaction.

'Hodge?' he asked, taking a final sip and handing the bottle back to Matilda.

'He didn't make it. I don't think the explosion was as powerful as yesterday's. It blew out the front window, but the majority of the partition wall is still intact. That's why you're still alive. I think Hodge was gone by the time he'd left the flat. You saw his wounds.'

A vision of Hodge's torso sprang into Lambert's mind, the lines of tiny puncture marks like an absurd decoration. Lambert had lost track of time. He didn't know how long ago the explosion had occurred and didn't want to ask Matilda in case she tried to insist he go to the hospital.

As if reading his mind, she updated him on the situation. 'We're still not letting anyone in or out. My guess is whoever's done this to Hodge is long gone. There are hundreds if not thousands of residents in the estate and it'll be a near impossible task questioning all of them.'

Lambert took another sip of water, the pain easing. He swung his legs off the stretcher, groaning at the effort.

Matilda reached out her hands, as if to hold him in position, before thinking better of it.

Lambert could hear the blood drum behind his ears and for a second wanted nothing more than to lie back down on the gurney and to spend time recuperating in the hospital. But he had to find Caroline Jardine.

He thanked the paramedics, who looked dismayed he was leaving their care.

'I need to get to a laptop,' he told Matilda. 'There's something I need to check out.'

# Chapter Thirty-Three

From the look of the faces in the incident room, it appeared the rest of the team shared Lambert's melancholy at the death of Trevor Hodge. Although the man who'd been responsible for at least three fires and possibly the deaths of Jonathan Turner, Maxine Berry, and Marcus Jardine was no longer at large, they were no closer to finding Caroline Jardine.

The team looked up as Lambert entered the room before returning to their laptops and phones.

The Fireman was dead, but there was still a missing officer.

He needed to go home, shower and change out of the clothes which were contaminated by his proximity to the explosion, but time did not allow for such frivolities. He'd left Matilda at the scene, working with the local CID to somehow make a dent in their house-to-house searches.

Lambert remembered the man's dying words and repeated them to himself, as if somehow they could be forgotten. He'd read the words before in the case files. They were common words, but the context in which he'd read them wasn't.

He logged onto the System and hesitated before entering the words. He hadn't yet shared with anyone what Hodge had told him, and now felt loath to enter the details onto the System where it would be forever linked with him. Instead, he searched through his saved documents and selected one of the old case files.

Trevor Hodge's dying words were 'the manor,' and Lambert remembered where he'd seen those words before. After speaking to Tillman, following the tip-off from Caroline's ex-husband Linklater, Lambert had studied the files of DS Alistair Newlyn, Caroline's ex-colleague who had committed suicide.

Like Caroline Jardine and DS Florence Colville's files from the weeks before Newlyn committed suicide, much of the file was blanked out. The case was an investigation into people trafficking, and Lambert had remembered the entry, as it stuck out in the case notes.

For one, the word was hyphenated due to a page break. Instead of 'the manor', the word was included in the document as 'the man-or', with the '-or' starting a new page. It could have been coincidence, but to Lambert it suggested Newlyn had entered the word purposely this way, as if he wanted someone to spot it. As if he wanted to prevent someone blanking out the phrase.

Alone, it meant nothing. The sentence read simply, 'possible connection to the man-or.' But coupled with Hodge's dying words it started to take on a greater significance.

Knowing he was almost definitely under surveillance, he couldn't risk entering 'the manor' as a search term. Instead, he began the slow process of reading a number of other files, starting with Caroline Jardine's most recent cases. He had to search for the phrase manually, reading each text from each case from beginning to end. It would take hours, so he began scanning the cover sheets of her cases trying to ascertain which was the best to study. An hour in, he realised the search was pointless. If his theory was correct then he imagined Jardine would have been as reluctant as he was to enter the details anywhere they could be traced. That left him with only one option. His time in the Group had taught him a number of cheats. He logged out of the System and used a different laptop to log in to HOLMES, the police database, using a proxy ID. He couldn't run a search on Jardine or Newlyn so instead he ran a search on the manor, relating to recent cases.

Again, the results were numerous, but after a bit of refining one case caught his eye. The local CID had been searching for a known paedophile, Kevin Clarkson, and following a tip-off, had found the remains of a body in an area called Waverley Manor.

Lambert ran a search for the location, but it didn't appear on the internet. He began reading the details of the case and quickly discovered 'the Manor' was a colloquial term. Lambert read the notes of the lead investigator, DI Greene, only to discover many of the notes were blanked out in a style reminiscent of Caroline Jardine and Alistair Newlyn's earlier files.

Lambert considered his options for a few seconds before deciding time couldn't wait. He picked up his phone and called DI Greene, who agreed to meet him at her office within the next two hours.

He was about to leave when Tillman entered – as usual, not bothering with the pleasantries of knocking on the door.

'Why aren't you in hospital?' Tillman demanded.

Lambert blanked the screen with a push of a button.

'Look at me, I'm fine,' he said.

'You don't smell it. It smells like there's been a fire in here.'

'What can I help you with, sir?'

'You may have noticed our main suspect in the disappearance of Caroline and Marcus Jardine is dead,' said Tillman.

'Funnily enough, I'd gathered that.'

'They've counted eighty-two wounds on his body. Eighty-two. Kennedy says he was still alive when you got to him?'

'Barely. He was lying on his front, enough blood on the floor to drown in. We must have got there seconds after the suspect left. We're trying to hold everyone at the scene but it's chaotic, as you can imagine. The residents are being less than cooperative.'

Lambert knew he should share the information about the Manor and his upcoming meeting with Greene with Tillman, but he couldn't bring himself to do so. At times he'd trusted Tillman with his life, but something had happened to the man of late. Lambert didn't want to share anything with him at present.

'What's your next step?'

'Hopefully we'll get lucky with the residents at the estate. We're doing our usual work with the CCTV cameras. That place is like a ghost area. Nothing is monitored.'

'Fine. I'll leave you to work your magic. I'm going back to the estate now to check in with Matilda, if you need a lift?'

'I need to speak to someone first,' said Lambert.

Tillman hesitated by the door, clearly wanting more information. When Lambert didn't offer it, he sighed and left the office.

## Chapter Thirty-Four

DI Greene worked out of the same central station as Sarah May. As Lambert drove to London, he realised he hadn't seen Sarah for some days and now ran the risk of running into her unannounced at work. After a brief altercation with a security guard, he parked in the station's underground car park and made his way up to Sarah's office. He groaned inwardly as he was beeped through the office door and was stopped by the first person he saw.

DCI Barnes stood with his hands on hips, staring at Lambert as if he was an apparition.

'DCI Lambert,' he said, 'to what honour do we owe your presence?'

Was it a coincidence Barnes was there? He worked in the building, but so did hundreds of others. But the way he stood there, and the accusatory way he glared at Lambert, suggested he'd been waiting for him.

'You're not here to see me, Lambert, are you?'

'No.'

It was almost certain Barnes knew about him and Sarah May. It wasn't a huge secret and the fact they were now both the same rank made their relationship acceptable. With what had happened today, and with Caroline Jardine still missing, a private visit to see Sarah would be frowned upon, but it would at least mask the real reason for his visit.

'Well?' said Barnes.

'Routine work.'

'Obviously I've heard about this Hodge character. He tell you anything that could help us find Caroline?'

'Not really, I'm afraid,' said Lambert, refusing to divulge any information.

'Her husband is dead?'

'According to Hodge. Naturally, we aren't taking his word for it.'

'Naturally,' said Hodge, folding his arms. 'Well don't let me keep you.'

'I'll keep you updated,' said Lambert.

'I appreciate that,' said Barnes, with a flicker of grief.

Lambert made his way to the large open-plan office where Sarah worked. It was ludicrous to feel nervous about seeing her and it suggested something which he'd been trying desperately to avoid. He turned to his left, sensing her movement in his peripheral vision. Sarah was talking to a fellow officer whose focus was on the open folder in her arms. She was on the other side of the office and, knowing he'd feel ludicrous calling over, Lambert simply stood there waiting for her to notice him. When she did he was disappointed to notice the smile on her face disappear. She said something to her colleague and walked towards him, her eyebrows furrowed.

'This is a pleasant surprise,' she said, fixing him with a stare which unnerved him and suggested the surprise was anything but pleasant.

'Business, I'm afraid,' said Lambert.

There was a subtle shift. He doubted many people would notice it but he could tell she was intrigued. If she could smell the smoke on him, she was hiding it well.

'Is there somewhere private we could go?'

Lambert followed her to one of the interview rooms where Sarah shut the door and pulled down the blinds.

'You hiding from someone?' asked Lambert.

'Oh, it's nothing. Mixing the professional and personal. Anyway, what was it you wanted to speak to me about?'

Lambert was confused by her response. She'd never been concerned about such matters before. 'Can we sit down? You're putting me on edge.'

Sarah smiled and Lambert felt a surge of relief sweep through him. Her face had softened and at last he was looking at the woman he knew.

'You've heard about Hodge I presume?' he said.

'News had filtered through. I heard he was stabbed multiple times in the chest?'

'Eighty-two. I was the first on the scene.'

Something changed again on Sarah's face. A look of panic this time.

'You were? I didn't know. You? Wasn't there an explosion?'

Lambert held out his arms. 'I'm still here, aren't I?'

Sarah moved towards him, glancing at the door as she did so.

'Jesus, are you OK?' she said quietly. 'Why didn't you call me?'

'It wasn't that big a deal.'

'Not that big a deal? It was an explosion. I can smell the smoke on you.'

'As I said, I'm fine. The explosion was just a distraction. It didn't even cause much damage to the flat.'

She placed her hand on his arm and he felt her tremble. 'You have been checked out though?'

'Yep, there's no need to worry, I'm signed off to work. I'm fine. That's not why I'm here though.'

He hoped he hadn't come over as too brusque. He appreciated her concern but he was still focused on finding Caroline Jardine. Sarah looked slightly taken aback but she didn't say anything. She retreated and sat back on the office chair to his left.

'What is it then?' she said.

'I'm here to see one of your colleagues.'

'Oh.'

Lambert smiled. 'Are you upset by that?'

'You've got to do what you've got to do,' said Sarah, matching his smile.

'It's only routine. Well, perhaps it was more than that. Hodge said something to me before he died. It was just a phrase. I remember reading about it in one of Caroline's old cases, and one of the officers here is working on something similar.' He didn't want to go into details and was grateful Sarah wasn't pushing for anything specific.

'Anyone I know.'

'DI Greene?'

Sarah shook her head. 'Don't know the name.'

'She's just been seconded here. She was working out of Watford.'

'Oh, OK.' Sarah hesitated. 'Why are you telling me this?'

Lambert wasn't sure he could answer the question. A sudden urge came over him to share his almost daily visits to Sophie's house, to announce his doubts over their relationship. 'I just thought it was a good excuse to see you.'

Sarah frowned, reading him easily. 'We should probably talk,' she said. 'But not now.'

# Chapter Thirty-Five

DI Greene's office was on the tenth floor. She'd been seconded from her role to lead a team working on a drug operation out of North London, having managed a similar operation in Watford. Lambert would have rather met somewhere less open. Despite the size of the building, it wouldn't go unreported he'd met with Greene.

Greene had a corner office overlooking a large open area with officers working on adjoining desks. He knocked and entered, Greene getting to her feet after Lambert's introduction.

'Please shut the door, sir. Can I get you anything to drink?'

Lambert shut the door, noticing one or two faces staring up at him as he did. 'Nothing for me, thank you,' he said, taking a seat opposite the officer.

Greene was a short, stout woman. Her brown hair was cut to give a severe fringe. Lambert had read her file and knew she was fifty-two. Her background was solid, though it looked as if she'd reached her pinnacle where rank was concerned, having been a Detective Inspector for the last twelve years.

'I have to say I was a bit intrigued when you called. I'm aware of some of your cases,' she said.

Lambert had been involved in a couple of high profile cases in the last two years, the downside of which was a dubious form of notoriety.

'I'm aware of some of yours as well, DI Greene. That's why I'm here.'

'Shoot,' said Greene.

Lambert appreciated her directness. 'What can you tell me about your recent case? The recovered body you found in Waverley Manor.'

Greene paused before answering as if deciding how much she was willing to divulge. 'About two months ago I was contacted by a con, John Smith. Smith was in prison serving a fifteen-year term for attempted child abduction. He was obviously hoping for a reduction in his sentence for cooperation, though he didn't specifically request it, and he didn't ask for a brief.'

'Why you?'

'It was a routine missing person case. Kevin Clarkson, married with two grown up children, had gone missing three months previously. We'd almost given up on it to be honest. You know how it is. Our thinking was that if Clarkson wanted finding he would turn up. He had no record, so no cause for suspicion.'

'Smith knew Clarkson.'

'Claimed to. Said Clarkson had been working the same circles as him some ten years ago.'

'Child abduction.'

Greene nodded, and her face twitched as if she had indigestion. 'During the interview, Smith broke down in tears. Started telling me about this place called the Manor. At least I thought it was a place. As he began to speak, I began to understand the Manor was the name of an organisation. Smith claimed they were the ones he'd been working for when he was arrested, and that Clarkson had been his go-between. Wouldn't divulge anything else, apart from one more thing.'

'Waverley Manor?'

'Yes. Supposedly, that's where they got their name. He said I'd find everything I needed there, and in part he was right.'

'You found Clarkson?' Lambert knew most of what she was telling him, having read it in her file, but still, it was good to hear it directly from her.

'A few days later and there we are, getting pissed on as our team searches this derelict area. This so-called Waverley Manor.'

'Tell me about it,' said Lambert.

Greene frowned again. 'It's little more than the remnants of an abandoned brick building, which we eventually discovered deep into the forest. Only the shell of a building remains. As you can appreciate, it was a risk, a lot of manpower and work for what was effectively the word of a felon.'

'Did you push Smith for more detail of this organisation?

'Of course. He was scared, that was clear, and when we discovered Clarkson I understood why.'

'How did Smith even get to hear about Clarkson's disappearance?'

'His family lawyer had been tipped off. We've interviewed him but there's nothing on him. It was local news, public record.'

'So what happened?' said Lambert.

'We struck gold early. We discovered the shallow grave in the first few hours, yards from the structure of the building. The body was wrapped in a polyethylene covering but it hadn't stopped the wildlife getting to it. The body's hands had been bound behind his back with a leather strap. We later identified the body as belonging to Kevin Clarkson.'

'What else can you tell me?' said Lambert.

'If you don't mind me asking, sir, can I ask what this is in relation to?'

Lambert studied the DI. She'd been open with him but she was holding something back. He decided to match her openness. 'You've heard of the Caroline Jardine case?'

'Of course. I can't see how it's related though.'

'Trevor Hodge. The arsonist responsible for the fire at Caroline's house, and almost definitely her abduction too.'

'He was murdered?'

'Yes. He obviously knew something. I managed to speak to him before he died. His last words were "the Manor."'

If Greene was surprised, she hid it well. 'I'm convinced there's more to that place.'

'What happened next?'

'I ordered the team to continue searching. They didn't like it and I couldn't blame them. It wouldn't stop raining and as far as they were concerned we'd reached our goal.'

'And you?' said Lambert.

'I thought there were more bodies. Still do, but the operation was shut down within two hours.'

'Who decided that?'

Greene scratched the back of her head. 'Sir, it was my direct boss DCI Jenkins' decision to pull me off the case. As you can imagine, I confronted him about it, but he wouldn't elaborate on his decision. He told me we'd .found Clarkson and the job was done.' She looked through the window of her office as if scanning for anyone trying to eavesdrop. Lowering her tone she said, 'there was something off about it all. I had an inkling it wasn't his decision but I couldn't make such an unfounded accusation. Next day, I've taken a day off and there's a knock at the door.'

The whole case was going through Lambert's mind from beginning to end. 'Anti-corruption?' he said.

Greene sat back in her chair. 'How did you know?'

Could it have been Duggan was working on this all along? 'What were their names?' he asked.

'You've met DS Duggan?'

Lambert closed his eyes. 'Jesus,' he said.

'He was quite taken with you as well. It seems they have been investigating one of our officers for some time. Chief Superintendent Sinnott.'

For one horrendous moment, Lambert had thought she was about to say Tillman. 'Sinnott?'

'He's the head of my department. Duggan believes he took me off the case.'

'Does he know I asked to meet you?'

Greene surprised him by blushing. 'I'm afraid so. I had no option.'

It was Lambert's turn to lean back in his seat. 'So Sinnott is linked to this Manor group somehow?'

'So Duggan believes.'

'And the second Anti-Corruption officer?'

'I think you'll have to meet her yourself.'

# Chapter Thirty-Six

Lambert didn't stop to see Sarah before returning to his car. The conversation with Greene raised more questions than it answered but it offered some hope. He'd agreed to meet her and the mysterious Anti-Corruption officer later that evening at a bar close to his flat.

He was in desperate need of a shower and change. Every time he breathed he was reminded of the fire earlier that day. His skin had a second layer of grime and ash. He reminded himself Caroline Jardine was still to be found and pressed his foot to the accelerator, swirling through the traffic.

As he approached his block of flats, he noticed a lady standing outside. Slim and elegant in a three-quarter-length trench coat, she had the kind of air and poise about her he recognised in a fellow officer. She was used to waiting. He could see it in her stance. He understood now, after Greene's revelations, that he'd been under surveillance all this time. It explained why he'd seen Duggan outside Gladys Hodges' care home the other evening and at the station.

He drove past the woman, keeping his gaze forwards so as not to attract her attention. He parked up and waited, studying the woman in his rear-view mirror. She stood perfectly still, her arms by her side. He could be mistaken;

she could be someone's girlfriend waiting patiently for one of the flats' occupants to make an appearance. But he didn't think so. He waited for ten minutes before he left the car and made his way down the road towards her, checking the parked vehicles for signs of life, looking out for Duggan's number plate. She looked down at the road as he approached. He stopped when he reached her.

'Can I help you?'

She turned to face him, clearly unmoved by his appearance or question. She stared intently as if summoning up a memory.

'DCI Lambert?' she asked.

'Who are you?' said Lambert, ignoring the question.

'My name is Florence Colville.'

Lambert didn't have to search his memory long to place the name.

'Formerly DS Florence Colville,' he said.

Colville had been the third member of Jardine's team who'd left the force shortly after their colleague, Alistair Newlyn, had committed suicide.

'I'm still a Detective Sergeant,' said Colville.

Lambert played the information through his mind and quickly decided it wasn't that surprising.

'You didn't leave the force,' he said.

Colville shook her head.

'Let me guess, you're working undercover?'

'Correct.'

'You're Greene's mysterious Anti-Corruption officer?'

Colville nodded. 'We need to talk, sir, somewhere safe.'

'Give me ten minutes,' said Lambert, leaving her outside as he went up to his flat to shower and change.

Colville had said somewhere safe, which suggested one of them was in danger.

Lambert stayed longer than anticipated under the shower. He scrubbed himself clean but still the smell of smoke clung to him and he wondered if it would ever leave. He doused his body in deodorant before changing and heading downstairs.

DS Colville was standing in the same position, rooted to the spot as if she was the security for the building behind her.

'Where's somewhere safe?' said Lambert.

'Somewhere public,' answered Colville.

'Follow me,' said Lambert, leading the woman to a bar on the High Street.

Colville took a seat at the back of the shop facing the entrance as Lambert bought them some soft drinks. As he returned, he noticed Colville sat with the same strange intensity she'd displayed standing outside his flat. She sat upright, stiff backed, staring ahead.

'What have you got to tell me?' said Lambert.

'What can you tell me, sir? I imagine you have some idea what's going on now?' she said, ignoring the drink placed before.

Lambert hadn't asked for her ID as he was sure she wasn't carrying any, but he had checked her file on the System before he'd left, and had verified her identity with a picture taken five years ago. She hadn't changed much in that time, physically at least. But the way she held herself suggested something had changed within.

'I'm not here to answer questions,' said Lambert. 'What the hell is this all about?'

Colville shifted in her seat.

'I was warned you'd be like this,' she said.

Lambert didn't respond. He sipped his sparkling water, refusing to be budged. 'What do you have to tell me?'

Colville barely reacted. 'Stop me if you know any of this,' she said.

Lambert nodded his head slightly, agreeing to nothing.

'You must be aware of Alistair Newlyn's suicide,' said Colville. 'You're probably aware Alistair was a former colleague of mine and Caroline Jardine's?'

Lambert didn't answer.

'Anyway, at the time of his suicide, we were investigating an organised crime group. Only, it was as if this group didn't exist. They were part urban legend. We believed they were responsible for a number of disappearances in the Greater London area. They were known as the Manor but we were never sure if that was the name of the group or a clue to their location. We heard the word only in dispatches.'

Lambert felt a surge of adrenaline at the mention of the Manor. 'How do you mean, 'dispatches'?'

'It was a name which kept cropping up in interviews and witness reports. We could never find anything concrete. No one would ever talk. Then, one day, we had a break-through. Or at least Alistair did. Sir, what did Trevor Hodge say to you before he died?'

'I'm here to listen to you,' said Lambert.

Colville frowned and continued.

'Alistair called me and Caroline to meet at his flat. He told us about an informant who knew about the Manor.'

'And that was the day you found him?' said Lambert.

'Yes.'

'What information did you get from him before you found him at the flat?'

'He gave us two names. One was Gerry Twain, a suspected paedophile who'd recently disappeared.'

'And the other?' he asked, thinking he already knew.

'That was the thing. The other name was a police officer. The officer was Chief Superintendent Sinnott.'

Greene's superior, the man she suspected had prevented her further exploration of Waverley Manor. Lambert paused, sipping the water, trying to analyse what he'd been told.

'He didn't give you the informant's name?'

'Not over the phone, no,' said Colville.

'OK, so let's backtrack. He mentions Sinnott on the phone and next thing he's committed suicide?'

'Yes.'

'That was four years ago?'

'Yes'

'So, you supposedly left the force a few months later but you moved to Anti-Corruption?'

'Correct, DCI Lambert.'

'And Sinnott's under investigation?'

'Following Newlyn's suicide we discovered his files, laptop and phone had all been wiped. We could find absolutely nothing to link him to Sinnott and, of course, we had no name for an informant.'

'So, what have you been doing for the last four years?'

'I've been trying to infiltrate the Manor.'

'And how's that working out for you?' said Lambert.

'Slow progress, as you can imagine.' She was obviously not prepared to tell him any more at that stage.

'Did Caroline know about you and your activities?'

'No, sir. She thinks I left. After Alistair's death they took her off the case. In fact, the case was closed. There was no legitimate reason to keep it running – that's when I went to Anti-Corruption. However, sir, there's one thing you should know. One thing I'm sure no one's told you.'

'What's that?' asked Lambert

'Caroline never stopped working on the case.'

'What do you mean?'

'There's nothing official but I know she's been investigating the Manor. She's been doing so covertly but she's left footprints.'

Lambert sat back. Things were starting to make some sort of sense, though the knowledge wasn't benefiting him at the moment. 'So following her kidnapping, you took an overview of my case?'

'Yes, sir. It followed close on the heels of DI Greene's case. I believe she told you that Sinnott is her department head. We're convinced he pulled Greene's investigation into Waverley Manor.'

'What else do you have on Sinnott?' he asked.

'Not enough. Alistair's suicide. Waverley Manor. And now we have Hodge's dying words.'

'He didn't mention Sinnott,' said Lambert.

'What did he say? DI Greene didn't share it with me.'

'His last words were "the Manor,"' said Lambert. 'I think it's about time we took a closer look at that place.'

# Chapter Thirty-Seven

Lambert arranged to meet with Colville and Greene back at his flat in two hours. He requested that Duggan not be involved for the time being though he was sure Colville would inform him.

He called Matilda and arranged to meet her beforehand. She appeared within the hour and he told her about Greene and Colville.

'So we're working for AC now?' she said.

'We're cooperating with them. It's our only option at this point.'

'Why don't you make it official? Tell Glenn you're going to this Waverley Manor. We could take a full team there. There's nothing Sinnott, or anyone else, can do about it.'

'Possibly. But it would mean notifying those involved. We don't know if the Jardines will be there. Seems unlikely to me. If Hodge had somehow betrayed his organisation then he wouldn't have taken Caroline to their main location. So, the plan is we'll do a reccy of the place. You and I will go in with DI Greene. Colville will stay on point at the car.'

'Why don't we just tell Glenn?' repeated Matilda.

Lambert had known Tillman a decade or so longer than Matilda. He understood she was questioning his loyalty and he didn't have a ready answer for her.

'At the moment, the fewer people who know the better,' he said, sensing the inadequacy of his words.

Thirty minutes later, Colville and Greene arrived. The four of them drank tea in Lambert's living quarters. Lambert glanced around him as they drank, wincing at the chaotic nature of the room, the mess he'd somehow created with a minimal amount of furniture.

'Drink up, it's getting late,' said Lambert.

He outlined the plan he'd shared with Matilda to the rest of the team.

'Greene, I want you to lead Kennedy and me to the site where you discovered the body. Colville, you'll be on lookout. Let's go.'

Outside, they got into Lambert's car and set off in silence punctuated only by the sound of the engine and the tyres on the tarmac. Lambert stopped at a lockout he used and filled the boot of the car with a set of portable floodlights, and a bag filled to the brim with torches and various tools he stuffed in on the off chance.

Back on the road, Lambert glanced at Colville in the rear-view mirror. 'How long did you work with Caroline for?' he asked the woman.

'About two years.'

'You got on well together?'

'Very well. We were a very secure trio, along with Alistair. Though Caroline was always the leading light.'

'In what way?' said Lambert.

'She had that burning ambition. You see it in certain officers. I'm sure you're aware of that.'

Lambert nodded to himself and wondered if that drive and ambition were keeping Caroline alive at the moment.

Colville still had that unusual intensity to her. Even in the relative darkness of the car he sensed her rigidity, the straightness of her spine as she sat almost to attention as he spoke to her. He wondered if she'd always been like that or if the incident with her former colleague had brought a new tension into her life, one which manifested itself physically.

He pulled off the main road an hour later, into a side lane guarded by an avenue of trees. As the car progressed, the road became more and more difficult to manoeuvre until eventually it was little more than a dirt track seemingly leading to nowhere. He switched on his hazard lights and brought the car to a stop. The temperature had plummeted a few degrees since they'd left. It was approaching midnight and Lambert put on a set of heavy-duty gloves, buttoning his coat tight against his neck.

'So this is Waverley Manor?' he said to DI Greene.

'You should be so lucky,' said Greene, with a high lilt to her voice Lambert had previously not noticed.

'There's still a good mile trek left. Through there,' she said, pointing a torch at a looming oak tree, magnificent and haunting.

'Are you sure you know the way?' said Lambert.

Greene shrugged. 'I've been here in the dark once before. We'll need the floodlights but I'm pretty confident we can find our way. To be fair, it's only the first quarter of a mile that's tricky, then the place opens up somewhat till you reach the Manor.'

'Sounds great. As agreed,' said Lambert. 'DI Greene, you're going to lead the way. Kennedy, you're with me, and DS Colville will stay on point.'

They retrieved the gear Lambert had collected from the boot of the car and headed into the woods. They made slow progress at first, Lambert and Matilda lighting the path with their high-definition torches.

The peacefulness of the area was impossible to ignore. Although there were many green areas surrounding the neighbourhood where Lambert lived he never felt truly able to escape the bustle of city life. When time allowed he'd occasionally take a walk in Beckenham Park Woods but even there he was reminded of the reality of the world just beyond the trees, by the occasional sound of traffic or the yell of a golfer shouting 'fore' from the soon-to-be-defunct golf course. No such sounds bothered them here. Maybe it was just the time of night, the clock approaching midnight, but as Lambert made his way through the brambles and low-hanging branches he felt a sense of isolation. The only sounds he could hear were the noises within his confined space: his own footsteps and those of his colleagues, and the scurrying wildlife just out of sight.

True to Greene's word, they soon approached the clearing. In the darkness it looked like an absence, a vast piece of land devoid of trees that looked out of place in the middle of the forest.

'Is this man-made?' Lambert asked Greene, shining his torch into the clearing.

'I don't think so. It's surrounded by trees on all sides. It must be a natural phenomenon.'

'Where's Waverley Manor from here?' asked Matilda, who was busy pointing her torch in all directions as if they were being followed.

'Across the clearing and then one last trek,' said Greene.

The clearing was not as flat and welcoming as Lambert had expected. More than once he lost his footing on uneven ground. Even in this vast openness the same lingering sense of isolation overtook him. Was Caroline waiting for them somewhere beyond the trees in the distance? He wondered if somehow the sound of their movement could carry in the stillness of the night.

The second trek through the woods was harder than the first.

'There is an actual building through here, Greene?' he said.

'Of sorts,' said Greene, slowing her pace as the trees encroached on both sides. 'It's the ruins of a building. The Manor is a misnomer. It's nothing more than some remnants of a small brick house. We couldn't find records of it anywhere. If it hadn't been for our informant we'd have never known it existed.'

'Here. Through here,' she said, turning her shoulder and pushing through the foliage.

Lambert followed a couple of steps behind Matilda until, for the second time that night, they broke through into a clearing, this one infinitely smaller than the once preceding it.

'There,' said Greene, shining a light on the ruins of an ancient building through which a solitary tree grew, its branches reaching out for the multitude of gaps in the structure.

'Welcome to Waverley Manor.'

# Chapter Thirty-Eight

Greene had been correct about the Manor: it didn't deserve the title.

They set up the floodlights illuminating the brittle remains of the brick building, the lights catching on the vines which interweaved through the structure. Lambert tried to stay positive but it felt as if they'd reached a dead end.

'Here's where we found Smith,' said Greene, showing them to a cordoned-off area fifty or so metres from the main site.

'Did you get much further in your search before it was called off?' asked Lambert.

'A couple of hours at most. We searched outwards from his grave but didn't discover anything before I was told to call it a day.'

They began the search nearer to the crumbling building itself. Lambert took the interior of the building, with its flooring of mud and foliage, whilst Matilda and Greene searched the perimeter.

Lambert shone his torch on the bricks of the Manor, hoping for the slightest indication they were in the right place. He pulled at the loose brickwork, revealing an abandoned bird's nest so brittle it fell away in his hands. As he scrambled around on his hands and feet, searching for God only knew what, he wondered what he was doing in this place. He chopped away at some dense vines with a small pair of shears, rubbing his hands against the brickwork as if searching for an opening.

Once again, negative thoughts overcame him. Experience told him searching a place like this would take days and conducting the search the wrong side of midnight with a team of three was not the way to go about it. He was standing gazing out from the interior of the building, moving his torch in a haphazard manner creating zigzags in the line of trees before him, when he sensed movement to his left. He shone his torch at some rustling leaves just in time to see the figure of a small mouse disappear into the undergrowth next to the far side of the wall.

Lambert followed the rodent, making his own rustling noise as he took large steps across the frozen ground. He squatted down, clipping away at the brambles which surrounded the wall. The mouse had disappeared but Lambert felt a different movement as he placed his hand into the vines. He pulled and pulled, brushing spiders and other insects off him, until enough of the vegetation came away that he could see the walls. Like the rest of the building the brown-red bricks had seen better times.

Lambert peered closer, shining his torch onto the lines of cement holding the bricks in place, as if the ancient masonry could relate something to him. Closer to the ground he noticed a small opening into which the mouse had presumably scurried. He clawed at it with his hands, pulling away chunks of frozen mud until he'd created an opening big enough to fit his hand through. He moved his hand through with trepidation, tentatively touching the other side only to be disappointed with what he found: more frozen mud.

'What are you doing?' said a voice from behind him.

Keeping his hand in place, he turned his neck back and snarled at Matilda. 'I'm not actually sure,' he said.

She approached further, shining her torch into the gap where his hand lay as if this was somehow of help. 'A secret passage?' she said, gently mocking him.

'Who knows,' he said, shoving his arm in further until his fingers made contact with something solid.

'Hang on,' he said, 'I think I've found something.'

'Yeah, right,' said Matilda, not believing a word of it.

Lambert drummed his fingers on the cold ground and shivered as something crawled across the back of his hand. He extended his index finger till he made contact again.

'Seriously,' he said, stretching his arm further into the hole. He managed to take hold of the object which was smooth and cold like metal. He flicked his finger until the object lifted and he was able to lock his finger around it.

'There's something here, some sort of lock or handle. Go round the other side and let me know what you can see.'

Matilda called Greene and together they made their way around the other side of the wall.

'See anything?' shouted Lambert a few minutes later.

Matilda returned and tapped him on the shoulder. At the same second, he felt something scamper over the back of his hand.

'We're going to be a while,' she said. 'The area behind is covered in brambles. Are you OK to hold on?'

'I'm not going anywhere, but I'd be grateful if you'd hurry up. I'm being eaten alive.'

Lambert lay on the damp ground and waited for his colleagues to cut through. He tried not to think of the various beings which seemed to be feasting on him as he waited.

Eventually, he felt a touch on his hand. 'We're through, sir,' said Matilda. 'I've got a hold of the ring-pull. You can let go and come back round this side.'

Lambert dragged his hand out, glad to see flesh still on his bones. He pushed himself up from the floor with a grunt of effort, his left trouser leg caked in mud.

Outside the house, on the other side of the wall, Matilda was crouched over, her hand on a metal object.

'What is it?' said Lambert.

'It looks like some kind of opening. A manhole cover if I'm not mistaken,' she said.

'Very well concealed,' added Greene, who looked as though the cold had got to her. She held her arms tightly by her sides, shivering.

Lambert knew better than to get excited. The door could be anything, most likely a disused access point for the sewage system.

They arranged the light around the opening and Lambert twisted the ring-pull, feeling the heavy creak of a lock mechanism opening. He pulled back the manhole cover which was heavier than he'd expected, and a wave of fetid air rushed him. He turned from the blast and laid the manhole cover on the ground.

'Torch,' he said to Matilda, blood rushing through his veins. He glanced into the opening, not keen to see what lay within the depths. The torch revealed a narrow tunnel drop. Metal rungs were hooked onto the curved wall, making up a makeshift ladder. Lambert peered into the hole, further ascertaining the length of the drop which he estimated to be thirty or forty metres deep.

'I guess one of us has to go down,' he said to Matilda, hauling himself back up.

'I guess so,' she agreed, not moving.

'Fine,' said Lambert, 'but you're coming with me. Greene, you stand guard.'

Greene perched the lights over the opening as Lambert dangled his leg over the hole.

He hesitated as he made contact with the first rung, pushing his foot into the hard metal, confirming it wasn't going to give way. He was almost disappointed when it didn't budge. He took a deep breath, and dangled his second leg into the darkness.

He stopped on each rung of the ladder, checking his footing. It was like being in a vacuum, the darkness of the opening sucking away the light and swallowing him whole. His head was telling him to return to the surface but still he crawled downwards, wondering if he would ever reach the bottom.

'Wait until I call,' he said to Matilda, continuing his descent until his feet landed with a thud. He stamped three times and shone his torch on the floor, confirming he was standing on concrete. It was a relief to be on terra firma but a sense of unease covered him, as he wondered what was down there. He counted to ten, controlling his breathing before calling up.

'Your turn,' he shouted up to Matilda, his voice echoing in the tunnel.

Matilda's progress was quicker and within a minute she was standing next to him on the concrete floor. To their left was a single archway. Lambert made cautious steps through the gap, which led to a cavernous room stretching to the ground above. Again, the flooring was made of concrete, suggesting the whole underground bunker was man-made.

They moved their torches around the room, uncovering three further openings seemingly carved into the rock formation. Lambert peered down the first of the three openings and noticed something odd on one of the stone walls.

'Here,' he said to Matilda, shining a torch on a light switch.

Lambert went to switch on the light but Matilda grabbed his wrist. He could tell what she was thinking. The explosions they'd endured over the last couple of days had taught them to wait. Lambert checked for wiring or any sign of a generator. However the switch was controlled, it must have been deep within the rock structure.

'Sod it,' he said, flicking the switch, surprised when a line of five dim lights sputtered into action along the corridor ceiling.

Five metres down the corridor they came to the first door. The thick metal structure gave the impression of a prison cell, but when Lambert pushed the door open he saw nothing more than a poorly decorated holiday flat. A further light switch illuminated the room. A king-size double bed took up much of the space. The stone walls were not painted but someone had fixed a large mirror opposite the bed and, to the side, a framed print of a nautical scene which Lambert vaguely remembered from his childhood.

'Do you think someone lives here?' said Matilda.

'There are certainly some home comforts.'

They left the room and moved down the corridor, discovering eight further rooms along the tunnel, each a mini replica of the first. In the last three rooms were a set of bunk beds. All in all, Lambert believed there was enough bedding to accommodate at least thirty people.

'This is bizarre,' said Matilda, reaching the end of the corridor.

'Could be some sort of military thing. A training barracks,' said Lambert.

They made their way back up the tunnel, switching off the lights until they were back at the starting point. They took the central tunnel next. It was mapped out similarly to the first. Again, the first door had a prison-like feel to it.

The feeling continued as Lambert pushed through the metal opening. This was no badly maintained holiday home. It was what Lambert had feared from the beginning: a prison. The stone-floored room was bare. No mirrors or ancient prints, just a soiled single mattress to one corner.

Lambert glanced at Matilda. It was something he'd become accustomed to within weeks of becoming a detective. Some places were off. The walls assimilated the pain and suffering which had occurred within. He had no scientific backing to such a theory but every officer knew it, and Lambert didn't need to use his eyes to know this was one of those places.

No light switch adorned the cell so they both shone their torches at the stone wall, the darkness of which seemed to absorb the light.

'Look, here,' said Matilda, pointing to a hook which protruded from one of the walls.

'Jesus, there's more,' said Lambert, lighting the opposite wall and revealing three further circular hooks.

Neither spoke, both understanding the hooks had been used to chain someone in place. Like tunnel one, tunnel two was full of identical rooms. It put paid to Lambert's theory of an army training ground. The second tunnel was a place of captivity, almost definitely torture. A wave of claustrophobia came over him and he stopped to take some deep breaths, trying not to smell the decay that emanated from the place.

They hurried back up the corridor, both reluctant to enter tunnel three.

# Chapter Thirty-Nine

At first, Lambert was thankful there were no doors along tunnel three. They walked through a low archway, as slowly as feasible, waiting for another surprise.

The tunnel led to a wide-open space. Again, there were no lights. As Lambert lit the area with his torch, all he wanted to do was turn and retreat, pretend he'd never seen what had appeared in his vision.

The room was a gigantic version of the tunnel two prisons. Mattresses were strewn across the floor and on the stone walls hung various hooks at different heights. Discarded chains and handcuffs littered the floor. They were standing in a place of unimaginable horror.

Knowing they shouldn't contaminate the crime scene, Lambert made them stand on the periphery, reluctantly shining his torch on every inch of space until in one corner he stopped, his light focused on a mound which seemed to be squirming. He made his way over, taking large steps so as not to contaminate the area further. He fought back rising nausea as he discovered what he'd feared. The mound was a pile of bones, sat upon a pile of waste swarming with insects. He'd seen some bad things during his career but nothing which could prepare him for this.

Matilda moved towards him but he stopped her in her tracks.

'There'll be time enough for that later,' he said. 'Let's get out of here. Seal the place up. Someone needs to answer some questions.'

—

They explained as best they could to Greene before sealing the trapdoor shut and covering it with discarded brambles. Greene looked distraught.

'Remember you were ordered to leave this place by your boss. It's not your fault, it's Sinnott's.'

'We need to get a team down here,' said Greene.

'We can't call it in yet,' said Lambert.

'You're kidding me,' said Greene, looking to Matilda for assistance.

'Whatever slim chance we have of finding Caroline depends on keeping this secret. We go public with this and whoever is responsible will panic. I need you to tell me you agree.'

Greene considered and nodded her head in agreement.

Colville was waiting inside the car. She listened intently to what they told her but didn't react, beyond a cursory question about Caroline.

They packed the car and covered their tracks as best as possible. Neither spoke as they drove back, Lambert lost in thought of what he'd seen beneath the ground. It appeared Greene had been correct in her assertion about the Manor. Trevor Hodge's dying words had been the only tentative link which had brought him first to Greene, and then the underground horror show. One thing seemed apparent, Caroline Jardine was not at Waverley Manor. The pile of bones they'd discovered were years old and even a cursory look at the discarded bones told Lambert they were not adult size. He kept playing over his options, and kept reaching the same conclusion.

'Get some sleep,' he told the officers. 'We'll reconvene here tomorrow at ten am, and no word of what we discovered to anyone. Even to Glenn, Matilda.'

Matilda nodded and drove off.

–

Back at the flat, Lambert was surprised to see Sarah May lounging on the sofa, a large glass of red wine in her hand. He'd thought about her at odd moments since their last encounter, his mind returning to the smell of her new perfume. She raised her hand in greeting as he entered the room and poured himself a glass of wine.

'I hope you don't mind,' said Sarah, as he sat next to her. 'I couldn't face being alone tonight.'

'You don't ever need to ask that, Sarah.' Lambert winced as he took his first sip of the wine.

'Don't I? I thought after what has been happening recently you might not want me here.'

Lambert pinched the bridge of his nose, the weight of what he'd seen at the Manor hitting him. He placed his wine on the floor and moved towards Sarah, too distracted to talk. As he kissed her, he realised her perfume had returned to her usual brand.

–

Later, he lay restless in his bed, unable and unwilling to sleep. He didn't want to face the risk of images from the dungeon at Waverley Manor coming to haunt him. He crept out of the bedroom, Sarah snoring gently, and brewed some fresh coffee.  On his laptop he logged into the System and ran more searches on the Manor, no longer caring if his searches could be traced.  He entered sub-streams: Waverley Manor, Caroline Jardine, Hodge, Berry, Turner. Greene, Colville, Duggan, Sinnott.

In the end he concluded there was only one definite lead at that moment, and he knew he had to pursue it alone.

# Chapter Forty

At some point during the night, he must have fallen asleep. He woke with a judder just before six am, sitting on the kitchen chair. His head was on the table next to his laptop as Sarah nudged him awake. She was already dressed. 'I need to get back,' she said. 'What are you doing sleeping at your desk?'

'Couldn't sleep,' he said, recalling the images of Waverley Manor which had plagued his fitful sleep.

She gave him a rueful look, a world of meaning in her eyes, and despite having spent the night together he sensed nothing much had changed between them.

He watched her leave, before heating some coffee in the microwave, showering and changing. He'd arranged to meet Matilda and the rest of the team at ten but it was unlikely he'd be back in time.

He drove to Beckenham first, back to his old house, thankful to see the light in the living room switched on. What would Sarah make of him being here, so soon after sleeping with her? He shook his head, trying to dispel the thought, unwilling to be distracted by personal issues when Caroline Jardine was still to be found.

Despite this resolution, his nerves jangled as he made his way to the front door. He knocked gently for the second time in recent memory feeling like a teenager on a first date.

'Michael,' said Sophie, opening the door. She'd obviously just woken up. She was wrapped in the well-worn dressing gown she'd had ever since they'd met, her hair dishevelled.

'I'm sorry to call round so early. I need to get something from the office.'

'Come on in,' said Sophie, running her hands through her hair. 'Come through, I'll pour you some coffee.'

Lambert did as instructed.

It was surreal sitting in the kitchen area. It was like he'd just returned from a long holiday, the place firmly rooted in his memory but somehow unfamiliar. Sophie hadn't changed any aspect. The same photos still hung on the walls, even one of their wedding. It was the new photos which changed the place. The pictures of the new baby, Jane, Chloe's sister.

Sophie poured him a coffee and sat at the table opposite to him.

'Rough night?' he said.

Sophie frowned but it was a light-hearted gesture. 'You could say that. She's kept me up half the night.'

If he closed his eyes it was too easy to imagine that it was ten years ago and Sophie was talking about Chloe. He remembered many a sleepless night, and would have given anything to have them back.

'I think I need some of that,' said Sophie, grabbing herself a coffee.

Lambert watched her glide across the kitchen, her aged dressing gown revealing more flesh than she realised.

She returned and frowned at him again. 'What you smiling at?

Lambert gestured to her gown, which was now fully open. He remembered with a stab of pain the last time he'd seen her naked, the day she'd told him she was pregnant with Jane. She pulled the gown shut, with a grin, and started biting the thumbnail on her right hand.

'What's so important in the office that you need to call so early?' she said, deflecting her embarrassment.

'Don't ask.'

On cue, the noise of Jane's crying filtered through the house. 'You can go up if you want,' said Sophie.

For a second, Lambert thought she wanted him to fetch the baby before realising she meant he could go up to the office. He followed her up the first flight of steps, not stopping as she headed into the nursery.

The office was situated at the top floor of the house, along with a bedroom and small bathroom. Lambert had moved in following Chloe's death and it looked untouched. The office still held one of his old laptops, and a wave of nostalgia overcame him as he looked out of the window at his neighbours' rooftops and gardens.

He opened the wardrobe, uncovering the safe that was built into the reinforced interior wall. He punched eight digits onto a keypad and the safe sprung open. As his current abode was only temporary, he hadn't had time to move the safe, and thought it safer leaving it at the house. He checked the contents and withdrew what he needed.

The Glock 22 was a legacy from his time in the Group. Although he'd been allowed to carry a weapon, the Glock had been purchased as a secondary, and unregistered, weapon. He withdrew the bag of clips and placed them inside his jacket, then strapped on the harness. He decided to place the gun in his inside coat pocket, rather than in the harness, as he didn't want Sophie to see the gun.

He closed the safe and made his way downstairs. 'In here,' said Sophie, as he reached the ground floor. Lambert checked his watch before hanging his coat up and returning to the kitchen.

Jane looked as if she'd just been fed. She sat on Sophie's lap and tilted her head to see him as she heard his approach. He couldn't help but smile at her, and again it was as if he'd been carried back to the past. It was almost too much for him to handle, and he was about to leave when Sophie's phone rang.

'Oh, I must get that,' she said, handing Jane to him without a second thought.

Lambert went to protest, his mouth hanging open, but Sophie had already taken the phone and departed. Jane stared at him as if amused by his predicament. 'I suppose you think this is funny, do you?' he said, provoking a giggle from Jane. 'You do, do you?' he said, warming to the game.

Jane started laughing and he saw so much of Chloe in the gesture that it was painful to watch.

'That was work,' said Sophie, returning. Instead of collecting Jane from him, she began filling the dishwasher.

'Work?'

'I'm thinking of going back,' she said, grinning at him as Jane played with his shirt.

'I need to go,' said Lambert, remembering why he was there.

'It's not a problem,' said Sophie.

'What isn't?' said Lambert, handing Jane back to her.

Sophie shrugged as if it was obvious. 'I see you, you know.'

Lambert felt his pulse quicken.

'The way you look at her.'

He relaxed, thankful she wasn't referring to the times he'd parked outside the house.

'You've noticed the way Jane looks at you too?'

'I haven't got time for this, Sophie. Really. I'm sorry.'

She gave him her standard withering look, telling him without words that he was talking nonsense. 'Well, when you do maybe we can talk about it?'

'OK. Bye,' he said. 'And bye to you too,' he added, pinching Jane's nose.

# Chapter Forty-One

Lambert sat in the front seat of the car and exhaled. He slipped the gun out of the inside pocket of his jacket and into the holster, before setting off.

His mind kept drifting to what Sophie had said at the house. The whole experience had thrown him. She'd said they could talk about it when they had the time, but he wasn't sure what exactly she wanted to discuss. With that, and Sarah staying the night, his mind was full of things it shouldn't be. He had to snap out of it. It was the sixth day the Jardines had been missing, and he was going to find some answers via the only way open to him.

He followed the route he'd programmed into the sat-nav, pleased to be making good time as the morning traffic gradually increased. He thought about what he'd planned to do constantly ever since his experience beneath the ground at Waverley Manor. He'd brought the gun as back-up, in case things went sour, but gun or no gun he was going to get the truth from Chief Superintendent Sinnott.

Sinnott lived in a hamlet in the Surrey countryside. From Lambert's research, he usually drove to a local train station, catching the train into central London. He'd accessed Sinnott's diary on the System, and he didn't have an appointment until after lunch. He also had a late evening gathering, so Lambert hoped this would mean he left for work later than usual.

Lambert was correct, though he'd arrived just in time. He parked across Sinnott's driveway, blocking any immediate departure, and made his way up the stone path to the front door. Sinnott lived alone, having divorced his wife of fifteen years some five years ago. Lambert could only hope he was alone now as he rang the doorbell.

Sinnott opened the door. He was on his phone, distracted, and held his finger up to Lambert as he finished the call. As he hung up, and glanced at Lambert, something in Sinnott's features gave him away. It was a simple gesture but it was enough. A glance of recognition, mixed with a hint of fear.

They'd never met face to face. Lambert had studied the man's file, and had prepared for the meeting by studying lots of photos of him. 'Chief Superintendent Sinnott?' he asked.

Sinnott played along with the game, guilt written all over his face. 'Yes?' he said, feigning impatience.

'DCI Lambert, sir. Sorry for calling at your house but I need your assistance.'

They were at an impasse. Both men understood Lambert could have called ahead and that Lambert was interested in how Sinnott would respond. 'Specifically?' said Sinnott, blocking the doorway.

'You may be aware I am working on the missing persons case. DI Caroline Jardine, sir.'

'Ah, yes. Lambert. I thought I recognised the name. How can I help you?'

'Apologies if I'm out of order, sir, but may I come in? Freezing the proverbials off here.'

Sinnott hesitated. He was under no obligation to invite him in but Lambert was a senior officer, and was investigating the disappearance of a fellow officer. Sinnott would need a good reason not to grant him access. In the end, he relented. 'Come through,' he said.

Lambert stepped through the doorway, side-stepping, not showing his back to Sinnott. Sinnott remained outside for a second, Lambert catching him glance down the drive.

'Is that your car?' said Sinnott, shutting the door.

'Yes. I could move it if you like.'

Sinnott shrugged. 'Follow me,' he said, leading him up a small staircase. Sinnott's house was impressive. He led Lambert across immaculate wooden floorboards, which shone as if freshly polished, to his office. Sinnott held the door open for him and made his move as Lambert stepped through the gap.

Sinnott was too old and slow to land the blow which had been aimed at the back of Lambert's head. Although Lambert hadn't been expecting it, he'd been on edge ever since Sinnott had answered the door. He moved his head in time, Sinnott's fist glancing his head but making most impact with the door. Lambert swivelled around and landed a punch square in Sinnott's throat, ending the dispute. Sinnott dropped as if he'd been shot.

Sinnott was breathless. He grasped for air, opening his mouth in panic. Lambert gave him a few seconds, allowing the first rush of air to filter into his lungs, before pulling his arms behind his back and cuffing him. He pulled tight on the cuffs, ignoring Sinnott's groans, and pushed the Chief Superintendent to the ground, waiting for him to recover.

As far as Lambert was concerned, the attack was enough to signify Sinnott's guilt. Once he heard the man's breathing return to normal, Lambert grabbed him from behind and shuffled him to one of the office chairs.

Sinnott grimaced, a line of spittle caught in the corner of his mouth. 'What the hell is this?' he said, still breathless.

'You attacked me,' said Lambert, still standing.

He paced the room, considering his next move. Sinnott's office was a beautiful wood-panelled room, resplendent with custom-built bookcases. Photos of Sinnott in dress uniform decorated the walls. Lambert studied each in turn searching for accomplices. Sinnott was pictured with giants of industry and politics. Lambert looked at his grinning face receiving an award from the Chief Constable. A second photo with the Deputy Prime Minister, and a familiar face in the background crowd. It was John Weaver, the Minister of Policing.

'You move in some pretty big circles,' said Lambert, taking a seat behind Sinnott's desk and opening the drawers of the carved desk.

'I'm expected elsewhere,' said Sinnott. 'You're in more trouble than you can imagine.'

'Save yourself, Sinnott. I've heard it all before. Tell me about the Manor.'

Experience alerted Lambert to Sinnott's response. A narrowing of the eyes, a pause before answering, was all he needed to confirm the man's complicity.

'What is this?'

'You've heard of the Manor?'

'Are you talking about Waverley Manor, where we discovered the body of that paedophile?'

'Don't plead ignorance, Sinnott. I've checked the files. You pulled DI Greene's investigation into Waverley Manor.'

'Yes, I freely admit that. She'd found Clarkson's body, job done.'

'But she thought there was more to it. She'd presented evidence of an organisation known as the Manor to her boss, yet you still cut the investigation.'

Sinnott remained defiant. 'Do you have any idea of the manpower and resources used to recover Clarkson? If you think I was prepared to extend this on the say of DI Greene then you must have me mistaken with someone else. It was a hunch, and hunches are bullshit.'

'It was more than a hunch, Sinnott, as you well know.'

'I have no idea what you're talking about, but I would suggest you release me whilst you have the chance.'

'Save it, Sinnott. I have enough to take you in. Anti-corruption have been after you for years. So why don't you help yourself?'

It was part bluff, but it was enough to defeat Sinnott. Lambert saw the resilience fade in his eyes. 'You can't prove anything.'

'Maybe not, but I will testify anyway. Your career is over either way, but maybe you can come out of this with some dignity.'

'You have no idea what you're dealing with, Lambert.'

'That's where you're wrong, Sinnott. I've been down there.'

'Where?'

'Waverley Manor. We've been back.'

Sinnott paused. 'You have me at a loss here, Lambert.'

'Don't give me that, Sinnott. We found the opening. The manhole cover hidden in the forest.'

Sinnott struggled in his seat, his arms flailing as if he was trying to break out of the cuffs. 'I don't know anything about that?'

Lambert leant across the desk until he was only inches away from Sinnott's face. 'Stop struggling,' he said.

Sinnott froze, Lambert drawing his head back as Sinnott's stale breath drifted towards him. 'You don't know about the underground prison? The torture rooms?' He reached forward again, this time pressing his forehead against Sinnott's. He struggled to contain his rage as visions of Waverley Manor swarmed his mind. He wanted to push Sinnott to the ground, to give the man his own kind of retribution, and if it wasn't for Caroline Jardine he wasn't sure he would have been able to contain the violence.

Sinnott understood. 'I don't know about any of that,' he said, pleading.

Lambert pulled his head back. 'Tell me what you know,' he said.

Sinnott smiled. It was the briefest of gestures but Lambert caught it. He leant forward and smashed his elbow into the side of the man's head.

'You don't understand, Lambert,' said Sinnott, spitting blood onto the desk.

'Explain it to me.'

'These people. The Manor. If they know I've been talking to you I'm as good as dead.'

'You're one of them, Sinnott, don't try to hide that.'

'No. I work for them, but I'm not one of them.'

Lambert sighed. He didn't believe the man but was willing to play the game. 'We can offer you protection.'

'Not from these people.'

'You need to start speaking, Sinnott, or these people will be the least of your troubles.'

'I don't have anything to tell you, and that's the honest truth.'

'You knew about Waverley Manor?'

'I was told to cut short the investigation. I have no idea about any underground prison.'

'Is Caroline Jardine alive?'

'I don't know. If I knew I'd tell you. You may not believe it, but I want her found as much as you do.'

Lambert laughed, fighting the well of violence growing within him.

'It's true,' said Sinnott, his voice a whine of protestation. 'You think I want to be involved with them? They got me young, Lambert. You should be glad they never got to you. They've dictated every aspect of my life since that moment.'

'Even if that's true, it's a coward's explanation. Look at you. At this house, your position. They helped you with that, I presume?'

Sinnott shrugged.

'Why didn't you go public?'

'And say what? I have nothing concrete on them, and they have people everywhere, including Anti-Corruption. If I ever opened my mouth then that would be the end of me. This is the end of me.'

'Who's in charge?'

'You don't understand. There are worse things than death, Lambert.'

Lambert had heard enough. He reached across the desk, grabbed Sinnott by the back of his head and slammed it into the desk. 'Where's Caroline Jardine?'

Blood trickled from Sinnott's nose. He spat a lump of blood-tinged phlegm onto the desk and smiled.

Lambert got to his feet. He pulled the gun from his holster and moved around the desk. He placed the gun against Sinnott's temple. 'Where is Caroline Jardine?

'Shoot me,' said Sinnott. His body was convulsing, but he thrust his chin outwards.

Lambert pushed the gun harder into Sinnott's temple. 'Come on, Sinnott, you must have some decency left in you. Just tell me where she is. You have my word we will protect you.

Sinnott stopped shaking. 'Stand me up, I'm in pain,' he said.

Wary, Lambert pulled him to his feet.

Sinnott moved his neck from side to side, as if warming up at the gym. 'I only know one name,' he said.

'Who?'

'John Weaver.'

'Weaver?' said Lambert, glancing at the photo on Sinnott's sideboard. He recalled meeting the Minister of State for Policing, Fire and Criminal Justice less than a week ago, remembered being underwhelmed by the politician, and his petty demands. It had a potential symmetry to it, but was difficult to accept at face value.

'Groomed me from the beginning,' said Sinnott.

'Do you have anything to back this up?'

'I'm sure you could find something if you looked hard enough. He's basically guided me through my career. You'll see him behind everything,' said Sinnott, collapsing to the floor.

Lambert let him fall, stunned by the confession. Could the MP, the jumped-up prick who'd warned him to catch those responsible as quick as possible, be behind the atrocities at Waverley Manor?

He only went to assist Sinnott when the man began smashing his face against the floor as if suffering some form of seizure.

Lambert pulled him onto his back. Sinnott's nose was smashed, as were a number of Sinnott's teeth. 'What the fuck are you doing?' said Lambert.

Sinnott smiled. 'Good luck, ' he said, before swallowing something in his mouth.

## Chapter Forty-Two

Lambert didn't hesitate. He bent down and opened Sinnott's mouth. 'What have you swallowed?' he said, thrusting his fingers down the man's throat.

Sinnott convulsed as he vomited. Lambert dragged back his arm but it wasn't quick enough to prevent the fluid covering his suit jacket.

The movement should have been quick enough, however, to stop Sinnott digesting whatever he'd swallowed. He was unconscious but breathing. Lambert placed him into the recovery position and considered his options, taking off his jacket and throwing it onto the office desk.

It was too risky to call for medical back-up, especially after what Sinnott had told him. Reluctantly, he came to a conclusion. Only one person could get him out of this situation.

–

By the time Tillman arrived, Sinnott was barely alive. His pulse was weak. A trickle of green froth fell from his lips. Lambert didn't want to get too close. It was possible whatever Sinnott had swallowed was poisonous to the touch.

Tillman was flanked by two of his team, the same silent men who sometimes accompanied him. Lambert had always presumed they were ex-military, but had never discussed the issue with Tillman directly.

'He's through there,' said Lambert, opening the front door.

Tillman's henchmen kept guard as the policeman made his way to the living area where Sinnott lay. Tillman stood stock-still and gazed down at Sinnott's prone body.

'You say he did this to himself?' said Tillman, his tone neutral, lacking judgement.

'From what I can gather. I think he had something in his teeth. He smashed his side against the floor and his mouth began to froth.'

Tillman nodded as if this was the most natural thing in the world. 'He was never any good,' he muttered.

Tillman made a call as Lambert paced the room.

'Who are you calling?'

'A medic team. We'll secure Sinnott until we know more.'

Five minutes later, a second pair of henchmen arrived, this time in a blacked-out transit van. They wore the same plain clothes as the two men guarding the front door and carried a gurney and medical bags. Within minutes they had Sinnott on a drip feed and strapped to a makeshift bed. Tillman nodded and they took Sinnott's body away as if he'd never been there, only to return minutes later to begin scrubbing at the mess on the floor.

'In there,' instructed Lambert.

They made their way through to the oak-panelled office where Tillman took a seat on a large leather-bound armchair. 'Tell me how the hell we got into this situation?' he said.

Lambert told him about the discovery at the Manor. How the case stretched back to the suicide of Alistair Newlyn.

'What tipped you off about Sinnott?'

Lambert shared what he'd learnt about DI Greene's investigation into Waverley Manor.

'Who knows you're here?' said Tillman.

'No one.'

Tillman snorted. 'Why doesn't that surprise me?'

'Sinnott admitted his involvement to a certain extent. He denied full knowledge of the Manor but his involvement is implicit.'

'And this Waverley Manor is secure at the moment?'

'We can't call it in, not yet. But we have some of the team watching it.'

'Who's on this team?'

'Matilda, DI Greene, and DS Colville.'

'It's never the easy way with you, is it Lambert?'

'What would you have me do different? I had to make a call. If we'd made the findings of Waverley Manor public then I don't think we'd ever find Caroline Jardine or her husband, if he's still alive. I am sure those responsible would go into hiding.'

Tillman stood up. 'And you think we'll find her now?' he said, through gritted teeth.

'Well I'm not going to stop trying. We need to arrest John Weaver.'

'That's what Sinnott told you?'

'He told me that's who he reports to. Weaver recruited him for the force. Groomed him into that position and has been handling him ever since.'

'Have you lost your fucking mind, Lambert?' said Tillman, taking a step forward. His face was deeply coloured and spit flew from his mouth as he spoke.

Rather than making him back down, Tillman's aggression brought out the same in Lambert. 'You're suggesting we forget this because he's a high-powered politician?' said Lambert, taking a similar stance to Tillman, bracing himself for physical confrontation, which was not unheard of from the man in front of him.

'What I'm saying, Lambert, is that Weaver is not the sort of man you just arrest. He has the sorts of connection you can only imagine.'

'I realise that, sir,' said Lambert with a dismissive sneer. 'I've seen the pile of bones his connections have helped him collect.'

Lambert took another step towards Tillman. They were within touching distance now, both holding their ground, snarling like pack-dogs.

Eventually it was Tillman who backed down, shaking his head and retreating to the armchair. 'Ever since I've known you, you've gone off record,' he said, with a false smile.

'I learnt from the best, sir.'

Tillman snorted again and accepted what Lambert said with good grace. 'If we want Weaver in custody, we're going to have to go off record again,' he said.

'What do you have in mind?' said Lambert.

'I'm not sure yet. The Jardine situation necessitates that we don't hold back. How soon can you get your team together?'

'Within the hour.'

'You're still staying at that slum hole?' said Tillman.

'My apartment?' said Lambert, not rising to the bait.

'Yes, your slum hole. We'll meet there in an hour. We'll need to see what Weaver's movements are like for the rest of the day.'

# Chapter Forty-Three

Lambert met with Matilda before returning to the flat. He recounted the incident at Sinnott's house and his conversation with Tillman.

'Why didn't you tell me? I would have come along with you,' said Matilda.

'I know, that's why. Only one of us needed to risk their career.'

'Ever the gentleman. So now you're getting Glenn involved?'

'Are you going to be OK working with him?' asked Lambert.

'Why wouldn't I be?'

'It's just with your…'

'Yes?' said Matilda, tilting her head to the side and enjoying Lambert's discomfort.

Lambert smirked. 'Oh come on, Kennedy, don't make me go through this. You know what I mean. Won't it be weird you two working together?'

'I've worked with him before,' said Matilda. 'We were seeing each other then. You may remember?' said Matilda, rubbing her face where the flames had destroyed her skin.

Lambert fell silent. He found it difficult to comprehend Tillman seeing anyone, let alone Matilda.

'You realise we've never once talked about that day,' said Matilda.

Lambert thought back to the explosion that had caused the damage to Matilda's flesh. It had been his idea to send her into the building undercover. He could picture the explosion and ensuing events in perfect clarity, could taste the bitter smoke which had engulfed the place.

'I'm truly sorry, Matilda,' he said, sensing how inadequate the words were. 'I just didn't know how to broach the subject.'

'A simple "how are you feeling" would have sufficed.'

'How are you feeling?' said Lambert.

Matilda smiled, and in that moment Lambert realised no amount of marks to her face could change her beauty.

'Look, sir, I know you blame yourself for what happened.'

Lambert raised the palm of his hand, begging her not to continue, but she ignored him.

'I know you've not asked for my forgiveness, and I'm not offering it.'

'OK,' said Lambert.

'There's nothing to forgive, sir. I was working. If you hadn't sent me in, something else could have happened to me. I might have got caught in the fringes of the explosion or been shot by one of those crazed gunmen. What's more, that maniac could have escaped. You couldn't have foreseen what happened.'

Lambert swallowed hard. 'I appreciate you saying that,' he said.

'For Christ's sake, it's not lip-service, Michael, I mean it. If we're going to continue working together you're going to have to get over your guilt complex.'

'I see,' said Lambert, matching the smile still etched on Matilda's face. 'Well, we'd better get going to the slum,' he said, standing.

'The slum?' asked Matilda.

'Just the word your boyfriend uses for my new abode,' said Lambert, ushering Matilda out of the coffee shop.

Matilda turned and through pursed lips said, 'Please don't use that term again.'

'Abode?'

'You know which term.'

—

DS Colville and DI Greene were waiting for them outside the entrance to Lambert's flat with an addition to the team. Colville stood motionless, her back rigid whilst Greene paced the front pavement, smoking.

It was the new member who spoke first. DS Duggan moved towards them, his black overcoat stretching beneath his knees, his styled hair not budging an inch despite the breeze.

'What the hell is this about, Lambert?'

The officer didn't have an easy way about him and with everything that had happened that morning Lambert would have liked nothing better than to take the man aside and to remind him about police hierarchy. He'd sometimes found this with the Anti-Corruption officers. Some felt as though the structure of the police force didn't apply directly to them. They spent so much time investigating crooked officers that they didn't trust anyone, and such lack of trust led to a lack of respect. Either way, Lambert couldn't let it slip.

'Listen Duggan, remember you're a guest on this investigation.'

'I'm not a guest. I've been working on this for four years,' said Duggan, his hand moving to his damaged right eye.

'The investigation at the moment is into Caroline Jardine's disappearance. You're a guest in that investigation. An investigation which I'm in charge of.'

Duggan went to protest but Lambert cut him short. 'If you want to continue being part of this, you'll follow my instructions.' Lambert didn't wait for a response. He opened the communal front door and made his way up to the flat. 'Make yourselves at home,' he said once they were inside.

Unfortunately, Tillman's description of his home couldn't have been more apt. What few possessions Lambert had with him were scattered about the place haphazardly. He couldn't remember the last time he'd washed the dishes, which were piled high in the sink and on the makeshift dining table. If any of the team were surprised by the habitat, they weren't foolish enough to express their feelings.

Lambert wasted no time. 'I spoke to Chief Superintendent Sinnott today,' he said, noting Duggan's lips forming in reaction.

Lambert raised his right index finger and continued talking. 'There were some complications but he has conceded he's linked to this so-called Manor.'

'Where is he now?' said Colville, who stood with her back against the wall, her perfect poise not affected by Lambert's revelation.

'He's in secure custody for the time being.'

'I haven't heard about this,' said Duggan.

'Why the hell would you have?' said Lambert.

'What exactly do you mean by secure?' said Duggan, not learning from the earlier confrontation.

'Secure in the fact that we're not going public with it yet,' said Lambert. 'There's more. Sinnott gave me a name.'

Colville inched a step forward from her position, the first obvious sign of excitement Lambert had seen from her.

'John Weaver,' said Lambert.

Duggan sat down on one of the dining chairs as if his legs had been dragged away from him.

'John Weaver, the Member of Parliament? The Minister for Policing?' said Duggan.

'You know him then?' said Lambert, wondering if Duggan was seeing his career fading away.

Duggan placed his hand on his forehead. 'What exactly did Sinnott tell you?'

'Not enough to make an arrest,' said Lambert.

'Then what the hell are we doing here?' said Duggan.

Lambert glanced over at DI Greene, who'd hardly said a word since they'd arrived.

'You've heard of Weaver?' he asked her.

'Of course I bloody have,' she said.

Lambert smiled, understanding she was as frustrated with Duggan's little performance as he was.

'The plan is this,' said Lambert. 'We're going to question him off record.'

'Off record?' said Duggan, getting to his feet and waving his arms about as if Lambert's suggestion was completely preposterous. 'You don't question someone like John Weaver off record. We'll all lose our jobs.'

'Well it's a risk I'm willing to take,' said Lambert. 'We have absolutely zero leads on Caroline Jardine's whereabouts. We all know what's been discovered at the Manor and, with Sinnott out of the picture, Weaver's the only one who can lead us to Caroline.'

'I don't go along with this,' said Duggan.

'You're part of it now,' said Lambert, 'so sit down.'

'No. No way. If we're going to speak to Weaver we do it officially or I'm out of here.'

'Oh just sit down, Charles, and shut up,' snapped DS Colville, who had moved from her position against the wall. 'Not everything can go through the books.'

Duggan sat down like a scolded child, and in that second the doorbell rang. Lambert glanced out the window to see the top of Tillman's head and two of his entourage.

'Oh, and there's just one more thing,' he said.

## Chapter Forty-Four

Tillman's entrance was as elaborate and over the top as Lambert had expected. He suppressed a giggle as the Chief Superintendent barged through the door to his flat like an actor entering the stage.

Lambert glanced first at Duggan then Matilda to assess their responses. Matilda didn't react but Duggan looked as if someone had shot him. He got to his feet and silently began shaking his head.

'You all know Chief Superintendent Glenn Tillman?' said Lambert, to the assembled group.

'No, no, no,' said Duggan finally finding voice. 'This won't do at all.'

Tillman hung his hands to the side. 'What's the matter, Duggan, I thought you'd be pleased to see me?'

They'd planned Tillman's entrance this way in the hope Duggan would be less likely to start a scene if others were present. It seemed they'd underestimated Duggan's level of antipathy to Tillman. 'Can I have a word with you both in the other room, DCI Lambert?' said the man from Anti-Corruption.

'We're all friends here,' said Lambert, refusing to be dictated to by the junior officer.

'Fine. If we're all friends here then everyone should be aware Chief Superintendent Tillman is currently under investigation by Anti-Corruption.'

'I think everyone already is aware,' said Tillman, stepping towards Duggan, his arms out to his side, making him look even bigger than he already was.

'I wasn't,' came a lone voice from the room.

'And you are?' asked Tillman.

'DI Greene.'

'Ah yes,' said Tillman. 'Michael explained your discovery to me. Pleasure to meet you. This AC investigation, if you'll pardon my French, is utter bullshit. Duggan here knows that but he can't bring himself to admit it.'

Duggan began shaking his head again, DS Colville placing her hand on the man's arm. 'Sit down,' she instructed, still with a silent poise.

'You must be DS Colville,' said Tillman.

'Sir.'

'Great, now introductions are over we need to work through the next stage of the plan.'

'There is a plan then?' said Duggan.

Tillman stared at Lambert as if somehow he was to blame for Duggan's continued outbursts.

Lambert opened one of the small windows. The radiators were on full blast and with the amount of people and hot air in the room the small confined place had become stifling.

'Sir, what can you tell us?' said Lambert, ignoring Duggan, who sat on the edge of his seat next to DS Colville.

'I'm sure Lambert has briefed you on the information gleaned from Sinnott, about our favourite politician the Right Honourable John Weaver? We need to question Weaver but, as you can imagine, it's not that simple unless you have something significant to back up your request.'

'Only the word of a senior officer, under detention, and no doubt duress,' said Duggan.

'Quite, a corrupt senior officer,' said Tillman, ignoring the jibe about duress. 'Furthermore, if we approach Weaver now he'll surround himself with lawyers, and any remaining chance we have of finding the Jardines will evaporate.'

Tillman laid out the plan for them, omitting the specifics he'd worked through with Lambert.

'I've managed to access Weaver's schedule for the day. He has a cross-town meeting this afternoon and I've managed to replace his transport team.'

The other officers remained silent until Greene spoke up. 'What exactly does that mean, sir?'

'It means, Inspector, that rather than going across town, Weaver will be taken to a safe place.'

Duggan got to his feet again. 'I really can't believe what I'm hearing,' he said. 'What the hell is a safe place? We're not in the armed forces.'

'A safe place,' said Tillman, 'is a place where we can question Weaver without interference from outside agencies.'

Even Colville looked perturbed by that statement.

'I hope you're not suggesting some form of....'

'Some form of what?' said Tillman.

'Some form of torture,' said Duggan.

Tillman laughed, his chest expanding so his shirt was close to breaking point.

'You AC guys do have a wild sense of humour, don't you? Who mentioned torture? We're going to question him without his lawyers present. Weaver's a sensible man, he'll understand the need to tell us what we need to know.'

'And if he doesn't?' said Duggan.

'He will,' said Tillman.

'You're going to go along with this?' Duggan asked Colville and the rest of the team.

Colville sat motionless. 'If it's the only way to find Caroline, then I'm behind it.'

'And everyone else?' said Lambert. He looked in turn to Greene and Matilda who both nodded their heads.

'It's down to you, Duggan,' said Lambert.

'I can't believe this is happening,' said the officer, who looked genuinely flustered. 'Why are you telling us this anyway? You could have gone ahead and taken Weaver yourselves. Why did I have to know?'

Lambert remained silent, waiting for the information to sink in. He'd told Duggan and Colville so they had a record.

'What better way to keep things above board,' said Tillman, breaking the silence, 'than informing Anti-Corruption?'

It was a question that had concerned Lambert on odd occasions during his career. If Anti-Corruption were there to monitor the actions of their fellow officers, then who was there to monitor Anti-Corruption?

Duggan held his arms wide, mimicking Tillman's earlier gesture. 'It looks as though I've got no choice,' said the man. 'But I'd hardly call it above board.'

'What's the matter with you, Duggan?' said Lambert, his patience close to breaking point. 'How long have you been after this group? Four years? We've got a fellow officer in dire trouble, close to death; this is our only chance of finding her and you're moaning about procedure.'

'It's not procedure, Lambert, as well you know.'

Lambert walked over. Duggan, who suddenly looked panicked, turning to Colville as though expecting a confrontation. He was correct. Lambert wasted no time and grabbed him by the throat.

'You didn't see those tunnels,' he said. 'You didn't see those underground rooms. And one more thing you didn't see, Duggan,' he said, pressing his fingers tighter against the man's throat, 'was the pile of bones.'

Lambert felt Matilda's hand rest against his shoulder and relaxed his grip.

'If you jeopardise this in any way then you'll find out the full extent of what a safe house means,' said Lambert, letting go of Duggan.

It was a huge risk that would probably lead to ramifications down the line, but Lambert's sole focus now was finding the Jardines.

Duggan coughed and spluttered, adjusted his shirt, and tried to regain composure and respect in the eyes of his fellow officers. He looked around the room and realised he'd failed in every way.

# Chapter Forty-Five

After assigning duties to the team, Lambert accompanied Tillman back to the NCA headquarters in Central London. Matilda had been disappointed not to be allowed to join them, but Lambert had sent her back to Chislehurst to head up the ongoing investigation with Bickland and Croft. Colville and Duggan had gone back to their respective roles and Greene had returned to Watford for the time being.

Lambert had promised the four officers to notify them as soon as they had Weaver in their own form of custody. Duggan was adamant any interview with Weaver was recorded, which Lambert supposed was a good idea, at least to begin with. Tillman had already signed off Sinnott sick for the day and no questions had yet been asked. He was being maintained in the same area they would take Weaver, albeit in the sick bay where the medical team were still working on him, monitoring the poison which was slowly leaving his body.

Silently, Lambert followed Tillman through the NCA building. He'd only been back just over a year, but every time he set foot in the place it felt like entering a prison. He watched his fellow officers battling away at their laptops and on their hands-free headsets. They provided a valuable service and he admired each and every one of them, but he was no longer sure he was part of the team.

It wasn't just the Manor that had shaken his faith. It was the corruption he saw on all sides. The number of people he could trust became fewer and fewer each day. And at the moment the chance of finding Caroline Jardine alive was diminishing. He could see no foreseeable future in his role.

Tillman held his office door open for him, then closed it after Lambert walked through the threshold. 'You know we're taking a great risk here,' said Tillman.

'When do we never?' said Lambert.

'Things have changed, Michael. We're not in the Group any more. That carte blanche has disappeared.'

'How do you get away with having a holding area then?' asked Lambert.

'You don't really need to know, Michael.'

Lambert didn't probe any further. He was sure the secure area had something to do with MI5. When he'd been in the Group they'd worked closely with the Intelligence Service and Lambert imagined Tillman still maintained a connection.

Tillman ran through the plan once more. 'The replacement driver is in place.'

DS Alan McCarthy was a name Lambert knew from his time in the Group. He was ex-military, a driving expert.

'Do you think Weaver will put up with a replacement driver, no questions asked?' said Lambert.

'His driver called in sick this morning,' said Tillman. 'Something he ate at the local deli didn't agree with him so Weaver will already know. McCarthy is well known and respected so I can't see a problem.'

Lambert smirked at the resources Tillman had to hand. He reminded himself, once again, never to get on the wrong side of the man.

'The problem will be when McCarthy goes off plan. There's a switch inside the car which locks the doors. McCarthy will tell Weaver there's a security risk and suggest they change course.'

'And if Weaver doesn't buy it?' asked Lambert.

'Not much he can do save for smashing through the reinforced glass. The doors will be locked and there's a divider between him and McCarthy.'

'Are you sure this is the only way?' said Lambert.

'If you have a better idea I'm all ears,' said Tillman. 'If we go through normal procedure, it would be days before we get any answers from Weaver, and in all reality we probably never would. You don't need reminding every minute is precious if we're going to find Caroline.'

–

Lambert left the office before Tillman. Despite having been seen arriving together at the NCA headquarters, Tillman thought it prudent they separate before reconvening in an unmarked car park four streets down.

It had started to rain by the time Lambert reached outside. The deluge had forced people to take shelter at bus stops or beneath the arches of office buildings and shops. Lambert had no option but to walk through the downfall as it battered against his head and coat. He upped his pace but already he sensed the water seeping into his garments, soaking his trousers and feet.

By the time he reached Tillman's car his hair was matted to his skull, the shirt beneath his wool raincoat sodden. He opened the car and sat in the driver's seat, switched on the ignition, and waited for the car engine to run for a few minutes before turning on the heat full blast.

Tillman arrived five minutes later, by which time the wet patches on Lambert's shirt were receding. Tillman, naturally, had brought an umbrella with him and his coat was bone dry as he placed it in the back seat.

'Got caught, did we?' said Tillman, with the infuriating lightness of tone and sarcasm Lambert was accustomed to.

'You could say that.'

Tillman placed his phone on a magnetic strip on the dashboard. 'This is McCarthy,' he said, pointing to a flashing dot on the phone's screen. 'He's still at Weaver's office. His route takes him past us. You know the drill.'

They sat side by side, not talking. Lambert had been here on many occasions before. He'd been Tillman's right hand man at one point. When he'd been part of the Group, they'd spent many boring hours waiting for the first sign of action.

But things didn't always go right when they were together and as this began to concern Lambert he drummed his fingers on the steering wheel. Were they doing the right thing? To all intents and purposes they were about to stage a kidnapping. If they had it wrong about Weaver more than their jobs were on the line.

'You think too much, Lambert,' said Tillman, as if he were there inside Lambert's head.

Lambert didn't want to openly question his superior. Instead, he turned his thoughts to Caroline Jardine. He pictured her in a single cell, somewhere below ground. He could imagine what she was going through because he'd been in a similar situation himself. Tied to a chair in a darkened room, awaiting the moment of his execution. But he'd survived and, if they did their job properly, there was a chance she could too.

'Right, here we go,' said Tillman, pointing to the red dot flashing on the screen of his phone. 'He's off.'

Lambert turned on the engine and switched on the windscreen wipers at maximum speed. The road in front of them momentarily cleared, only to be obscured by the pelting rain a split second later. Adrenaline buzzed around him, reminding him the job could be electrifying at times. Tillman rocked gently in the seat next to him, preparing himself, and Lambert felt a rush of camaraderie.

'Right, here we go,' said Tillman, as Weaver's car rounded into their road.

Lambert took deeper breaths as the car passed them. He exchanged looks with Tillman, both of them counting the mandatory seconds in their head before Lambert pulled out into traffic.

With the tracking device installed they didn't need to hurry, but Lambert wanted to keep the car in sight. The rain continued its deluge and battered the bonnet and windscreen of the car like tiny bullets. Lambert kept his gaze on the traffic, the windscreen wipers working over-time as Tillman studied the map. The planned route was already on display but experience told them the driver could change the route at any moment for whatever reason he saw fit. Lambert eased the car into a lower gear as he noticed Weaver had stopped at the traffic lights a few hundred yards ahead.

'Four more turns and he's going to turn left instead of right,' said Tillman. 'It's unlikely Weaver will notice and if he does McCarthy will just give him some bullshit about mixing up routes.'

The sound of screeching tyres stopped their conversation mid-sentence as it immediately became apparent something was wrong.

# Chapter Forty-Six

Lambert could only watch, stunned, as a moped carrying two passengers cut in front of them and began meandering through the stationary traffic. Tillman reached for his phone and began calling McCarthy, but within seconds it was too late, as the moped pulled up alongside Weaver's car. The figure on the back of the moped drew a gun and started raining bullets through the rear passenger window. Lambert went to pull away but Tillman placed his hand on his arm.

'Just wait. There's nothing we can do now.'

The traffic lights turned green and the moped drove away. Lambert yelled in frustration and pulled out into the oncoming traffic, narrowly missing a car driving the other way seemingly unaware of the events unfolding behind him. Lambert ignored the protestations from the other drivers as he moved towards the traffic lights.

'Turn right here, Lambert,' said Tillman, when they were a hundred yards away.

'What the hell are you on about?'

'Turn now,' said Tillman. 'We can't be seen there.'

Lambert knew he was correct, and reluctantly turned right until they were out of view, then parked up. 'We need to see what's happened,' he said, controlling the adrenaline swarming his body.

'You go, on foot, I'll meet you here,' said Tillman, pointing to a road four streets down from the traffic lights. 'McCarthy has a second phone in his inside jacket pocket. Dead or alive we need to retrieve it before the police show.'

Lambert understood. He dragged his coat from the backseat, wrapped his scarf around his throat, and made his way into the pouring rain. The reason they'd stopped away from the incident was the same reason he'd wrapped the scarf around his face. In such a busy area CCTV cameras would have captured everything. A chance still existed that Tillman and Lambert would be caught on camera following Weaver. But for now, he had to get to the scene and retrieve the phone without being caught.

He tried not to think of the implications of what had happened as he ran across the pavement. Someone had purposely taken Weaver's life – which suggested whoever was responsible had somehow been notified.

A crowd had gathered around the car. Thankfully no police were present yet. The hit had been professional, perfectly so. There was little chance McCarthy had been spared. A professional knew an eyewitness, however deranged with terror or however perfect the hit, was still a risk.

Lambert merged with the crowd, his surveillance training kicking in as he weaved through the throng until he could see the full extent of the crime scene. At close range it became apparent even the extra strength glass in Weaver's car was no match for the powerful shotgun blast that had ripped through it. On the back seat sat the corpse of the politician, John Weaver, a bloody stump where his head used to be. In the front seat, McCarthy slumped against the steering wheel, a gaping hole in the back of his head.

Lambert scurried round the other side of the car, keeping his head low, trying to avoid any face recognition software that could be used from the CCTV footage. He gently nudged a couple of onlookers towards the vehicle, pretending to trip as he did so. The gun blast had also shattered the driver's side window. With a strained effort Lambert leant his hand through the jagged gap and didn't hesitate as he felt the dampness of McCarthy's chest. He reached into the jacket pocket and retrieved the phone positioned there as Tillman had promised.

He backed again into the crowd, purposely tripping up a number of the gawkers who had their phones out, parasites feeding on the misery before them. He shook his head in disgust and began to walk away, his pace slow and measured, not wanting to announce his presence to whoever was watching.

–

Tillman was waiting with the car running. Lambert dived into the passenger seat and Tillman pulled away before he had time to put on his seatbelt.

'You got the phone?' asked Tillman.

'Yes. I'd be surprised if I haven't been compromised.'

'At least there's no initial connection,' said Tillman, who was subdued and lost in thought.

Lambert wondered if he was thinking the same thing: if Weaver wasn't safe, none of them were.

'Where are we going?' said Lambert.

'Only one place we can go. The safe house.'

'What about the others?'

Tillman shook his head as he braked hard at a set of traffic lights. He rode the clutch and glanced nervously around him, no doubt looking for the sight of two men riding a moped.

'I should blindfold you and knock you out,' he said, wheels spinning as soon as the lights turned amber. 'Once you know where this place is, it becomes compromised.'

'Thanks very much,' said Lambert.

'It's for your own safety. But one thing's for sure, none of the others can find out about it.'

A mile into the journey Tillman finally asked about McCarthy.

'Sorry,' said Lambert, shaking his head.

Tillman lowered his eyes and gritted his teeth, saying no more on the subject.

'If it's a message, it's as clear as can be,' said Lambert.

'It's a message all right. But they've assassinated the wrong people.'

'We need to go public,' said Lambert. 'Even if we can't find Caroline, the least we can do is expose the Manor and the atrocity there.'

'There's one person we need to speak to before we do that,' said Tillman. 'Whether he likes it or not, Sinnott is going to give us some answers.'

# Chapter Forty-Seven

They drove for a while until they reached the Hammer-smith Bypass and headed towards the M4.

'Where's he being held?' said Lambert.

'I could tell you, but I'd have to kill you,' replied Tillman.

'Very droll.'

'I'm serious. You don't have the clearance.'

'Does anyone have the clearance for this? Surely you're holding him illegally?'

'I have my own connections, Lambert. There's nothing Duggan or Colville can do about this, if that's what you're worried about.'

With Tillman's connections in MI5, Lambert was sure his superior was utilising some form of loophole to warrant the keeping of Sinnott in custody.

'We need to tell the others something,' he said, repeating himself.

'We'll speak to Sinnott first. See what we can get from him and then we'll let the others know.'

Lambert thought of the piles of bones they'd seen at the Manor site. He wondered what amount of missing persons cases they'd be able to solve, the brittle comfort they might be able to offer the families who'd lost loved ones to whatever brutal regime had been at Waverley Manor.

Tillman came off the M4 before Reading and began driving into the countryside. Lambert was used to the concept of the safe house. He'd had access to them himself when he'd been part of the Group. But the name itself was a contradiction, for whoever was held at a safe house was usually far from being safe. And although he'd never seen interrogations go beyond what was legal, he'd always had concerns about the concept that people could be taken and questioned without the knowledge of others.

As the rain subdued, Tillman pulled up a dirt track to a secluded farmhouse surrounded by trees. Lambert was confident he could make his way back to the house from memory and was sure Tillman realised this.

The wind outside the car was brutal. Lambert followed Tillman towards the entry of the ancient-looking farm-house. There were echoes of the Manor, which troubled Lambert. Was it possible the Manor had started as a safe house? With Sinnott's and now Weaver's involvement, it was already clear members of the police had been involved. What if what lay beyond these walls had the same depths?

The atmosphere through the front door was little different to that outside. Cold air billowed through the unheated building.

'Through here,' said Tillman, opening a side door leading to a narrow passage. 'Turn your back, please,' he added.

Lambert did as instructed hearing the electric tone of a keyboard as Tillman entered a ten-figure password. The security door buzzed open and Tillman held his arm out for Lambert to go first. A brief hesitation came over him as he wondered if this too was a set-up, if Tillman had been part of it all along and he was stepping into his own Manor.

Tillman gave him a look as if warning him not to be so ridiculous, and he stepped through the threshold.

The interior was in stark contrast to the outside. It had the clinical cleanliness of a hospital ward. The walls were tiled white and the floors scrubbed clean.

Lambert followed Tillman down a brightly lit corridor to the room where Sinnott was being held. A man and woman, both dressed in white coats, attended to the man who sat upright on his bed. Two drip bags fed into his body whilst various wires protruded from his chest into a machine, presumably measuring his heart rate.

Sinnott's face was drawn, his skin tinged yellow. His eyes were bloodshot and he didn't even look up at Tillman and Lambert.

'Give us the room,' said Tillman, to the medical personnel.

His voice was enough for Sinnott to look up. 'You're back.' Sinnott's voice was coarse, gravelly, as if his throat was bone dry. He lifted his head and glanced towards Lambert. 'You should have let me die,' he said.

'That can still be arranged,' said Tillman.

'Good,' said Sinnott, with no irony.

'Jonathan Weaver is dead,' said Lambert.

Sinnott was too ill to express much emotion. If he was shocked he didn't reveal it.

'Shot down in broad daylight,' continued Lambert.

'What do you want me to say?' said Sinnott.

'You don't know about these places, do you?' said Tillman.

Sinnott chuckled, the sound emitting from his throat sounding painful. 'Of course I know about them. Do you think you and your little Group were the only ones in on the secret? Nothing that's happened in the force in the past twenty years has gone past me,' said Sinnott, trying his best to muster some pride.

'Then you'll know what can happen here?'

Sinnott blinked. 'I know the extent of what's supposed to happen here. Are you threatening me, Tillman?'

'No one is threatening anyone,' said Lambert, concerned as to how the interrogation was going.

'I wouldn't quite put it like that,' said Tillman, falling easily into the bad cop role.

'I've told you all I'm going to,' said Sinnott.

Tillman leant over the man, his face close enough to touch. 'Do you know how many times I've heard that from people in this room before?' said Tillman.

Sinnott tried to sit up in a brutal show of strength. 'You don't frighten me, Tillman. Don't you think I know about you? I know everything about you. What's that saying – all mouth and no trousers? You're on a tight leash, whether you know it or not. Whatever you say now, I know you won't go any further than you're allowed.'

'I'm afraid you don't know me very well at all, then,' said Tillman. As he spoke he placed his heavyset hand on Sinnott's shoulder.

At first it looked innocuous and then he began to squeeze. Lambert had been taught the same technique before. Tillman was working a specific pressure point.

Sinnott closed his eyes, took a deep breath and, eventually, let out a scream.

# Chapter Forty-Eight

'That's enough, Glenn,' said Lambert, as Sinnott's screams continued.

Lambert laid his hand on Tillman's shoulder, surprised at the granite-like feel of his flesh. Tillman was turning red with exertion as he dug his hands into Sinnott's shoulder. 'Tell me,' he mouthed.

Lambert shared his superior's frustrations. It was at times like this he felt most impotent. Somewhere, Caroline Jardine was being kept and the trembling man on the gurney in front of them was the only link they had to her whereabouts. They were just one step from finding out where she was, from closing the case. But still Sinnott wasn't budging.

Reluctantly, Tillman released his grip. Sinnott lay back on his pillow, exhausted from the confrontation. From the monitor attached to his chest, it was clear his pulse rate had exceeded one-forty. He looked close to death and Lambert doubted he would survive another confrontation.

'How does this benefit you?' he asked.

'It doesn't,' said Sinnott.

'Then why not tell us? Who would have the authority to order a hit on Weaver?'

A sigh left Sinnott's lips, a faint sound, almost inaudible. 'It beats me. I've told you before, Lambert, the only person

I know from the Manor is Weaver. He recruited me, I reported to him. I sorted things out for him. That's where my connection ends.'

'You always were a snivelling fucker,' said Tillman. 'I knew there was no way you'd have risen to this rank without outside backing.'

'You're probably right,' conceded Sinnott. 'What does it matter now?

'I'll tell you why it matters,' said Tillman, moving towards him.

Lambert held out his arm and felt a blow as he stopped the charging Tillman.

'You must know who the other members of the Manor are,' he said to Sinnott, holding Tillman in place.

'I know they exist,' said Sinnott. 'Some are in the force, most outside.'

'Give us some names,' demanded Tillman.

Sinnott struggled to shift himself upright. He leant towards them, this time his turn to display anger.

'I've told you before. The only person I know is Weaver. It seems from what you've said he was not in charge.'

Lambert sighed. 'And the Manor itself? Waverley Manor I mean, you knew what was going on there?'

Sinnott lowered his chin. 'I had a vague idea.'

'A vague idea?' said Lambert, growing agitated at Sinnott's nonchalant tone.

'It was my role to deflect attention. I'm not proud of it but if I hadn't done it I would have joined those unfortunate souls beneath.'

Lambert struggled to understand what he was hearing. He pulled Tillman away and they stepped outside of the room.

'I think he's telling the truth,' said Lambert.

'Do you now?' said Tillman.

'What has he got to lose at this stage? If he survives this he's going to prison for the rest of his life. And if what he says is true, and what we've seen today with Weaver suggests it is, then chances are he's not long for this world.'

'He knows some names,' grunted Tillman. 'There'll be bodies he's protected and I intend to find out who they are.'

'You're only going to get yourself into trouble,' said Lambert.

Tillman shrugged and Lambert understood that was unlikely to ever happen.

'Someone knew we were going to question Weaver,' said Tillman.

Lambert nodded.

'Aside from McCarthy, the only people who knew about our plan were those who'd gathered at your flat.'

Lambert had been thinking the same. It was hard to accept but it seemed likely one of the team had given up their plan.

'It has to be Duggan,' said Tillman. 'He has a connection to both Sinnott and Weaver.'

Lambert agreed. He tried to think of reasons why it couldn't be the man from Anti-Corruption but each time he came up blank. It couldn't be Matilda, and it seemed highly unlikely Colville and Greene were involved.

'We need to call it in,' said Lambert. 'Recover those bodies from Waverley Manor.'

'Once we do that we'll never find Jardine,' said Tillman.

'I'll call Matilda. Get her to track Duggan. Once we have him in our sights I'll talk to him myself.'

'We should bring him here,' said Tillman.

Lambert shook his head. 'I'm having no more part in this, Glenn. Let me speak to Duggan. Once I have his response we'll release the information, sort out what's happening at the Manor and go from there.' Lambert took out his mobile phone. 'No signal,' he said.

Tillman shook his head. 'All signal is disabled from within,' he said. 'There's a wired phone on the wall through there.' He threw Lambert a set of keys. 'Call Matilda and get to Duggan before it's too late. I'm going to have a few more words with former police officer Sinnott here before I come and join you.'

# Chapter Forty-Nine

Matilda answered on the second ring.

Lambert was standing in a sterile room, the only decoration the fixed phone he held in his hand. The room was airtight. A faint outline of a door was etched into one of the walls but it wasn't soundproof. From the other room, Lambert heard Sinnott's cries and hoped Tillman wasn't going too far. He didn't agree with what was happening but had to focus all his attention now on finding and speaking to Duggan.

'I've been calling you for hours,' said Matilda. 'What the hell happened?'

'They came out of nowhere. Before we knew what was happening Weaver was gone. Where are you at the moment?' said Lambert.

'I'm here with DS Colville and DI Greene.'

Lambert cursed under his breath. 'Where's Duggan?' he said.

'He left for work earlier, said he needed to speak to someone,' said Matilda. 'You don't think...' she added, obviously coming to the same realisation as Lambert.

'Someone must have notified the killers about Weaver. If it wasn't one of you three, then it had to be Duggan,' said Lambert.

It was Matilda's turn to curse.

'We need to speak to him. Call him and act as if nothing's happened. See if he'll meet you. Back at the flat if possible,' said Lambert.

'OK, I'll call him now. When will you be back?'

'Depending on traffic, I should be back within the hour. Let me know as soon as you've spoken to him.' Lambert placed the phone back on the wall and headed back the way he'd came, until he reached the secure area where he'd entered the safe house. One of Tillman's team guarded the exit. He stared Lambert down, blocking his way.

'I'm leaving,' said Lambert.

The man, who dwarfed Lambert in height and width, continued to stare as though he'd spoken a foreign language. He picked up a walkie-talkie and uttered some words. A second later, a buzzing noise preceded the opening of the door. Lambert stepped through, thanking the guard with a mocking nod and headed towards his car.

–

Tension built in Lambert's head as he made his way back to the flat. He'd stumbled on something larger than the simple disappearance of Caroline Jardine and, as such, the answers were further from reach than ever.

Why would Duggan be working with DS Colville if he'd been a member of the Manor all along? Surely, if their powers extended as far as Sinnott seemed to think, Duggan could have closed this investigation down earlier? Maybe he was another pawn, and had been placed by Weaver into Anti-Corruption to protect the Manor's activities, but it didn't ring true to Lambert.

As he joined the South Circular, Matilda called. 'Duggan's going to meet us back at the flat,' she said. 'He's coming by car.'

'How did he sound on the phone?' asked Lambert.

'If I'm honest, he sounded gutted. But it could be that he's just a great actor. Apparently Weaver's death is the talk of the office. As you can imagine, there are a number of conspiracy theories. Duggan's been called to work on the case so he says he can't stay with us long.'

'He'll stay as long as we need him,' said Lambert. 'We're going to have to go public about Waverley Manor as soon as we've spoken to him. We can't let it wait any longer.'

'Where's Glenn?' said Matilda.

'He's still talking to Sinnott. Once we've cleared this up with Duggan we'll have to make his arrest official.'

Matilda began to speak then hesitated. 'I'll see you back at the flat,' she said, hanging up.

The seasonal rain returned as Lambert reached Clapham. It fell from the sky in sheets, pummelling Lambert's windscreen and restricting visibility to metres ahead. Lambert wished he had some sort of trace on Duggan. For all he knew, the officer could be miles away, utilising an escape plan.

Lambert made a mental note to check his archived files, to re-examine them from both a Duggan and a Sinnott perspective. Lambert parked up as Duggan was arriving at the flat, as promised.

This simple development suggested Lambert was heading down another dead end. Unless Duggan was bluffing, if he was going to present himself for potential interrogation, it seemed highly unlikely he was guilty of being associated with the Manor.

Lambert sprinted across the street to his flat through the torrent of rain still spewing from the sky. The four officers were assembled in his living room, sitting as if at a wake. Matilda shot him a nervous look as he entered the room. Duggan sat next to her on the Seventies-style sofa within touching distance.

'You all know about Weaver,' said Lambert, deciding to get straight to the point.

They all nodded. Sullen, like a group of teenagers.

Lambert assessed them all for a response. The slightest twitch of guilt. He saved the majority of his attention for Duggan, but the man looked as crestfallen as the rest of his companions.

'I need to ask you all,' said Lambert, 'if you shared the information about Weaver with anyone else?'

'What do you mean?' said Greene.

'It can't come as much of a surprise that I'm asking you,' said Lambert. 'When we left here earlier this morning only the five of us and Tillman knew about our mission to interrogate Weaver. The only additional person to know was DS McCarthy who is no longer with us. So, I'm suggesting there was a leak and unfortunately the first place I have to look is here. So I'll ask you all again if any of you shared the information about our mission?'

'Of course not,' said Greene.

'No,' said Matilda.

Colville and Duggan shook their heads.

'You need to think carefully,' said Lambert, 'even if it was just a loose word with a colleague. We need to trace this to discover how they knew about Weaver.'

'Oh, come on. This is bullshit,' said Duggan. 'You really think one of us would be unprofessional enough to have shared the information?'

If it was Duggan, he was doing a plausible job of denial.

'OK, well what suggestions do you have for me?' said Lambert, not pushing things for the time being.

'You mentioned McCarthy,' said Greene.

Lambert nodded and poured himself a cup of coffee from the pot one of them had brewed.

'He was the driver but he was in on the plan?' said Greene.

'Yes. Tillman switched him.'

'Someone would know about that, obviously. Have we looked at the other driver? The one he replaced. Or whoever's responsible for Weaver's timetable? That change alone could have alerted lots of bodies.'

The thought had crossed Lambert's mind. So had the realisation that it would be almost impossible to check on all of them.

'The case is being treated as a terrorist attack,' said Duggan out of nowhere. 'MI5 are handling it for the time being.'

'Great. That's going to close off all doors of investigation then.'

'What about Sinnott?' said Duggan.

'We're going to bring him in shortly. We have to work under the presumption the Manor now know about us.'

'That's not good,' said Colville, who sat upright on one of the dining chairs. In the gloom she looked almost like a mannequin.

Lambert was running out of options. He could take Duggan in and interrogate him officially. But he had more to lose than gain by doing so. He was confident he was not involved.

Making their investigation into the Manor public would send everything into turmoil, especially considering Weaver's assassination. It wouldn't take MI5 long to link the two cases. But they couldn't sit on it any longer. He doubted the Manor would risk retrieving the bodies from the underground dungeon. But anything was possible at this juncture.

'I'm going to call it in,' he said. 'Greene, you go with Matilda to Waverley Manor and supervise everything. We'll see what the fall-out is once we've uncovered the Manor's little secret.'

Quiet descended over the room as they thought about the implication of what they were doing and why. As they realised the mystery of Caroline Jardine's disappearance would probably never get solved.

# Chapter Fifty

Lambert stayed at the flat as Matilda took charge of events at Waverley Manor. He stared at the accumulation of files on the System, running routines until he felt he could search no longer. Everything returned to Trevor Hodge. Why had he replaced the Jardines with the corpses of Berry and Turner? This was the biggest anomaly to the case. If, like Sinnott had suggested, Hodge had been under instruction by the Manor to eliminate the Jardines, why had he gone against their instructions? He'd sounded genuinely mortified whilst confessing that Marcus Jardine had died. Lambert could only hope this meant he'd tried to keep the Jardines out of harm's way, for negotiation reasons if nothing else, and that somewhere Caroline was still alive.

Sarah called and he let it go straight to voicemail. He would have loved to have spoken to her, to share the turmoil he was enduring, but things were complicated. Their last meeting hadn't gone well. A sense of unease hung over their conversation and their unsaid words suggested things were coming to an end. However, he only waited five minutes before checking her message.

She sounded hesitant, unsure of herself. 'We need to talk,' she said, at the end of the message. 'Call me when you're free.' The words were simple enough but Lambert sensed the hidden meaning.

He cursed to himself as a light appeared in the corner of his eye, glowing in a haze of blazing shades. Lambert controlled his breathing and let the exhaustion take him. The swarm filled his vision and he closed his eyes, hoping he wouldn't sleep for long.

–

It was dark when he woke. Four am. He showered and changed in a hurry and headed towards Waverley Manor. He checked his voicemail messages on the car's Bluetooth as he drove. Sarah hadn't left a message but there was one from Tillman, stating he'd officially charged Sinnott and that they'd moved him to the NCA headquarters. Matilda had also left a couple of messages updating him on progress at the Manor.

Lambert's mind once again moved in various directions. After checking in at Waverley Manor, he intended to resume his work on the System. It was possible there was an indication of a link between Hodge and the Manor he'd overlooked, or had simply not been looking for previously.

Floodlights guided him to his destination. A large police presence was stationed at the perimeter of Waverley Manor. Lambert parked up after showing his warrant to one of the uniforms.

Matilda had done a great job organising the site. Two uniformed officers guarded the pathway which led to the ruins. One gave Lambert a torch, but the path had already been lit so Lambert took little time reaching first the large clearing, where a second team of officers were congregated, and then the Manor itself.

Numerous sets of floodlights illuminated the crumbling building and surrounding area of Waverley Manor. In the crisp winter night, the floodlights gave the area an ethereal feel. He could have been dreaming had it not been for the disgruntled face of DS Bickland approaching him.

'Heads up would have been nice, sir,' said the junior officer, in his south-western drawl.

'Things have been moving at an incredible speed, Sergeant,' said Lambert. 'Where's Kennedy?'

'Down in the depths. You'll need a SOCO uniform if you want to go down there.'

'Tell her I'm here,' said Lambert, not keen to explore the labyrinth again any time soon.

Bickland headed off and Lambert paced the area, watching the officers at work. More officers would join the teams tomorrow. Aside from the complicated search beneath ground, the whole area would be turned upside down. Lambert was convinced more bodies would be found, and by the time they'd finished there wouldn't be an inch of land untouched.

'This is going to look great on your record,' said a voice from the shadows.

Lambert moved towards the sound. 'DCI Barnes,' he said, as the face of Caroline Jardine's boss revealed itself.

'Not going to help find my officer though, is it?' said Barnes, ignoring Lambert's offer of a greeting.

'I haven't given up hope yet.'

'You're more a fool than I realised then,' said Barnes. 'You were involved in Sinnott's arrest?'

'Yes,' said Lambert, ignoring the accusatory jibe.

Barnes shook his head, eyes facing the ground. 'He was never any good. Never had any respect for the man, and never met anyone who did, but this? Shit, if anything I'm amazed he had the balls for it.'

Lambert wasn't about to share any information with Barnes, however much he was clearly angling for it. He remained silent and let the DCI continue.

'And that MP prick. Weaver? Jesus Christ, what had Caroline stumbled onto?'

'I don't suppose she ever shared any information with you?' said Lambert.

Barnes looked up from his study of the earth as if surprised Lambert was there. 'Your DS gave me some background on what you've been looking at. I knew about Alistair Newlyn's suicide way back, but thought that was old news. I'm surprised Caroline had time to continue looking into this. If only she'd come to me about it.'

Matilda rescued him from Barnes' regret. She approached like a ghost, wearing the white overalls of the SOCO team and her headgear under her arm. 'Kennedy,' said Lambert.

'Sir,' said Matilda. 'Sir,' she repeated to Barnes.

Barnes ignored her. Lambert understood his frustration. He shared it, but knew words would not suffice in the current situation.

'You'll keep me updated,' said Barnes to Lambert, as if Matilda wasn't there.

'Of course,' said Lambert, as Barnes headed down the floodlit pathway back to the clearing.

–

A stepladder had been placed at the entrance of the trapdoor. Lambert made his way down, LED lights reflecting against his SOCO uniform.

Matilda had limited the amount of officers allowed into the underground cavern. She had assigned one pair to each tunnel. Lambert followed her down the third pathway, where they'd initially discovered the pile of bones. Battery-powered lights flooded the area with illumination, but that did little to alleviate the horror of the place. If anything, it highlighted the terror of what had occurred.

Lambert saw clearly the patches of blood, and the various instruments hammered into the walls. The area where the bones were collected had been cordoned off. One of the SOCOs was filming from every conceivable angle and would continue to do so for some time before they even contemplated moving the evidence.

'Through here, sir,' said Matilda, pointing to an area to the left of the room they hadn't noticed the previous evening.

With the floodlights in place it seemed inconceivable they had missed it. It was a second trap-door which had been propped open by one of the team.

'We've three officers down there now,' said Matilda.

'Dare I ask?' said Lambert.

'It's just one room. Smaller than this but piled high with remains.'

Disbelief almost overcame Lambert as he edged down the second stepladder into a circular room, again lit by powerful beams.

One of the hooded figures of the SOCO team turned to look at him and, through the plastic visor, Lambert recognised the face of Lindsey Harrington.

'You've certainly stumbled on something here,' she said, her words muffled by the face protection.

Lambert remained silent, words failing him.

'How long have these bodies been here for?' he asked eventually.

'It's hard to say at the moment. But it's possible some of the remains have been here for decades. One thing I've started to notice though.'

'What's that?' said Lambert.

'Many of the bones I've seen are deformed in some way. I'm afraid there are the usual breaks and abrasions that haven't fully healed. I'm sure you've seen that before, horrendous though it is. But one thing I've seen here I haven't encountered before. Some of the bodies aren't fully grown. Or their growth's been hampered in some way. If I had to guess, I'd say some of the bodies down here never left this place.'

Lambert felt nauseous. 'You mean they were born here?' he said, not wanting to believe what he was hearing.

'I'm afraid it looks that way,' said Harrington. 'They were born in the darkness and, unfortunately, were left to die in it.'

# Chapter Fifty-One

Lambert retreated from the underground bunker.

Although it could be seen as a success uncovering such a place, Lambert felt like a failure. If what Harrington had told him was true then some, if not all, of the bodies would never be accounted for. Furthermore, aside from Sinnott, who had now been officially charged, there was no one to assign blame to. Worse still, nothing about the situation led them to the whereabouts of Caroline Jardine.

The sun had risen by the time he was back above land. Without the floodlights on, the surrounding area of Waverley Manor had a drab and common countenance. His fellow officers busied away above ground as if in shock. Lambert saw months, if not years of work spiralling out in front of him. Whoever was responsible for the atrocities beneath ground, it extended beyond just one person. Sinnott had denied detailed knowledge of the place and despite himself Lambert believed him. He wondered too if Weaver really had any part to play or if he'd been a scapegoat, a diversion tactic.

As he headed back through the clearing on the now well-trodden pathway, he thought about DCI Barnes' frustration at the operation and how things seemed to be moving away from Caroline Jardine. To some people it had become bigger than finding the officer but to Lambert it was still his only true goal.

Mia Helmer stopped him as he reached where his car was parked. 'DCI Lambert,' she called, her hand raised as if they were best friends.

Lambert stopped, anger surging through him as the petite woman moved towards him. He told himself she was just doing her job but this didn't calm him.

'Ah, DCI Lambert,' she repeated, catching up to him. 'Would you care to comment on the latest developments?'

'No,' said Lambert. He was still acutely aware of his feet planted into the ground as if ready to push up; in attack or retreat.

'Have you located Caroline Jardine? I can't get any answers from anyone,' said Helmer, glancing round at the uniformed officers.

'You shouldn't be here,' said Lambert.

'Oh come on, don't give me that. The public has a right to know what's going on.'

Lambert thought about what he'd seen, about what Harrington had said about the babies born into the living hell of the Manor, and finally snapped. 'Get her out of here,' he said, to one of the uniformed officers.

'Sir?' said the officer, moving towards Lambert.

'Get that confused look off your face, officer. This person does not belong here.'

'Don't be ridiculous,' said Helmer, showing her press card in defence.

The officer hesitated, glancing at Lambert before deciding the best course of action was doing as instructed. 'Please follow me, madam,' he said to Helmer.

'I will not,' said the journalist.

Lambert took in a deep breath. 'If she refuses again, arrest her,' he said, heading to his car.

He heard Helmer's protestations from the shelter of the vehicle but managed to tune them out. Try as he might, however, he couldn't get the images of the bunker out of his head. He feared Caroline Jardine was in a similar place. He slammed his fist against the steering wheel. He needed to help her but didn't know where to start. Maybe he should have let Tillman interrogate Sinnott further after all. He shut his eyes and tried to think, but the images from the Manor kept returning, Harrington's words haunting him. *Born in the darkness, and left to die in it.* It had a cadence to it. A refrain he couldn't quite place but he was sure he'd heard the words before.

He trawled his mind trying to recall every aspect of the case. He worked methodically from beginning to current end. And then he remembered where he'd heard similar words before. Gladys Hodge had been discussing the death of her daughter and how her husband had never fully recovered from the loss. Lambert had asked her what had become of him and she'd answered, 'he got lost in the darkness for a final time and never returned.' At best it was a tenuous link but it gave Lambert hope.

He started the car and headed towards the nearest town. He needed to get online to check the System to discover more about Trevor Hodge's father.

–

Lambert didn't bother ordering coffee. He walked straight past the counter of the chain coffee store and found a seat at the rear of the shop. Out of instinct, he faced the door before taking the laptop out of his holdall and accessing the System via a secure dongle.

Gladys Hodge had said her husband was alone in the darkness. She'd also informed him the man had been something of a loner following the death of his daughter. But, in retrospect, Lambert was convinced she'd meant more by the statement. She was a keenly intelligent woman and it wasn't beyond her to have given him a cryptic clue.

He accessed as much of the information as he could on her husband. According to the records, he'd died of natural causes aged a mere fifty-five. He'd suffered a fatal heart attack whilst at work. He searched for more detail on the man. He'd had no criminal record. He'd been on the electoral role since age eighteen and had been up to date with his National Insurance contributions.

Lambert began cross-referencing his sources, searching for something that would explain Gladys's statement to him. Had Leonard Hodge been involved with the atrocities at Waverley Manor? Was it this which had led to Trevor Hodge setting fires? Had he found out about his father's shameful secret? There was very little to go on. He didn't have a criminal record so there was no report of him on HOLMES or the System for that matter. However, the System had one advantage over HOLMES. It had access to social media databases, which were still legally a grey area. Again, Lambert had reached a dead-end, Leonard Hodge having died too early for either Facebook or Twitter.

He ran a few more searches, deciding he would have to speak to Gladys Hodge if no answers were forthcoming. It was a long trek over to Dartford and time was certainly of the essence. He tried every trick he knew, even entering typos on purpose and searching for the results, but still he came up blank. He cursed loudly in the coffee shop, receiving a dirty stare from one of the baristas who was obviously still unhappy he hadn't purchased something. He left without thanks, jumped in the car and headed towards Dartford.

It wouldn't make a difference, after all. Matilda had everything under control at the Manor, Sinnott was safely in custody and was Tillman's responsibility now. He played the words in his head as he drove. *Alone in the darkness.* Each time he did, the images of the last two days sprung to mind. He couldn't let such things distract him now. He was convinced Gladys Hodge had meant something and he was going to find out what.

–

It was midday by the time he arrived at Gladys Hodge's care home. As he parked up he was momentarily distracted by the remembrance of seeing DS Duggan's car in the street the other night. He'd yet to question the man over why he'd been following him, and decided he'd find out the next time they met.

The white T-shirted receptionist nodded to him as he walked into the main reception area.

'DCI Lambert, isn't it?' said the man.

'Sharp memory. I need to speak to Gladys Hodge now,' said Lambert, skipping pleasantries.

'She's up in her room. You wait here, I'll get someone to show you up.'

'That's OK. I know the way,' said Lambert.

He controlled his pace as he made his way up the stairs, despite being desperate to run. He knocked on her door and shuffled his feet as he waited for an answer.

'Come in,' came the confident reply from behind the barrier.

Gladys Hodge sat by the window, a different novel from the last time in her hands. Instead of a semi-naked man on the cover, this particular tome had a picture of a raven-haired woman in a green dress. Hodge shut the book and stared at Lambert as if she'd been expecting him.

'My son's dead,' she said to him, as if somehow he was to blame.

In his desperation to see her, he'd somehow forgotten she would be in a period of grief.

'I'm very sorry for your loss.'

'You were with him when he died?' said Hodge.

Lambert nodded. 'I did everything I could to save him.'

'And that's why you're here? To pay your condolences?'

'In part,' said Lambert.

'I know the circumstances. Someone stabbed him. Multiple times from what the officers said to me. It was all my fault.'

'How was it your fault, Gladys?' said Lambert.

'Because I called his number, I led you to him.' Hodge squeezed her eyes shut and for a second her body contorted as if she was trying to expel the pain from her body.

'Please don't feel that way, Mrs Hodge. Nothing about that phone call had anything to do with your son's death.'

'Do you think that matters?' snapped Hodge, shaking herself out of her remorse. 'Just tell me why you are here.'

'It's your husband I'd like to speak to you about,' said Lambert, still standing, having not been offered a seat.

'That fool,' said Gladys with a sneer. 'What do you want to know about him for?'

'It was something you said to me. About how after your daughter died Mr Hodge never fully recovered.'

'Of course he never recovered,' said Gladys. 'If you think anyone recovers from the death of their child you're insane.'

Lambert nodded, not about to besmirch Chloe's memory by mentioning his own grief. 'It was more than that,' he said. 'It was a phrase you used. That he'd retreated back into the darkness.'

Lambert studied Gladys and noticed the flicker of recognition in her eyes as he said the words.

'You have a good memory,' said Gladys. 'Remember I said he was a simple man, Mr Lambert. Simple in heart and mind.'

'What was the darkness you talked of?' said Lambert.

'I'm surprised you didn't ask me at the time. Apart from his daughter, the only thing my husband loved was his work and once she was gone he retreated more and more. Some days he wouldn't even come home.'

'What did he do for a living?' asked Lambert, sensing he was close to something.

'As I said, he was a simple man and, as such, he had a simple job.'

Lambert rubbed his face, his patience close to snapping.

'Didn't I tell you?' said Gladys with a cruel gleam in her eyes. 'He was a guide.'

'A guide?' said Lambert, not liking what he saw in Gladys's face.

'Yes, he was a guide. And where he worked, he died. His body was found there.'

For Christ's sake, thought Lambert. 'And where was that, Mrs Hodge?'

'In the caves of course.  My husband was a guide at Chislehurst Caves.'

# Chapter Fifty-Two

Lambert wasted no time. He called Croft and Bickland and instructed them to meet him at the caves with a rescue team.

'Mrs Hodge, did your husband ever take your son to the caves?' he asked.

'Yes, all the time. At least...'

'At least?'

'He stopped taking him after our baby daughter died.'

'Thank you, Mrs Hodge. And, again, my condolences for your son's death,' said Lambert, things becoming clearer.

'Wait, I don't understand,' said Gladys.

'Thank you, again,' said Lambert, shutting the door.

He was at the caves within an hour. Croft and Bickland were waiting for him, a team assembled. Bickland was in deep conversation with one of the members of staff outside the entrance as Lambert walked over.

'Sir, this is Miles Nicholls. He's the current manager of the caves. Mr Nicholls, this is DCI Lambert.'

Nicholls shook hands with Lambert. 'Ah, maybe we can get some sense here?' he said.

'Mr Nicholls, thanks for meeting us,' said Lambert.

'I haven't had much of an option. Your colleague here tells me you think someone is stranded in our caves.'

'It's possible. How long have you been working here, Mr Nicholls?'

'About eight years.'

'And what can you tell me about the caves?'

'In what way?'

'How deep are they? Would it be possible for someone to stow away in them? That sort of thing.'

Nicholls sighed. 'Well, for one, they're technically not caves. They're completely man-made. They're effectively chalk and flint mines.'

'And how big is the place?' said Lambert. He'd heard of Chislehurst Caves before, but they'd never crossed his radar.

'There're about twenty-three miles of tunnels,' said Nicholls.

Lambert closed his eyes, for a second pretending he wasn't there.

'Twenty-three miles?' he said, hoping Nicholls had made a mistake.

'Yep.'

'And I presume it's all mapped out?'

'It is.'

'What's the temperature like down there? Would it even be possible for someone to be living there?'

'It's a completely static temperature all year round. Seventeen degrees. Certainly warm enough to live by.'

'So, do you think it's feasible for someone to camp down there?'

'I wouldn't say camp. Once you're inside, it's pitch black. Of course, you can bring artificial lighting with you.'

'Could you go undetected though?'

'That I very much doubt.'

'You have guided tours though?'

'We do but they only go into the fringes of the caves. They were used as air raid shelters during the war. We even used to stage pop concerts down there in the Seventies.'

'Show me,' said Lambert.

Nicholls began walking to the front of a building. Lambert nodded over to Bickland and told him to follow. Croft saw the gesture and accompanied him. Nicholls led them through a souvenir area with old pictures of the mined area. The place reminded Lambert of an old railway station.

'Through here,' said Nicholls, leading down a passageway that led to the entrance of the caves.

Nicholls lit three oil lamps and handed them to the officers. 'This is what we give to the people on our tours.'

'You obviously mark people in and out?' said Lambert.

'We use a ticketing system to allow them in. Each tour guide obviously maintains the correct number of people on their tour, and ensures the correct people return.'

'Have you ever had people wander off?' said Lambert.

'It happens. As you can see, there are loads of different tunnels. The guide usually goes down on his own so we've had people wander off. Some even purposely do so but they always return.'

'May I?' said Lambert, taking the torch from the man. He shone it onto the granite walls, the undulations. 'How many different tunnels are there?'

'Depends on what you classify as a tunnel. But there are hundreds, if not thousands, of sections on the twenty-three miles.'

'Have you walked it all?' asked Bickland.

'No, not personally. Some of the guides have claimed to.'

'And could there be a section uncharted?'

'You mean where someone could hide?' said Nicholls.

'Yes,' said Lambert.

'I've never heard of such a place. I suppose it's feasible. You'll have a lot of ground to cover. One of my guys is on shift soon. Clive Friedman. He's been with us for over twenty years. He's probably your best bet.'

'When's he on shift?' said Lambert.

'In about fifteen minutes' time.'

'OK, Mr Nicholls, I'm afraid we're going to have to close the caves off to the public for the time being. I've a strong reason to believe there's a missing person being held somewhere down here.'

Nicholls didn't seem too bothered by the direction. 'Seems unlikely to me,' he said, 'but if that's what you want, fine. Our next tour is due when Friedman gets in. I'll go upstairs and tell them you've cancelled it. If you'd like to follow me.'

—

Friedman was a bullish man, similar in size and stature to Tillman, only ten or fifteen years older. When Lambert told him his theory he looked at him as if he was mad.

'I would know if someone was down there,' he said.

'You regularly traipse the twenty-three miles, do you?' said Bickland.

Friedman turned his head to face Bickland and gave him a dismissive look. 'No, but I could still tell.'

'How exactly?' said Lambert.

'The smell for one thing. If someone was living down there for a few days the smell would drift. It's hard to describe but when you've been going down there for all those years you become attuned to little things like that. Little differences.'

'And you believe you've seen every area? Every inch of these caves,' said Lambert.

'In my time, yes.'

'Are there are other ways to enter them?'

'Of course. There were some houses built on top and places where you can enter the labyrinth if you know where to look.'

'What's the best way of searching the place?'

'Well, if you insist on going ahead, I would suggest we get the rest of my colleagues in and we can make a methodical search of the place in sections. That way, we'll get it covered quicker. Not that you're going to find anything,' he added, for good measure.

'How quickly could you get that arranged?' said Lambert.

'If everyone's available, the next hour and a half? Two hours to be safe.'

'If you could do so that would be wonderful,' said Lambert.

'Leave it to me,' said Friedman, walking away.

Lambert followed the man back into the car park and placed his hand on his shoulder, making sure he was out of earshot from the rest of the team.

'You've been working here twenty years, Mr Friedman?' Lambert asked.

'That's right.'

'Did you ever come across a man by the name of Leonard Hodge?'

Friedman's eyes narrowed. 'I'd only been in the job a couple of years at the time but I knew him. Strange creature. A loner.'

'Do you remember his son?'

Friedman nodded, his lips pursed. 'Even stranger creature. Never said boo to a ghost. That last year before Leonard died he was down here every day, even when his father wasn't around. The boss at the time used to let him. He'd take a lamp and a torch and off he'd go, wandering the place as if it was his backyard.'

Lambert paused, remembering what Gladys had told him. 'He was found down here? Leonard?'

Friedman looked to the ground. 'I didn't find him, thank God. He must have been down here days. They say he had a heart attack but I think he starved himself to death.'

Lambert nodded, imagining the self-control it would take to remain underground long enough to die from starvation.

'Thanks, Mr Friedman. Please, let me know when you have your team together.'

Lambert instructed Bickland to find more officers for the search. Caroline Jardine was down here. He was sure of it. He called Matilda and updated her on the situation.

'Do you want me to come over?' she asked.

'No. I think you're more than busy enough over there,' said Lambert, 'but I'll keep you informed.'

With Nicholls' help, they managed to split the search into eight sections. Lambert led the main search from the entrance in Chislehurst and walked the tunnels with

Nicholls. Barnes had sent extra bodies from his team and the noise of hundreds of officers trawling the caves reverberated across the stone interior.

They soon passed from the tourist area into less patrolled sections. If Hodge had taken Jardine, Lambert was under no illusion that he would have left her there in plain sight. As deserted as the caves usually were, Nichols informed him the majority of tunnels were in occasional use. Some kind of role-playing group used the caves for their activities. Lambert had spoken to the leader of the organisation, who claimed not to have come across any sign of other people using the space.

Lambert shone his torch onto the rocks as he moved through tunnel after tunnel. He tried to imagine the men who had mined the area hundreds of years ago, the planning needed for such a mammoth project.

At least the caves were blessed with a lightness of air. As Nichols suggested, the caves had a constant temperature which meant the Jardines would not have perished through cold. After a few hours, the search parties began crossing into one another's territories. Lambert noticed the looks on his fellow officers' faces. They either thought it was a waste of time or had given up hope.

'We're nearing the end of our section,' said Nicholls. They were four miles into the cave and faced a long trek back. Was it a mistake? Lambert remembered the plaintive cries of Trevor Hodge on the phone stating Marcus Jardine was dead. That had only been hours before Hodge died, and he hadn't mentioned Caroline. Why go to the trouble of switching their bodies, only to take their lives? No, he was convinced Caroline was being held captive somewhere, and this had to be the place.

'Have you shown me everywhere?'

'The teams have covered every inch as far as I can ascertain.'

'If you were going to hide somewhere, where would it be?'

Nicholls checked his map and began walking. 'There are a couple of other places we could try. It's a long shot, though.' He led Lambert through more tunnels, moving as if he was outside, making swift turns without a second thought until he came to a halt. He shone a torch against a cave wall, moving the beam of light up and down as if searching for something. 'No,' he said, almost to himself.

'What is it?' said Lambert.

Nicholls ran his hand along the cave wall. 'There's a gap here. I thought it might be big enough to squeeze through but I'm afraid I was mistaken.'

Lambert hadn't noticed the gap but up close he saw it. It was about big enough to stick a head through but he wasn't about to try. 'Anywhere else like this?'

'A couple. There's an opening, probably about two or three miles from here. I have to warn you though, it's down quite a low tunnel. You'll be on your hands and knees by the end.'

Lambert's optimism faded as he followed Nicholls down the winding tunnels. It seemed inconceivable Hodge would have gone to all this effort. How would he have forced the Jardines along these corridors? 'Is there another entrance anywhere near here?' he asked, as the walls started narrowing.

'No. Unless…'

'Unless?'

'It's highly unlikely, but there are some houses built on the land above. Who knows, there may be some secret entrance,' he said, with a mocking smile.

'It's not a joke.'

'I know, sorry. It's not beyond the realm of possibility. There have always been rumours about such things. Legends I guess. Anyway, here's the spot.'

Nicholls had stopped at an opening which was about the same height as him. 'It gets narrower,' said Nicholls. 'I believe there is a second opening about eight hundred yards down.'

Lambert called out Caroline's name as he followed Nicholls into the tunnel. The hard ground was taking its toll on his knees and soon he was crouching as the tunnel narrowed and the roof of the cave dropped. 'Lucky I'm not claustrophobic,' he said.

'You will be,' said Nicholls, as they dropped down a level.

Lambert was on all fours now and progress was slow. They were packed in so tight he feared they would have to go backwards when they left the tunnel.

'Through here,' said Nicholls, shining his torch into an opening the size of a small human.

Lambert controlled a mounting panic, the confines of the tunnel echoing his earlier confinement in the MRI scanner only days ago. 'Check it,' he said to Nicholls.

Nicholls inched forwards as the tunnel narrowed. At the opening the cave roof was higher and he managed to get to his feet through, albeit with his back arched. Lambert whispered a prayer to a God he didn't believe in as Nicholls peered into the opening. He made his way through the gap, stepping in sideways until all Lambert could see was his left leg dangling from the opening, as if the cave had somehow swallowed him whole.

Seconds later he shuffled back out. Lambert shone his torch at the man's face, which was crestfallen. 'You better get in there,' said Nicholls. 'We've found them.'

## Chapter Fifty-Three

Lambert told Nicholls to call in their location to the other teams as he brushed past him. Nicholls didn't elucidate on what he'd seen beyond the gap and Lambert didn't ask.

'Take this,' said Nicholls, handing Lambert a second high-powered torch.

Lambert took a deep breath and squeezed himself through the opening. His first response on viewing the scene was to close his eyes. Somehow the smell hadn't filtered through to the tunnel but it hit him full force now, his eyes watering. The opening led to an enclosed area twenty metres in diameter. To the right of him lay the corpse of Marcus Jardine. His eyes were still open and they appeared to stare back at Lambert as if in accusation.

To the right of him, Caroline Jardine lay on the cold floor. Her arms were bound, a chain linking her cuffed wrists to a holding hook fixed on the cave wall. She looked lifeless and Lambert approached with trepidation. 'Caroline,' he whispered, as he took the short steps to her body.

He reached for her neck and almost let out a cry as he found a weak pulse. Relief and elation rushed his body, despite the sight of her deceased husband nearby. He shone the torch into her closed eyes to force a response but she didn't open them. Her face was drawn, her lips bone-dry. He tipped water from his canteen onto them and the majority of drops bounced off as if they were impermeable.

'Caroline,' he repeated more urgently, as he shook her body in an attempt to revive her. He felt his own hands shake as he continued his attempts to wake her. His elation at finding her was dampened by the possibility that he was too late.

She still didn't respond so Lambert used his walkie-talkie to check in with the response team. It was then he noticed the small opening in the cave roof above him. 'Nicholls, get in here,' he shouted.

Nicholls peered into the cave. It was clear from his face that he'd rather be anywhere else.

'Up there,' said Lambert.

Nicholls glanced towards the roof of the cave, using a second torch to clarify what he was looking at. 'Well, I'll be,' he said.

'Could you deduce where the entrance is?' asked Lambert, his hand still placed on the cold flesh of Caroline's neck.

'I'm sure I could. Let me call my colleague.' Nicholls lifted his mouth to his walkie-talkie before pausing. 'She is…?'

'Yes, she's alive, Nicholls, but we need a rescue team here as soon as feasibly possible.'

–

Thirty minutes later a face appeared at the roof opening above them. Lambert had never been more pleased to see the pudgy face of DS Bickland in his life. 'Rescue team here,' said the officer. 'We're trying to work out how to get down there.'

The rescue process was a difficult one. With the body of Marcus Jardine in the corner, the area was still a crime scene. The fire services had been deployed and were busy trying to find a way of hoisting Caroline's body through the small opening in the cave wall, whilst a paramedic tried with no success to bring Caroline round.

Eventually the fire team lifted her out. Lambert watched her ascend with a growing sense of dread. Once she was safe he called for the team to winch him out as well. He couldn't face traipsing back through the narrow corridors of the caves and didn't want to let Caroline out of his sight.

Once out, he found himself standing in the corner of a field, surrounded in darkness. Bickland helped him out of the hole. 'We had to move that,' said the DS, pointing to a large boulder which had covered most of the hole.'

'Where are we?' asked Lambert.

'Some field near Chislehurst. This opening isn't sup-posed to exist.'

Caroline Jardine had been lifted into the back of an ambulance, which was making slow progress through the muddy field.

'Where are we taking her?' said Lambert.

'Princess Royal.'

'Set up some teams there. Who's gone with her?'

'Croft.'

'I'm going to follow. You take charge here. We have a murder case below. I'm sure we've contaminated the area by now but manage the SOCOs and keep me updated.'

Lambert instructed one of the patrol car officers to drive him to the hospital. 'Siren on and step on it,' he instructed the officer. 'I want to get there at the same time as her.'

As the officer sped through the country lanes, Lambert called Tillman. 'We need an armed presence at the hospital. Someone went to all this trouble to have Caroline killed. As soon as they find out she's alive they are bound to try again.'

'Leave it with me,' said Tillman, hanging up.

The driver glanced at Lambert, looking away when Lambert matched his gaze. They made good time and caught up with the ambulance as it headed into Accident and Emergency.

Lambert still had his gun in his jacket pocket. The case had affected him in ways he couldn't imagine and carrying a gun was unwise when in the clutches of such emotion. It was a risk but he couldn't act without it at the moment. He jumped from the car and surveyed the area as the ambulance doors opened.

'Sir,' said Croft, heading out of the ambulance first.

'Has she regained consciousness yet?' said Lambert.

'Not yet. She's severely dehydrated, as you would expect. They've been working on her non-stop since we left.'

Two paramedics carried Caroline off the ambulance on a gurney. She was connected to a drip feed and in the artificial glare of the A&E lights Lambert could see the full effect of the days of confinement. Her skin was ghostly pale, her clothes soaked in her own waste.

'We have a room for her?' asked Lambert.

'Yes, sir. She's going straight to intensive care.'

Lambert called over the officer who'd driven him to the hospital. 'Follow me,' he said. 'You too, Croft.'

As a trio, they followed the paramedics into the building. Caroline was rushed through and was seen immediately by one of the A&E team, Dr Morgan. 'We have a room on the fourth floor waiting for you,' she said.

Croft walked side by side with the doctor, whilst Lambert took the rear, remaining on constant lookout for an attack. He only started to relax once Caroline was safely in intensive care and a team had been stationed outside her room.

Dr Morgan joined them outside the room after examining Caroline in full. 'She's a lucky lady. Any later and I think you would have been too late. She is severely dehydrated but I can't see any significant trauma to her body. Obviously, we'll keep on high alert but I would hope she regains consciousness in the next few hours.'

Lambert thanked the woman and instructed Croft to manage the officers who'd recently arrived to provide support. 'I want this whole floor airtight,' he said.

Tillman arrived an hour into his vigil. DCI Barnes, whose mood hadn't lightened since Lambert had last seen him at the Manor, accompanied him. Lambert updated the pair on the situation, and the security he had in place.

'Can I see her?' asked Barnes.

Lambert hesitated. He didn't want to antagonise the man. He understood what he must be going through, having lost colleagues before, but he didn't want anyone seeing Caroline before him. 'I'm afraid not. Doctor's orders for the time being.'

Barnes looked at Tillman for confirmation and Lambert's superior shrugged his shoulders. 'It's Lambert's case,' he said – his only words.

Barnes cursed under his breath and stormed down the corridor.

'Touchy,' said Tillman.

Lambert didn't respond.

'You think Jardine will have anything additional for us?' asked Tillman, for once sensing the mood.

'Let's hope so. Even if it's confirmation on Sinnott and Weaver,' said Lambert.

Tillman nodded his head a few times. 'You think there's more?'

After witnessing the aftermath of Waverley Manor it was obvious the group behind the atrocities extended beyond the officer and the MP. Sinnott claimed never to have seen the Manor itself and they would probably never fully discover what Weaver knew about the place. 'Too many unanswered questions for me at the moment,' he said.

'Matilda's got her hands full at the Manor,' said Tillman.

'I'm not leaving here until Caroline is conscious.'

'No one is asking you to. You've done well here, Lambert. Very well. Uncovering the Manor, finding Jardine. It's another huge feather in your already brimming cap.'

It didn't feel like it. Marcus Jardine was dead, as were Berry, Turner, and Hodge. And how could he consider anything a success after what he'd seen at Waverley Manor? That would never leave him, and he would do everything in his power to track down everyone responsible, even if it took him the rest of his career.

A nurse left Caroline's room and exchanged a nervous glance with them before heading off down the corridor. Lambert got to his feet and checked the small window into Caroline's room. A second nurse was monitoring the various machines surrounding Caroline and didn't look in any undue distress, so he returned to his seat.

Dr Morgan returned a few minutes later with the nervous-looking nurse in tow.

'Everything OK?' said Lambert.

'Nothing to worry about. Give us some time,' said the doctor, not making eye contact.

Lambert paced the corridor, waiting for Doctor Morgan to leave the room.

'Would you sit down? You're making me nervous,' said Tillman.

Lambert was about to sit when Morgan opened the door. 'Mrs Jardine is awake. I can only give you a couple of minutes with her.'

Lambert nodded. 'Sir, I'd appreciate it if you kept guard,' he said to Tillman, who didn't respond beyond a slight raise of his eyebrows.

Caroline was still prone on the bed, lying to her right, but Lambert could make out a slight spark of colour in her eyes. 'Caroline, my name is Michael Lambert. DCI Lambert. I was the one who found you.'

'Teresa?' said Caroline.

The word came out as a rasp, little more than air, but Lambert sensed the tragic hope and despair to the question. He knelt down so he was at her eye level. 'Teresa is fine. I've met her. She's a remarkable little girl.'

Caroline's eyes watered as her lips curled upwards. 'Barnes,' she croaked.

'DCI Barnes?' said Lambert, confused.

'Yes.'

'He's fine. He's been desperate to find you.'

Caroline wriggled on the bed as if fighting to stay awake. Dr Morgan moved towards her and Caroline shook her head. 'No,' she said, every word a battle. 'He's the one you want.'

# Chapter Fifty-Four

Lambert rubbed the back of his head as Caroline slipped back into sleep. 'Is she OK?' he asked.

'She's fine. She obviously needs the rest,' said Dr Morgan.

Lambert was struggling to come to terms with what Caroline had told him. 'Could you wake her again?

'No,' said Morgan, with an authority she hadn't displayed previously.

Could Barnes really be the one they were looking for? His concern and passion to find Caroline had been convincing, but it seemed his motives for finding her were different to Lambert's. 'Could I ask you to both remain here for a couple of minutes?' he said, to the three medical professionals.

Dr Morgan looked extremely put out by the request. 'Two minutes,' she said, her glare suggesting this was final.

Lambert left the room and dismissed the officer standing guard.

'What is it?' said Tillman, once the officer had departed.

'She gave me one name. DCI Barnes,' said Lambert, with a whisper.

Tillman knew better than to repeat the name. 'Is she still awake?' he asked, seemingly processing this development.

'No, but I'm convinced she meant it. How well do you know him?'

Tillman sounded as if he was still struggling to come to terms with what he'd been told. 'Never encountered him before this. We should check on his relationship with Sinnott and Weaver. If what Caroline is saying is true then they must have been working together. Fuck, I wonder what he'd have done if you'd let him in the room. Shall I call him and tell him to get back?'

'I'd be surprised if we see him again,' said Lambert. 'Unless…'

'Unless?'

Lambert had been formulating a plan ever since Caroline had shared the information with him. 'I think we need to pretend Caroline is dead.'

Tillman paused. Lambert waited for a chance to explain but Tillman didn't question the decision. 'What about the medical team?'

'I'll explain the situation. We'll have to get Barnes here as soon as possible, and you'll have to sound plausible.'

'Plausible is my middle name, Lambert.'

Lambert returned to Caroline's room and explained the plan to Doctor Morgan. 'We'll need to move her to another room, and she'll have to be covered with a sheet as if she's deceased.'

'You're serious, aren't you?' said Dr Morgan.

'It's the only way I can draw the man responsible back to the hospital. If he thinks she is alive he'll abscond.'

Morgan held his gaze, letting out a deep breath. 'There's another room on floor three available. We can move her there. The less people we have to pass the better.'

'Thank you. Could you give me five minutes and I'll dismiss my officers.'

Lambert left the room again and nodded to Tillman. He summoned over one of the uniformed officers and told him that Caroline Jardine had died. 'I want you to reposition those on duty outside the main building downstairs and monitor everyone who enters and leaves. Leave two on duty. One on either side of this corridor,' he said.

Once the hallway was clear, Tillman called Barnes. 'Answerphone,' he mouthed.

'Leave a message.'

Tillman sounded convincing as he told Barnes Caroline had died. He didn't summon the officer to the hospital, which would have sounded too obvious, but protocol would suggest he should return.

'We need to move her,' said Lambert. He'd left the two officers on duty in case Barnes tried to get confirmation.

He called Croft before moving back into Caroline's room. 'We're ready to go.'

Dr Morgan repositioned the bags feeding into the prone officer. 'We'll need to be quick,' she said, placing a sheet over Caroline's body.

'You two stay here,' he said to the nurses, wanting to limit the chances of someone giving the game away.

Tillman stood as they left the room, Dr Morgan wheeling Caroline along. They made their way down the corridor, past one of the uniformed officers, Lambert hoping Caroline would remain asleep.

Lambert accompanied Morgan and Jardine in the lift to the third floor, trying to shake the notion that Caroline was actually dead beneath the white cover. Croft was waiting and led them to Caroline's new room. There was no viewing window and a sense of relief swept through Lambert as they entered the room and Croft removed the sheet.

'She's alive?' said Croft.

Lambert explained what had happened. 'I need you to stay with Caroline. Explain the situation to her if she wakes, and try to get more information from her if possible. Ideally, I would like this door left locked. Could we do this?' he said, turning his attention to Morgan.

'I'll see what I can do. I still need Mrs Jardine to be monitored.'

'Could you do that for us? I'm sure it won't be for too long.'

Morgan sighed. 'I'll have to sign myself out but I can do that, I suppose.' She returned five minutes later with a key.

'I'll leave you to it. Do not let anyone other than myself or Tillman into this room,' he said to Croft.

Lambert made his way back to the other floor. He couldn't believe Barnes had made such a fool of them. The revelation made him reassess everything from beginning to end. He had to concede Barnes was one hell of an actor. The thought made him shudder as he contemplated what Barnes and Sinnott had accomplished over the years. Instinctively, his hand reached for his gun. He stopped and used the breathing exercises he'd taught himself for his sleep issues. Now was not a time for emotion. That could come later. He had to stay focused. Whatever happened now, he couldn't let Barnes get away.

'He's coming in,' said Tillman, who was waiting outside the first floor lift entrance. 'I have a team waiting in the car park in case he doesn't like what we have to say to him.

If he is involved in this then I don't think it's worth any preamble.'

'Meaning?'

'Meaning as soon as we have him in our sight we pounce.'

Lambert would have liked to have told Barnes that Caroline was alive, to gauge his reaction, but Tillman was right. If Barnes was part of this, then he was potentially capable of anything. 'OK. Let's wait until he's up close.'

Lambert dismissed some of the uniformed officers as they waited for Barnes to arrive. With Caroline supposedly dead, there was no real need for such a police presence and he didn't want to give a reason for Barnes to retreat.

Lambert paced the corridor as they waited, his mind drifting to Caroline Jardine. A fluke had led him to her whereabouts. If he hadn't remembered Gladys Hodge's words about the darkness then chances were they would have never found her. She would have rotted away in the cave, and Teresa would have become an orphan. Once again, he tried to control his mounting rage, deciding Barnes would pay one way or the other for what he'd done.

'He's arrived,' said Tillman. 'The fucker's parked by the exit and is walking across the car park. My team have eyes on him.'

It was far from a sign of guilt, but Barnes would have been able to park much closer if he'd so chosen. Tillman had told Barnes to meet them on floor two, where Caroline had initially been positioned. Although two uniformed officers were still posted either side of the corridor, neither knew Barnes was under suspicion.

'He's not taking the lift, he's heading for the stairs,' said Tillman.

'Sir, why don't you monitor that area? I'll wait for him here. As soon as he approaches you follow him in,' said Lambert.

'Yes, sir,' said Tillman, lacing each word with exaggerated sarcasm before jogging along the corridor.

Lambert tried to relax as he waited for Barnes. He pretended to read from his mobile phone. He didn't glance up as he heard the door at the end of the corridor open.

'Lambert,' said Barnes, his voice echoing in the empty corridor.

Lambert kept his eyes on his phone a few heartbeats longer before glancing up. Barnes was only a few metres inside the corridor. He stood stock still, his feet planted in a wide stance. Lambert lifted his hand, tried his best to paint a distressed look on his face. As Barnes hadn't moved, Lambert pushed himself up from his seat and made his way towards him. He kept his pace slow, pretending to be unconcerned by Barnes' appearance. He noticed Barnes twitch, guilt written all over. He was in flight mode and this put Lambert on edge. He twisted his torso, feeling the weight of his gun in his inside jacket.

'That's far enough,' said Barnes.

Lambert kept walking. 'What's that?' he said, as lightly as possible. He wanted to be nearer, wanted to provoke an admission of guilt.

In one deft move, Barnes produced a gun from inside his jacket. 'I said that's enough,' he said, pointing the gun at Lambert's chest.

Lambert took a couple more steps forward before standing still. He had no idea what had tipped off Barnes. 'What the hell are you doing?' said Lambert, pleading ignorance.

'I'm not an idiot. She's not dead, is she?'

'Caroline? I'm afraid she is. What the hell are you doing with that gun, Barnes. Has it been issued to you?'

'As a matter of fact it has, but that won't stop me using it. I want out of here, Lambert, and you're going to help me.'

Lambert kept calm. It was not the first time he'd had a gun pointed at him and he doubted it would be the last. 'What the hell is going on, Barnes? Why are you pointing that gun at me?' He'd raised his voice for two reasons. First, he wanted to sound incredulous and cause doubt in Barnes mind. He'd succeeded in this, as Barnes' forehead creased in confusion. Second, he wanted to signal Tillman.

His boss didn't let him down. He barged through the swing doors on cue, charging like the bull he was at Barnes.

Barnes was slow to respond to the noise. He turned his head, feet still planted, and tried to adjust his position as he saw Tillman's body charging him down. He went to turn the gun on Tillman but Lambert was mirroring Tillman's movements. He was on Barnes in seconds. He pulled at Barnes' wrist, whilst inflicting a series of blows to the man's groin and kidneys with his knee.

Barnes somehow managed to keep his grip on his gun as Tillman joined in the attack. Lambert kept the pressure on Barnes' wrist as the officer faded onto the ground. He felt the man's grip weaken, only to hear the sound of a single bullet leave the gun a second later.

Lambert didn't hesitate as the shot rang out in the hallway. He continued placing pressure on Barnes' wrist and eventually the gun slipped from his grasp. Lambert took the opportunity to cuff Barnes' hands behind his back before pushing him to the ground.

Tillman glanced up at him, a pained look on his face. 'You OK?' he asked.

Lambert checked himself for injuries, for a delayed reaction to a gunshot, but knew he hadn't been hit. 'Fine, you?'

Tillman got to his feet as Lambert turned Barnes over. Barnes screeched in pain as Lambert dumped him on his back, his hands twisted behind him. Lambert ignored the cries and checked him over before noticing a bullet hole in the corridor wall.

'I guess we should read him his rights,' said Tillman, as the uniformed officers rushed the scene from either side of the corridor.

'Easy there,' said Lambert to the confused officers. He pointed to the gun which lay abandoned on the floor of the ward. 'Let's cordon this area off. I want SOCOs here to process that gun. Chief Superintendent Tillman and I will be taking Mr Barnes here into custody.' He emphasised the "Mr" with a sneer as he hauled Barnes to his feet, enjoying the cries of pain as he did so.

## Chapter Fifty-Five

The following day, Lambert was back at the hospital. After showing his ID to the two armed officers positioned outside her room, he was pleased to see Caroline Jardine sitting up in bed. The transformation was remarkable. The colour had returned to her face and she already looked close to full recovery.

Sinnott and Barnes were both in custody under Tillman's supervision and Lambert would interrogate both men later – after he heard Caroline's version of events.

'I guess I have some talking to do,' said Caroline.

'I guess so,' said Lambert, taking a seat next to her bed. 'Let's start with your investigation into Waverley Manor.'

Caroline confirmed what Colville had told him. She'd continued investigating the Manor covertly ever since Alistair Newlyn's so-called suicide. She hadn't been aware that Colville had remained in the force, joining Anti-Corruption, which was a testament to the department's effectiveness.

'And where did your investigations lead you?'

'Nowhere to begin with. I knew there was a conspiracy within the force so I had to be careful who I spoke to and who I trusted, which was basically no one. I had my theories. I was continually researching the cases involving the Manor. It was becoming increasingly dangerous to access the files and every time I managed to get a glimpse, more and more parts of the files were blanked out.'

Caroline's experience mirrored Lambert's own. He suspected the corruption went beyond Barnes and Sinnott and doubted the full extent of the organisation would ever be revealed.

'What else?' said Lambert. The conversation was being taped and he didn't want to lead Caroline in any way. She would have to supply the names, the links to the Manor organisation.

'I'd long believed the Manor was more than a place. It was either a code name, or some form of group. I kept reaching a dead end, then I came across the case DI Greene was working on. She'd found a body at Waverley Manor and I noticed the case had been pulled. I considered contacting her but I wasn't sure if she was involved. I decided to make my own reccy of the place. I went to the area in the daytime. I hiked most of the way in instead of driving in case the place was being monitored. I was glad I did because that's when I saw him.'

'Who?' said Lambert.

'DCI Barnes.'

Both of them fell silent as Lambert let the news settle. 'Was he alone?'

'No. I believe the man he was with was the Minister for Policing, John Weaver. It was then that I was foolish.'

'How so?'

'I began to rush. I retreated from the site sure that Barnes was involved. At the office, I ran a search on Barnes' connection to the Manor. I used a proxy to sign in but I don't think I hid my tracks well enough.'

Lambert had conducted a similar search himself. Barnes' name appeared more than once in cases related to the Manor. 'When was this?'

'About three days before the fire at my house.'

'Were you ready to go public on your findings?'

'Not quite. I was trying to find someone in Anti-Corruption I could trust.'

'Did you come up with any names?'

'No.'

Lambert paused, again considered the involvement of the AC officer, DS Duggan. 'Tell me about the fire.'

'I'm afraid I don't remember the fire.' Caroline rubbed the back of her head. 'He must have struck me and I think he drugged me somehow. Next thing I know I'm in that fucking hole.'

Lambert noticed the slight tremble in the woman's hand as she spoke. 'I'm sorry to ask you...'

'My husband? He was already gone by the time I came round. At least I think he was. I called out to him, tried to reach him but the chains held me back. I screamed myself hoarse. I tried everything to get him to answer me but he just wouldn't move.' She spoke as if she had to defend herself, her eyes watering.

The autopsy report stated Marcus Jardine died from a blow to the back of his head, similar to the impact Caroline had received, rather than from slipping as Trevor Hodge had claimed during his phone call. Lambert suspected the Fireman had given more force to Mr Jardine due to his bulk. 'Did he speak to you, Hodge?'

Caroline visibly shivered and Lambert couldn't help but be impressed with her defiance. 'On a couple of occasions. That snivelling bastard apologised, can you believe that? He fucking apologised for killing Marcus. What sort of psycho is he?'

Lambert explained that Hodge had died in an explosion of his own making.

'Why didn't he just kill us, let us die in the fire?'

'That's what we need to determine,' said Lambert, thinking he already knew the answer.

—

Matilda and Tillman joined Lambert in the interrogation room at the heart of the NCA's building. Barnes had been placed in a jumpsuit, his wrists and ankles cuffed. He'd been under armed guard, and placed on suicide watch ever since his arrest.

The disruption hadn't seemed to outwardly affect him. He gave each of the officers opposite him a glassy stare, his mouth fixed in a permanent smirk as if he was the interviewing officer and not the detainee.

'I've just interviewed Caroline Jardine,' said Lambert.

Barnes' smirk grew and for a second Lambert wondered if the man had lost his mind. The gun attack was enough to put Barnes behind bars but Lambert needed more answers. He tried to hide his desperation as he continued to speak. 'What can you tell us about Waverley Manor?' he asked.

Barnes' smirk continued to grow. Lambert understood the provocation and regretted it was having the desired effect. They'd given him some time alone to reflect on his situation and at this point Barnes would have considered every angle.

Barnes continued staring as if they were circus exhibits. 'You don't understand anything,' he said, after a long pause.

It was a familiar refrain Lambert had heard from psychopaths all his life. 'Explain it to us, then, Barnes,' he said.

Barnes' tongue protruded from his mouth half an inch as he nodded at Lambert's demand. 'I want to make a deal,' he said.

Lambert sensed Tillman physically tense next to him as if he was ready to strike. 'What do you have to offer and what do you want?' said Lambert.

'I can give you everything. Everyone.'

'And.'

'Freedom.'

Lambert smiled. 'We both know that's not going to happen.'

Barnes leant towards them, his face now contorted into a sneer. The transformation was incredible. Lambert was facing a completely different man. 'Not literal freedom, you fucking cretin,' said Barnes.

Lambert paused. It was pointless getting embroiled in an argument with the man. 'Explain it to me.'

'Change of identity and movement to a secure prison. Some place they can't track me.'

'They?' said Lambert.

'The Manor, of course.'

They adjourned as Tillman made arrangements for Barnes' demands.

Lambert sat with Matilda in the canteen, restless. 'How are we doing at Waverley Manor?' he asked.

'Body count is up to forty-three now. All children.'

It was as Lambert had expected but hearing it out loud made him recoil. All he could do now was to find some justice for them, however meaningless that sounded.

'There's more, I'm afraid,' said Matilda.

Lambert exhaled, unsure if he could take any more information. As he looked at Matilda he realised he hadn't considered the burn scars on her face for some time and the thought gave him some fragile comfort. 'The other room?'

'Yes. The bodies there... Jesus, sir.' Matilda shook her head, her face whitening. 'There were babies, sir. There were fucking pregnant girls.'

Lambert felt his eyes watering. He was continually surprised by the extent of human deprivation but this was a new one, even to him.

'Come on, Sergeant. Let's go get this bastard.'

–

Barnes sat back as far as his chains would allow him, trying to give off an air of nonchalance as Tillman read him the agreement. 'I guess that will suffice,' he said, once Tillman had finished.

'Begin then, before we change our mind,' said Tillman.

'Gladly, though you'll never understand.'

Lambert knew he would never forget the minutes that followed. Barnes explained the Manor was an organisation decades old. 'Waverley Manor is just one of many locations,' he said. 'Don't ask me about the others, because I don't know. It's safer that way, you understand,' he said, as if somehow the three of them were complicit.

'I don't understand anything you are saying, Barnes,' said Lambert.

'You wouldn't. None of you would. It takes someone with a greater appreciation of the world to understand what we achieved there. Someone more evolved.'

Lambert felt nauseous. His mind wandered back to the previous day in the hospital and regretted not taking the gun and emptying every single round of it into Barnes' head. 'Where did you find the children?' asked Lambert, sickened by the question.

'I don't need to tell you about missing children, Lambert. The key, obviously, is to search the correct areas. Find places where a lost child means nothing. We've been doing this for years, we're masters.'

'You're fucking monsters,' said Matilda.

'Calm your bitch down, Tillman,' said Barnes, smirking.

Lambert was impressed by the restraint shown by Tillman. 'Let's everyone calm down,' he said. 'How did you become aligned with the Manor?'

'A case I worked on early on in CID. Theo Barnes, no relation. Our department were investigating him as a suspect for child abduction. I eventually earned his trust and after a few years I was initiated into the Manor.'

Barnes began reeling off a number of names, none of which Lambert recognised. Barnes claimed they were senior members of the Manor, though said there was no such thing as a hierarchy.

'What about Caroline Jardine?' asked Lambert.

'Ah, Mrs Jardine. We should have eliminated her along with Newlyn. Should have thrown in Colville for good measure but we feared the attention. One suicide was conceivable. More than one death, too suspicious.'

'So why now?'

'I knew she was on to me.'

'So you arranged for Trevor Hodge to murder her?'

'And wasn't that a fuck up, Lambert, eh?' said Barnes, as if the situation was one big joke. 'That was my fault. I knew of Hodge from old. We'd used him on many occasions. He's surprisingly effective at what he does. Setting fires, explosions and what have you. Apparently, though, he's not effective at killing people.'

'You need to elaborate, Barnes.'

'I'll elaborate. He was supposed to start a fire at the house. Make it look like an accident whilst making sure the Jardines died. He promised he was up to it but obviously he wasn't. I guess his conscience got to him.'

'So he wasn't hired to kidnap the Jardines?'

'Nope.'

'So you killed him?'

'Me?' said Barnes, incredulous.

'No, you wouldn't get your hands dirty would you, Barnes?'

Barnes squirmed in his seat, his mouth forming into a cruel grimace.

'But you ordered it, didn't you? He knew too much,' said Lambert, revelling in the man's discomfort.

Barnes' lips twitched but he didn't answer.

'What about Berry and Turner, the bodies found at the Jardine house?' said Lambert, changing tact.

'Beats me. I didn't know anything about his suicide fetish. My guess is he replaced the bodies and hoped you and I would be fooled by the switch. There's a lesson for us all there, Lambert. Be careful who you hire.'

# Chapter Fifty-Six

It had started in a restaurant and it ended in one. Michael Lambert sat opposite Sarah May, a sense of melancholy running through him as they discussed their separation. Sarah smiled at him with that lopsided grin which he'd been so taken with from the moment he first saw it. For a second he wanted to backtrack, but that was the coward's way. They'd come to an agreement and Lambert knew deep down it was the correct decision.

It was two weeks since Barnes' arrest. A total of fifty-one bodies had now been discovered at Waverley Manor. It was national news and Lambert was doing his best to stay out of the spotlight, despite Mia Helmer's stream of articles accusing him of botching the investigation.

Tillman was happy to take all the plaudits for the discovery at Waverley Manor, whilst Matilda was coordinating the identification of all those lost children, and the coroner was considering the deaths of Berry and Turner. By all accounts it was likely Trevor Hodge would be tried posthumously for their murders.

Lambert had his own role. Barnes had given them a list of ten senior members of the Manor and Lambert had already made seven arrests. Along with Sinnott, Barnes had been placed in a secure unit with a brand new ID. He was in solitary confinement and would not mingle with the general prison populace for some months. Despite his cooperation in apprehending the others responsible, he would be spending the rest of his life behind bars.

'I suppose I should give you this back,' said Sarah, handing him a set of keys.

Lambert glanced downwards as he accepted the key ring, remembering a happier time when she'd given him a set of keys to her flat in Bristol. The agreement had been mutual. However much he tried to deny it, Lambert had not recovered from his split with Sophie. They'd tried and failed, and in the end they both concluded the relationship had run its course.

'You can always speak to me,' said Sarah, getting to her feet.

They embraced and for the second time in minutes Lambert almost backtracked.

'Bye, Michael,' said Sarah, kissing him on the cheek.

Lambert watched her leave the coffee shop, for once dumbstruck.

–

Lambert met up with Tillman back at the NCA head-quarters. 'There could be a promotion in this for you,' said Tillman. He was dressed in black, like Lambert. He appeared to have lost some weight and was clearly enjoying his time in the media spotlight. Lambert was sure Anti-Corruption's decision to drop its ongoing investigation into him had its part to play, even though he wasn't convinced it would be the last time either of them heard from the section.

'What, and be a desk jockey like you?' said Lambert.

'One step at a time, Lambert. Where are we on the list?'

'We're trying to track down William Spencer and Phillip Tan. It looks like news of the arrests has spread and they've absconded. We've notified the airports and docks, their details are with Interpol. Once we get them, we're finished with the list supplied by Barnes. Then the real work will begin.'

Interrogations had already started on the detainees. Each of the eight men were of high profile in their chosen field. Sinnott and Barnes were thankfully the only policemen. Lambert would spend months putting together a case against those arrested. Some were already twitching to make deals, and as Barnes had suggested there had been hints of other locations. Lambert had already spoken to Tillman about passing the case onto another officer but he wouldn't hear of it.

'It's a terrible case, Michael, but I'm glad you're at the helm.'

'Steady, sir, I thought that almost sounded like a compliment.'

–

They met Matilda in the car park and she drove them to the funeral. They'd kept news of the service as quiet as possible, but a large congregation had come to pay their respects to Marcus Jardine.

Lambert sat at the back of the church as various family and friends spoke about Marcus and his impact on their lives. Lambert had never met him, but was moved by the offered words. He bowed his head at the end of the service as Caroline retreated down the aisle of the church, accompanied by her father, ravaged by pain and tears.

Outside he walked with Tillman and Matilda, following the congregation along the pebble-dashed pathway to the spot where Marcus was to be buried.

The weather held as Caroline watched her husband lowered into the ground. Lambert looked away as she tried to control her grief, only for it to overwhelm her as she sprinkled soil onto the coffin and collapsed into the arms of her parents.

–

Caroline had invited the three of them to a small gathering back at her parents' house. Lambert avoided the assembled group as best he could, standing on the edges of the main room. He sipped at a glass of warm red wine, surveying the guests whilst Tillman and Matilda made an attempt to mingle.

To Lambert's right, a sideboard laden with family photos caught his attention. In particular a picture of Caroline Jardine holding Teresa as a baby, Marcus Jardine with his arm round her, smiling at the new addition to the family.

'Thank you for coming, Michael,' said Caroline, appearing at his side.

Lambert was always lost for words in such situations and offered a feeble smile instead. He'd got to know Caroline well over the last couple of weeks. Despite her ordeal and ongoing grief, she'd been keen to assist him with her knowledge of the Manor. He'd been present for an emotional reunion with DS Florence Colville, where he'd felt like an intruder as they both poured out their grief for Caroline's lost husband and their late colleague, Alistair Newlyn.

'How's little Teresa?' he asked, his eyes moving to a second picture of an older Teresa possibly taking her first steps.

Caroline smiled, her eyes still red. 'She's doing well. As you can imagine, it's a very difficult concept for her to grasp that she'll never see her Daddy again.'

'Sorry, ridiculous question,' said Lambert, crestfallen at having made such an insensitive comment.

'Michael, it's OK. I'm being serious. I'm getting some help and we're gradually going to introduce her to the idea. But I'll make sure she never forgets him.'

Lambert didn't know how to respond. 'I promise I'll do everything to put away all those responsible,' he said, fearing his words were inappropriate for the situation.

Caroline nodded and smiled again, though Lambert sensed she was on the verge of tears. 'Excuse me,' she said, retreating into the throng of family and well-wishers.

Lambert waited for an acceptable time before making his excuses and leaving. He made some calls as he drove away from the wake, agreeing to meet with one of his contacts later that evening. He had somewhere else to be now. He drove on autopilot, thorough streets he'd travelled down hundreds of times before. He passed Chloe's old pre-school, picturing her as a two-year-old full of life, and tried his best to cherish the memory, rather than dwell on what was to come later for her. Across the mini roundabout and onto the main road, a right at the cinema, his mind elsewhere as the car almost drove itself, until he was back in the his old street, parking the car, and for once not dawdling inside like some deranged stalker.

He didn't know if they were home, and it didn't matter for the time being. He clicked the car shut and rushed across the road to his old front door. He pressed the doorbell without hesitation and welcomed the butterflies as he heard footsteps.

The door opened and Sophie stood gazing at him. In her arms she held Chloe's sister, Jane, who gave him a quizzical look as if she remembered the last time they'd met.

'Michael,' said Sophie, as if unsure it was really him. As always, she saw right through him. He understood she knew why he was there. He watched for a sign as she analysed him, was relieved when her eyes widened and her face broke out into a smile.

'You better come in then,' she said.

# Epilogue

The men stared at one another. The first, a brutish man who looked like a wall of muscle, went to speak, but the second man cut him off. 'No names,' he said, pouring sugar into the boiling water before stirring.

The first man nodded and picked the pan off the stove. The pan was nearly a metre high and was full to the brim but he carried it with such ease it appeared empty.

'This way,' said the second man, heading down the corridor.

The corridor was known as the Beast ward. It was reserved for those prisoners unable to be part of the general populace, occasionally because they were a risk to the inmates, but usually because they were at risk from their fellow prisoners. It was where the rapists and child molesters lived and word had spread a particularly nasty specimen had been added recently.

The gates, which were usually locked shut, had been mysteriously left open, and both men were able to walk through to the Beast ward with no difficulty. They walked at an even, purposeful pace. Both had been recruited through various secret channels. Promises had been made about reduced sentences but after what they'd heard both men would have gone through with the job even without such motivation.

A prison guard was waiting around the next corner. He stood outside one of the Beast rooms. He was young, and looked nervous, as if he thought the pan of boiling water and sugar was for him.

'Napalm,' said the wall of muscle to the guard. Napalm was the nickname given to the substance in the pan.

The second man had only seen a napalm attack once. Sugar was added to the boiling water as it made the burning liquid stick to the skin. The napalm attack he'd witnessed, a revenge gang attack, still appeared in his nightmares. He could hear the screams of the victim; could smell the sickly-sweet smell of burning flesh. Despite that, he didn't hesitate as the guard unlocked the door.

The man was lying on a bed which made it easier. The wall of muscle ran towards the figure as the second man gave him the message. 'Barnes?' he asked.

The man sat bolt upright in bed, clearly understanding the situation. He was supposed to be there under an alias and hearing his name out loud had clearly shook him. 'What is this?' he said, trying to intone a sense of authority into his words.

'Tillman and Lambert say hello,' said the second prisoner, as the wall of muscle deposited the message over the top of his head.